WORDS OF OUR ENEMIES

A Novel

Bruce Colbert

Published by:

Blue Jade Press, LLC
Vineland, NJ
www.bluejadepress.com

"In the end, we will remember not the words of our enemies, but the silence of our friends."

Martin Luther King, Jr.

For Ray Gill

Chapter 1
Memphis

It was one of those humid early spring days you get in the South. The shot itself wasn't particularly difficult to make as he'd made so many like it, but it still required fast movement and enough accuracy. He'd killed North Vietnamese generals from two hundred yards half way up a tree while they were in mid-bite of their rice bowl.

What he had agreed to do had little real challenge in it. The distance and the field of fire would pretty much ensure that he'd kill the man with the first bullet without the need to fire a second.

As a boy, he'd shot cheetahs on the run with his grandfather's clumsy Enfield. Now he used a Remington hunting rifle which presented no problem.

He hardly even needed the wobbly scope someone had mounted on the metal barrel. In fact, he thought this killing shot would be easier if he simply removed the scope and just used the barrel sighting.

He remembered how he had hunted the herds of bounding gazelle with his father, and how he had been taught to anticipate the jump of the animal when it detected the human scent, and then calmly fire a bullet into the middle of the jump through its chest.

As he walked up the stairs in the vacant building, he could hear rats scurrying in the adjacent rooms. Of all the dangerous animals he'd faced over the years, rats made his skin crawl and gave him the worst fear for some strange reason. The empty room he'd selected for the shot was on the third floor. It had several large windows that faced the balcony across the street and into the courtyard. There wouldn't be any obstruction that hampered his sight line, and with some straining, he pulled up the warped window. A clearance of ten inches was all that he required to place the barrel on the windowsill and make the shot.

The building had been a cotton factor's office. There were great empty tables with sides continuing up for six inches where the raw cotton was placed inside to be examined for its fiber quality. You could still see bits of the thin white fibers and whole bolls of raw cotton all over the scarred floors.

The company had produced its own farm calendars that had photographs of the cotton picked by a 1920's John Deere machine. Every month was a black and white snapshot of years before, and in one picture there was a black Model T Ford truck parked next to a cotton gin.

He walked around the room, and found a small table to put next to the window where he could lay his own Zeiss binoculars and a box of live rounds. To make this shot effective, he had chosen soft point bullets that would spread on impact, and literally remove most of the man's skull. It wasn't a pleasant sight, no, but it was a necessary evil because the thankless task had to be done, and by a true professional.

He could execute a shot to the chest because it allowed him some margin of error; the bullet could land three or four inches away from the exact spot he'd chosen and still be effective. However, he felt that he wanted to make a shot to the head. He thought, "Maybe I'll blow off his jaw and that will finally shut him up forever. "His silence was what they all wanted to end this chaos he'd created.

There would be no revolution without him. It would all wither on the vine and things would get back to the way they should be. Across the country and in Washington, cooler heads would continue to prevail. It was really all he had to know.

The man remembered meeting an ex-convict, a two-bit felon on the run and how the man had come to trust someone he'd never met before, someone else who shared his extremist views about eliminating the whole black scourge of the country.

"Mow those fuckers down, one loud mouth nigger after the other," the Birmingham bar-fly told him and he had agreed. The drifter said he would be first in line to shoot the head nigger himself. It was something he had wanted to do for a long time, and now he was ready to kill the bastard. He had already bought the gun to do it.

This man obviously deranged and emotional wasn't up to the daunting task which unfolded before them. Yet, it was these limitations of character that made him of use. It was at that very moment that this loudmouth redneck became everything they wanted, and so he called the Germantown telephone number to talk about what lay ahead at length and then agreed to proceed.

They believed that this delusional character he found in Birmingham wouldn't notice the difference in the rifle he had. The bolt on his particular Remington would be temporarily obstructed with a thin piece of wire that he had inserted in the mechanism, and even if he wants to make the shot, he won't be able to engage the firing pin.

The gun will be useless in his hands, and as he struggles with it, the shot will be made from the abandoned building next door. He'll then know that someone else has done what he wanted to do, and flee quickly in confusion.

They had given this pawn money and told him to get to Little Rock and escape to Canada where he would meet some people who will provide him with his cover and a new Canadian identity. The man can then continue on his journey to Europe in an effort to disappear from the authorities for the crime he won't be committing.

Someone would be staying in the room next to him during his stay in the flophouse to closely monitor his moves. They'll confiscate the rifle wherever he drops it, switch it with the other Remington, and hide it where the police can find it in a bag that he owns along with some of his clothing. They will transfer his fingerprints from tape onto the water glasses in the room he uses for his cheap whiskey. He's caught inside a web he won't escape.

"His infamy has been guaranteed and it'll blind him to us, and he'll be putty in our hands."

He would become the sacrificial lamb they had hoped to find. He could be easily manipulated to shoulder this heinous crime.

Through the Birmingham bar conversations and the barrage of free whiskies that continued this unlikely bond was formed between these two disparate men who would enter the lion's den together. However, at the last instant, one gladiator would turn on the other.

That's how it'll play out. The government and the courts will have their murderer, and children for the entire millennia will learn his accursed name. For the world, he's the one, the murderer, and what they've done will pass unnoticed.

The real assassin in the empty building put his rifle and the rest of his equipment, except for his trusty field glasses, under a nearby tarpaulin he had brought with him. Quick of senses, he noticed that there had been some movement on the balcony across the street. It had been a housekeeper in an apron who was pushing a cart from room to room, opening doors with a master key and putting clean towels and soap inside the vacant rooms. He was able to see the black woman's face in almost perfect detail as it had been magnified enough through the binoculars. She was rather light-skinned, around twenty-five or so, and attractive, he thought to himself.

He let the binoculars rest on his chest, and let out a sigh. Thus far, his own life had many turns in the road. Who could have foreseen the direction that it's taken? He smiled at the irony and slowly prepared to leave the empty building for what must be done the next day.

As the man climbed down the rickety and narrow building staircase, he thought about the first time that he had been called upon to kill another man. He was but a boy who hadn't even reached his seventeenth birthday on the farm. Some of their neighbors had been slaughtered by rebellious natives in their beds so every movement you made in those days was with a gun.

He had been in the shower in the tiny bathroom stall at the back of the farmhouse when he had heard a loud noise coming from the living room. Instinctively he grabbed and cocked the revolver that he had on the shelf across from the shower then walked straight from the shower spray into the carpeted parlor, still soaped and dripping wet.

The black insurgent, holding a carbine, was so shocked at the sight of a naked white man in front of him that he hesitated a moment before raising his rifle. That split second had given the man enough time to fire a single shot from the pistol, striking the rebel in the forehead and killing him instantly.

Smiling on the last broken building step with his hand on the front door knob, he thought of that long ago boy and the awful bloodbath he had faced.

Chapter 2
Arrival

I was living in New Orleans when Rusty talked me into coming to Memphis with him, and since on most levels New Orleans wasn't working for me, it didn't take much for him to convince me to leave the sweltering city. I had been living in a studio apartment on Milan Street in the Garden District with three of us sharing one broken down double bed and an empty kitchen. He had a guest house where he lived part-time on Lee Garrett's horse farm and because he played on the Memphis polo team and exercised the ponies, Lee had let him stay there without rent.

It was a pleasant enough place, furnished with rustic pieces, and a modern Pullman-style kitchen. The one room cottage worked for him and the offer worked for me too. That morning he headed out on his British BSA motorcycle and I followed him in the beater car that I had, and we threaded our way northward through the sleepy Delta towns.

The route was more or less due north along the Mississippi and because he liked to speed with the motorcycle, he was always ahead of me. After three hours on the road, I had come into Greenville, or one of the other larger Delta towns I can't remember, and saw him having a beer at some roadside café-bar, the BSA parked out front.

We took a detour in northern Mississippi, just outside Tunica, and I followed him to the rambling farmhouse of one of his childhood friends, Will Atkins. We sat on the back porch of Will's parent's home and had lemonade with a little gin in it along with some fresh ham sandwiches Eugene, the black man who looked after the house and farm office, made for us.

Will finished Ole Miss three years earlier, and had been drafted into the army. He served in Vietnam with the 101st Airborne, much to the consternation of his family. He refused a commission and had been a common rifleman. But since he suffered from recurrent migraine headaches, he had been medically-relieved from squad reconnaissance duties in the jungle. He was reassigned to division headquarters sending troops into the bush each day and night to make contact with the hidden enemy.

That raging war had made him an angry young man and the whole experience colored his world in harsh shades that few of his contemporaries could understand, including Rusty.

Will was engaging company for the visit, and we discussed the military ever so briefly, both with disdain as I had served the same master since I was in the Marines and had been trained with the Navy Engineers.

Rusty told me later that Will had been mustered out at Fort Leavenworth. The process had taken maybe five months, during which time he had spent most nights high on whatever hallucinogens he could find, and they were plentiful among the discharged troops.

His family had a large cotton plantation, so he found his way into the cotton brokerage trade, and was leaving Tunica in three weeks' time, so our paths might indeed cross again in Memphis.

The main reason I went to New Orleans in the first place was to land a job as a reporter with the Times Picayune Newspaper. The man who had arranged for an interview with the brash managing editor had no way of knowing that they had been cutting staff since their bold overexpansion in the late Fifties. They would no longer be trying to compete with the larger national dailies, so that went nowhere. Other thoughts about attending law school at Loyola, or most other ideas, gave way to the lethargy of living in the sinful place which seemed to encourage indolence and excess.

I had been in New Orleans for maybe four months when I met Rusty. He had briefly been with a band playing French Quarter dives for nickels. I heard them at one of the bars I frequented in those days and struck up a friendship with two of the band members. He came in late to them after their doped-out drummer had quit, and though a half-hearted musician Rusty looked the part with a red-haired ponytail and green velvet Nehru jacket. He popped enough pills for him to be believable. From some wealthy family in Memphis, he often lamented that they were too religious. He called his own father Nigger Jim after the central character in the Tom Sawyer novel and for months they had spent most of their conversations on the telephone arguing about everything. Salvation was an important topic discussed.

I had survived on occasional work I picked up in the classifieds like passing out handbills on street corners. The work allowed me my nights free to roam the Crescent City and to savor its supposed hospitality which at worst was drunkenness, narcotics and prostitution. It was a tough and uncompromising town for those that traveled its underbelly and that hadn't changed in fifty or even a hundred years.

There was some level of excitement that came with the territory and I had found myself sleeping with a young woman from Honduras. I would find out later that she was only fifteen, though I had thought all along she was in her twenties from the way she had dressed and acted. It came as a shock, but I'd figured it was all part of the experience of not knowing in life. It wasn't something I would repeat or share with anyone. It was simply some strange path that I had taken.

The Memphis experience was different. It brought me into the world of the disappearing South and the people who ran it; the white ones that is. It was the same in New Orleans of course, the color bar, but there always seemed less tension between races there and it was rather common to mix in the circles that I came to know.

Lee Garrett, himself, would become one of those people who lived like a patrician and acted as if this world would never change. There was no reason for it to change. It functioned well as it was and he behaved as if there would be no tomorrow, and for him there wasn't.

Lee's father had a lumber fortune from his own father and his mother was a Ferguson, one of the first families in the Kimberly Clark lineage living in splendor outside Philadelphia. His lone sibling, his sister Sharon, would make tsunami waves with her raucous adolescent drunk and profane behavior at debutante parties. Then afterward more waves with four or five marriages. She eventually ended up with an ordination as an Episcopal priest in some prison ministry in Latin America, where she would marry an inmate prize-fighter serving a twenty-year term for manslaughter. He killed a man in a deadly barroom brawl.

Sharon's first husband was a professional polo player and large-scale farmer in the Outback of Australia whom she met while on his American tour. He had stayed for a time at their large farm at Germantown training polo ponies and playing with Lee's team against others from several southern cities.

Marrying him, she went back to the Northern Territories where she stayed three years and gave birth to a daughter. In the middle of their fourth year on the lonely dust-chocked farm, she sought a divorce from this casual sportsman and returned to Memphis with her young daughter. The divorce was easily granted and she never saw this man again, even for visits to the child which he never attempted.

When I met Sharon, she was a reporter for the Press Scimitar which was the afternoon paper that mostly covered social events, with perhaps a few other feature assignments. I hadn't known she could write, or ever had any training, however, I'm certain her family contacts alone had impressed the editors. Who best to write society articles as vacuous as they might be than someone whose family is held in high esteem by a narrow and wealthy segment of the population?

When I shared the polo field guest house with Rusty, I had talked with Sharon maybe three or four times, and she and Rusty seemed to have this durable friendship based on his history with her elder brother. She was an hourglass-shaped dark-haired woman with a loud laugh who would come unannounced to see Rusty at the guesthouse. She was quick-witted, yet there seemed to be a hidden macabre side to her, though she was always civil in conversation with me and often very funny. It was a self-deprecating humor that few women had. Most were not as confident in their own skin as Sharon clearly had been with her great wealth and prominence. Her parents had fifty million dollars when that was a lot of money and she nonchalantly roamed around a 500-acre horse farm with a twenty-stall barn and a groom's furnished apartment above.

At the time I met her, she was dating a much younger man who was an actor at the local Little Theatre where she often served as a reviewer for the newspaper. He was perhaps ten, or more, years younger. He was decent enough, though clearly overwhelmed by the enormous wealth of that family. He always had a pained look on his face when he would be introduced at polo games, or garden parties, and for many, he was simply a halfway attractive untutored man who feared horses. If they had contemplated marriage, most people believed it would be quickly doomed, but marriage did come along as well as a second child for Sharon.

The child, a healthy bouncing boy, arrived around the same time as the marriage ceremony in the downtown Episcopal cathedral. The stocky church rector, the Reverend Harold Morrison, who had many years of service and dubious sexuality, officiated for a small crowd which consisted mostly of Sharon's family and her husband's parents who had driven from their home in rural Marked Tree, Arkansas. She wore a diamond engagement ring which had been her grandmother's and she paid for both the wedding rings and the reception, which would be black-tie for some ungodly reason at the Hunt and Polo Club founded by her grandfather.

They would live in a ten bedroomed white-columned farmhouse where visiting polo players from around the world were sometimes housed. The dinners often had fifteen, or more, seated at a massive dining room table. It was a kind of opulence that the area wasn't used to seeing. There were a few big cotton merchant homes in midtown left over from the Twenties, but nothing of this particular scale.

One afternoon Lee invited Rusty and me to lunch. The three of us sat in the cavernous windowed dining room eating plates of cold chicken served by the woman cook who came to the table in a print housedress. The conversation was centered around horses. In fact, Lee acted as if it were only he and Rusty at the large table sending one or two passing comments my way that had to do with New Orleans. He struck me then, and even now, as one of the most singularly self-absorbed men I have ever encountered in a relatively well-traveled life.

Rusty had been seeing a young woman that he had met at one of the drive-through restaurants where they roller skate out to your car with the burgers and fries. They had hit it off and had been seeing one another for almost a month now. She was tall with honey blond hair and very pretty. She had started her freshman year at the state university campus in Memphis, so they were frequently together. He would give me a call every week and ask me to spend a night at another friend's house to give her some time to get used to having me at the guesthouse. It became a painful romance for me, though I couldn't protest considering his largesse with the extra bed.

I think they had been intimate for several weeks when Rusty came into the driveway with a ripped shirt and a nasty cut that split his eyebrow. He looked as if he had fallen off a motorcycle at a stop sign, at least that's what I assumed. He could hardly get out that he was a victim of a violent attack at a pizza joint near the university where he had met this girl for lunch. The father had driven there unbeknownst to the two young lovers, and seeing them huddled together in a booth, the large man had pounced on Rusty, pummeling him several times before the daughter had pulled him off his victim.

It just so happened that the night before, the young woman was in a rage arguing with her father and had confessed intimacy with Rusty. Her father made good on his vow to beat that vulgar miscreant half to death. As the father left the restaurant, he warned Rusty that this was only the beginning of what he could expect after deflowering an innocent Christian woman. For Rusty, that threat ended the relationship, and the nights we spent sharing the guesthouse pretty much returned to earlier pot-filled smoky nonchalance.

A woman that Rusty had introduced me to several months ago at a downtown restaurant visited us late one afternoon. At the time, she seemed rather shy and an unassuming petite young woman with dirty blond locks. She drove around town in a dented white VW bug she had called Minnie Pearl for some strange reason.

It was the last gasp of the Sixties, and it seemed that this part of the country had completely missed the surging counterculture wave that had the rest of this generation rising up in smoke with peace, love and the sickly-sweet scent of sandalwood. She didn't even wear patchouli. Her scent might have been the slightest hint of Shalimar, or 'sure screw' as the women at my university termed it. Instead she smelled more like some absent horse flesh, actually, and her calf-length boots were always muddy.

I had never seen a woman dressed quite this way before. She seemed almost like a caricature, jodhpur-crossed legs with silver spurs swinging with the canned restaurant music. When she drove away that night I saw that she had an English saddle in the backseat, a gift her father had given her for her graduation from college. It was a Hermes, she had breathlessly whispered to me at the noisy table with great pride of ownership. I simply nodded unknowingly since I knew little about horses or what went on their broad backs.

We spent several hours together and found common ground politically as well as other ways. This casual beauty showed me that she was so different from what I had experienced with other women. I asked to see her again, and smilingly she agreed.

Martha Whitcomb was a newly minted lawyer and the only female barrister in the district attorney's office. She toiled for a long-time for a family friend who was her father's University of Virginia fraternity brother, and later his brother-in-law.

It all seemed a rather neat arrangement. Everyone who had worked with her said she was precise and intelligent, and quick to humor. She possessed a wide circle of colleagues and close friends. She was one of two sisters; the other a pianist and private school music teacher who was even more attractive, taller and with their mother's piercing cornflower blue eyes. Her father, naturally, was an attorney and most of his practice was in the banking world with the occasional state government commission. As a family they were comfortably upper middle class and belonged with others such as themselves to the University Club. They were the ones with Confederate officer forbearers who were invited to join the bastion of the Memphis Country Club, which was the center for the town's older inherited money.

There were exceptions that were invited into that inner sanctum, and Lee Garrett was one though his Philadelphia and New York pedigree was rather deep and unassailable. The wealthy Jews in town congregated at the Colonial Country Club for those single synagogue events in the city.

Through Lee, I did find myself at a Cotton Carnival secret society party and was thrown together with this same horsey woman lawyer who, in her spaghetti strap summer dress had sunburned arms from jumping horses all afternoon in the scalding pastures. Her face was attractive and freckled, and she liked to smile widely, even when there seemed no levity about. It was like a nervous reaction someone might have, like unconscious coughing.

Her father's family were from Columbus, Mississippi, where they had been landowners twenty years before the Civil War. Those with awful Reconstruction losses had moved into town and ran a series of hardware and appliance stores until the Depression. They had lived in the same white house for a hundred and thirty years. She told me this as we were standing on the roof of the Peabody Hotel looking down at the busy street watching the cars dropping off excited ladies in evening gowns.

"You know, whenever I'm standing at the edge of a roof like this, I always think about jumping," she said with a strange seriousness in her lilting voice. "Don't you?"

I laughed, "No, it never occurred to me. That's why I never get too close to the edge. I don't want to entertain that thought, ever."

"Only self-destructive people have to worry," she continued,
"people like me."

"You're self-destructive?" I inquired, half curious.

"Oh yes, and I'll bet you are too. It's something I sense about you."

With that, the conversation ended. She looked down onto the busy street and yelled to a woman who had hiked up her satin gown and was running between the moving cars to get to the hotel front door.

"She'll be late for her own funeral," she said.

She then turned to me and straightened the single red carnation I had pinned on my white dinner jacket lapel and disappeared into the crowd that was beginning to fill the rooftop ballroom.

The outside evening temperatures were still too damn hot for late spring, and the automobile emissions from the street didn't help the situation either. Rusty joined me wearing a dinner jacket that was wrinkled and didn't fit him.

"I would stay away from her, honestly. She's not worth the trouble, wound too tightly and ready to snap." He snapped his fingers in the air for emphasis, and through the crowd I could see her glance back at the two of us smiling slightly.

Two weeks later she invited me to her parent's home for a Saturday lunch. It was a large Tudor style home built in a midtown enclave of similar homes that bespoke of older stucco and brick construction. She was living there with her father for a time, since her mother had gone to Silver Hills to dry out for a month or two. Lately, the Dewar's had done its awful deed with her mother Carolyn, and her father, Alfred had recently made the

14

thankless drive to the well-regarded private treatment center outside Lexington once more. This would be Carolyn's third time and the promising sobriety had lasted almost two years before the heartbreaking relapse occurred.

A black woman who introduced herself as Lucille opened the front door and directed me to an anteroom den, or sunroom, where I sat until the others might summon me. Before I had even asked, she brought me a cool glass of lemonade, and told me everyone would be down shortly.

I waited patiently while looking at the bookshelves which held a fine collection of leather bound classics and two shelves devoted to law books. I got up from the chair and opened one of the William Faulkner novels, squinting to read an ink inscription.

"My grandfather knew him, Faulkner. It's his writing on that First Edition," Martha informed me as she entered and saw the book in my hands.

"The horse and the man, always inseparable, To Brewster from Bill," I read impressed. The stained leather binding felt as if it held history.

"I saw him once, actually." she told me, "I was thirteen riding in my first fox hunt. We had all gone after the fox but didn't get it and were back at the clubhouse for the brunch. Faulkner was sitting right there by the fire, and he spoke to me, and asked me how I liked the chase."

"What a wonderful memory," I offered.

"It was the fall of 1960. He was more famous than anyone I have ever known, or probably will know."

I laughed. "I envy you that."

"Well, I was too intimidated to speak. I just said, 'fine,' and ran around the corner as quickly as I could." She took the book from my hand and looked at the gold embossed title, "Sanctuary".

"Faulkner came twice to ride with the Long Green Hunt, and after the last time, he was dead within six months."

"A marvelous experience," I told her.

"You know, he was a rather smallish man with a steel-grey mustache, trimmed neatly with his nice smile," she explained.

"Whenever I would read his books after that, I could hear his voice in the writing, as if he were speaking directly to me as he had by the fire then."

"Did your grandfather like him?" I asked, curious.

"Oh, he adored Bill Faulkner and when Faulkner was given the Nobel, my grandfather literally wept. Some say it was the only time that anyone had ever seen him cry."

"Talking about Faulkner?" a booming voice asked from behind me. I turned towards the voice and Martha's stocky father extended his meaty hand to me in salutation.

With a firm grip, he began to talk of his own boyhood in Columbus. He was the oldest boy in his grandfather's house of maiden aunts at the time. His mother, who was the oldest of four daughters, was widowed with three children; him and his sister Lulu who was just a toddler at the time, and an infant brother.

By now, we were seated at a long dining table and Lucille had started to serve lunch with the first course being a soup that was served cold.

"I sat at this man's knee, and my grandfather would tell me stories of the civil war," her father reminisced, "and I could never get enough of those tales."

He put his spoon down and leaned over the varnished wood table toward me, smiling all the while, and added, "Can you imagine, he joined the Confederates at fourteen years old? They took him as a drummer boy for the infantry."

"Daddy, I don't think Jeff wants to hear all that, really," Martha said with a quick roll of her eyes.

"But I do. Please tell me," I urged her father.

He laughed. "I defer to my daughter, except for this."

"As a boy, my grandfather marched into the cannon and musket fire at Shiloh against Grant's troops and beat on that drum for the three assaults against the Union lines."

He coughed for a moment and took a long drink from the water glass that the cook had placed next to his plate.

"On the final assault at Hornet's Nest against the worst gunfire imaginable, he took a musket ball wound in the arm, but switched his drum stick to the good arm, and kept at it toward the blue lines until retreat was sounded."

"Please, please, let's enjoy lunch," Martha finally pleaded.

"The rest for another time perhaps," her father stated, and he changed the subject to my life where I provided the table with the briefest version I could manage.

As a veteran trial attorney, he was a perfect and insightful listener and only interrupted once or twice to ask some friendly questions, or to make some comments of similar import on his own life. He served his tenure with the army in Panama before the Second World War and then his captaincy in California at the Presidio where he'd been hospitalized with severe arthritis.

At first glance, the prominent man seemed rather open, but that was his cunning and strength; that engaging, wholly male personality which underscored a manipulative core. His wife, Carolyn was more obvious in the countless ways with which she sought to use people toward her ends. Whatever dysfunction her daughters had was probably inherited mostly from her devious and cloying behavior.

I would come to like both of Martha's parents. But after knowing them more intimately, I became fearful of any real trust. Everything was appearance with them, and I appreciated that this behavior was how they had made their place in this world. At the end of everything that occurred, it would be easy to forgive what I did within their prescribed lives. I'd never understand these disparate people.

Martha's parents were self-made. They were blessed with a peculiar attractiveness and the rabid pretense to achieve more was their calling card. I imagine it covered a profound lack of self-esteem they embraced in the Depression South. They grew up where they could've been labeled crackers or worse, people who had never seen a cotillion or worn a dinner jacket until they found their later fortune.

It would be maybe two months or more before I would meet her mother, and even then, under the most controlled circumstances. We met for a cup of coffee in her sunroom on the way to somewhere else with an audience of fifteen minutes at the longest.

Carolyn had been raised on a hardscrabble farm in Western Kentucky and had a scholarship to Ole Miss where she had met Martha's father in the normal sort of collegiate manner, at some dance or weekend football game. They were never intimate in those days though they had married right after Pearl Harbor and lived apart except for his hospitalization in San Francisco where she had lived with a general's family at the Presidio. Later the couple returned to the South when Alfred began his studies at the Virginia law school, and subsequently Carolyn finished her degree teaching primary school for a time before Martha came.

Martha was born in Charlottesville and they moved to Memphis before her third birthday when her father joined a prestigious law firm downtown. He was the only associate who hadn't gone to either Yale or Harvard. They were a bluestocking bunch of stiff-necked guys.

I continued to live out on the Garrett farm with Rusty and found an editing job on the Memphis morning newspaper. I was temporarily filling in for an editor who had been diagnosed with cancer and advised to spend at least six months at home in a stress-free environment.

The job worked rather well, and the hours and pay seemed to balance the life I had adopted. I was going to the clubs and alcohol was an important part of the polo and scion crowd which I'd joined as an observer and perhaps would-be scribe.

After nearly ten months, Martha thought we might share an apartment, and though it would certainly upset her parents, she did it anyway. It was her single pathetic attempt to be close to the hippie movement and do her own thing. We found a two-bedroom apartment in the stucco Kimbrough Towers next to Overton Park. It proved to be a spacious sunny living space built in the early Fifties and now the preserve of mostly everyone's aging grandmother. Getting into the elevator along with Martha she would soon be recognized and forced to engage in conversation with some blue-haired women who simply loved her mother, which was untrue. They wanted to know all about Martha's every moment in the last decade.

Martha had broken the southern family tradition and had gone away to Smith at the insistence of her mother and had followed it with law school. This peculiar difference fascinated the old ladies on the elevator. Time after time as we moved ever so slowly to the twelfth floor, the story would be repeated. No one ever asked me anything, not even why I might be standing next to her. Martha preferred to keep that portion of her own world in total ignorance of our sinful cohabitation, hypocritical as her attitude might be.

In truth, she was only half-liberated, the part of her brain concerned with law and fairness. Everything else in Memphis was forced into this archaic category of what a southern woman should or shouldn't be. Martha didn't play the part well, the two realities bled into each other until they hemorrhaged.

She would do some pro bono work for blacks that she knew and liked, mostly the older and more malleable couples she had known over the years, like those who had done her parents' yard work or served at garden parties. They would call on her when their grandson, granddaughter, or second cousin got into trouble with the police or some city inspector. Maybe they had their driver's license suspended because they hadn't paid the yearly renewal fee. She would help them straighten it out, and do it cheerfully. She would lend them money too, without any thought that it would ever be paid back because usually it wasn't.

She helped one maid's daughter get an abortion. Martha made phone calls among her college friends who knew of these opportunities and drove the young girl to the rural clinic, waited there for two hours until it was done. Afterwards, she delivered the girl home after putting the whole medical bill on her credit card. That was the kind of woman she was, but there were other inexplicable disconnects and the family shadow had covered both daughters in a truly unhealthy manner. It was almost Shakespearean.

Her sister married a local real estate developer's son while she was still at a women's college in Virginia and soon after, a son was born. Her husband had walked away from the lucrative family business to raise hunting dogs an hour outside of Memphis. He had bought a small farm and it was a bit bohemian. The farm work soon became tiresome, and he put his wife and son inside a mobile home until he had built a log house on the property.

The upshot of Martha's sister's marriage was that she hated everything about it, including her husband. About midway through the fifth year, she left one day with a professional shooter with an English sporting arms company who had been touring the states as a shootist from Great Britain. The hunting professional was featured at the National Field Trials at nearby Ames Plantation when he stayed with the couple as a guest for two weeks. He was rugged and rather dapper and certainly continental for rural Tennessee. He had this movie-quality West Country accent that made women fawn and think of the lauded actor Oliver Reed with his unfamiliar international brand of heightened masculinity.

Martha's sister left her toddler son with a black maid while her husband was on a trip to Georgia to pick up new black Labrador dogs for obedience training. She left a hand-written note in her Episcopal girl's school cursive that explained little about her departure. It was perhaps two paragraphs long.

After the incident, and the gossip that obviously followed, her mother Carolyn's drinking escalated until it veered completely out of control, and the already twisted way she saw the world became even more grotesque.

The family owned a lake house outside La Grange, and her parents often stayed there over the weekends after Memorial Day. The property had a man-made lake of thirty acres that had been created for three friendly couples who were sophisticated and accomplished people that attended the same Episcopal church. It was rustic and comfortable.

By this time, we were accepted as we were, though it was never spoken of in mixed company much like her sister's hasty marital absence, but they were much relieved when we were married that next summer.

I would fish at sunset in a Sears aluminum runabout by myself, and if I was lucky, we would fry the catch with hush puppies and enjoy the warm southern night. Her father and mother were always kind to me, and honestly there was little I disliked about them as people. Their personality quirks were the same as others I known and usually acceptable. They never criticized me in front of their daughter or others, and they behaved with far more decorum than had ever been seen in my own coal town family.

I, of course, heard all the civil war stories her father told of his own family and learned in time that his grandfather had been returned to Columbus wounded after Shiloh pretty much losing use of his right arm. Less than a year later however as Grant's column was marching through Columbus he became enraged. He had found his own father's ancient pistol and stood in the middle of the road aiming it at the blue Federal column. Grant's soldiers were ready to shoot but one of the officers had called out that it was a crippled boy and a mounted rider quickly knocked the gun out of his hand from horseback. A squad then collected the teenager and forcibly returned him to his home.

They were never particularly wealthy or landed people in this reconstructed South, and his sister Lulu married a handsome local civil engineer whom some said was a Klansman. Later after I had met the uncle that description seemed greatly far-fetched. He was a gentle and generous man who was quick with a joke on himself as he appeared rather clumsy and impractical.

I found work with the Memphis mayor's office. Since I had been a journalist, he made me one of three assistants, all of whom who were relatively young men from families he had known. Martha's father happened to be one of them. Lee Garrett had also been a friend of the present mayor but something untoward had happened between them, and now they were distant antagonists.

21

Lee had influence he could use to make life difficult for the mayor though for some reason he held back. Perhaps the time wasn't quite right to strike at him, or the circumstances hadn't yet presented themselves clearly.

After two weeks with the mayor, there had been a police shooting in South Memphis where a black man had been killed by white police officers in some type of standoff at a convenience store. The police had been summoned by the store owner who was white. He told them two men inside the store had behaved suspiciously and that he believed that they were planning to rob him. When the officers arrived at the scene, supposedly a shot had been fired at them from the store doorway. One officer subsequently opened fire, killing a black man with his gun. His companion was unarmed. It had been the third police shooting that year where white officers had shot and killed black men, some of whom were unarmed.

After the second police shooting, a task force from the Justice Department had been sent to Memphis to investigate. They first met with the chief of police and the officers involved inside the Mayor's office to discuss the preliminary findings which pointed to what some called 'cowboy tactics' among the police.

The mayor himself was a lawyer who had earlier been a two-term city councilman but had no criminal justice background. Wyeth was simply a sharp business lawyer and successful local politician with no other agenda.

The mayor's meeting with the Justice Department lawyers was cordial. Although a tacit threat may have been made in the conference room that this unwarranted police incident was never to be repeated, no actual charges were issued against the officers. In fact, this would be the last chance for the Memphis city government officials to stay free of Bobby Kennedy's lieutenants and for Wyeth to hold onto his ambition for higher office.

One of the Justice Department lawyers who was from Atlanta stopped Wyeth in the hallway to tell him point blank that the Johnson Administration could make an example of a segregated southern city with a black disadvantaged minority population, and Memphis might be that city. They would send a large disruptive army of federal marshals if anything else happened with the city police. The mayor clearly understood that this was his last chance for civic order.

I would see Rusty from time to time, and we managed to have a rib dinner one evening at the Rendezvous downtown across from the Peabody. He was still living out at Garrett's horse farm and working with the polo ponies, but he said that Lee was becoming stranger and stranger. Lee had a Yale degree in philosophy and had found his way into the family business though he also had invested in outside companies with his own capital along with other partners. Most of them fit neatly into the Wharton Business School and Wall Street mode: tailored, sharp and abrasively intelligent, and all focused with little ambition beyond amassing millions. But this last bunch Rusty had noticed were far rougher, and it was hard to fathom what Lee found in common with them, or where their capital had come from. He had talked to one of these men who had watched him while he was breaking green horses. This man dressed and behaved like some mafia thug and looked at everyone with a menacing face.

Rusty had been perplexed with Lee though not for long. A truly sybaritic man rarely given to introspection on almost any front, horses, women and drugs consumed Rusty's present and seemingly future interests.

Chapter 3
Wedding

Since Martha knew Lee's mother Anne, she hosted a pre-wedding party at the farm and it was a quintessentially lovely event. I had never been around such casual opulence before. We ate at linen covered tables on the house terrace looking across the resplendent green lawn that stretched with bluegrass for eight acres. As we sat there with our cold chicken and walnut salad, we watched a herd of polo ponies shining in the sunlight as they slowly worked their way nearer the house.

Mrs. Garrett acted like the patrician woman she was, and fortunately Martha's mother had only drunk the light white wine that was served at the tables.

Lee showed up for only a minute on his way to the barn or somewhere else. He had been charming to Martha and her parents, and wished us well before turning on his heel. Even Rusty appeared and made some pleasant though long-winded toast before sitting down and attacking his chicken hungrily.

Looking at Carolyn, I caught her once or twice furtively looking around to see if anyone was staring at her and perhaps whispering about the abandonment of her grandson.

As long as I have known Carolyn, I don't think she was ever able to get past that incident without almost complete mortification. Her own family were unschooled and poor dirt farmers. She herself had not only been educated but her husband became this successful striver and had distinguished himself in important legal corridors. They dined regularly with prominent people, and she was close friends with a woman from one of the former city boss's extended family. Carolyn had been one of a dozen women who had been invited to Albert Gore's summer barbecue in Franklin while accompanying a Federal judge and his wife who drove. Everyone there with the Washington crowd assumed that she had gone to school on the East Coast, and she never corrected them. That single incident may have been why she insisted on sending Martha to Smith, where now she might share the same laurels as her mother.

On most days, Carolyn was easy to like. You could see inside that she was a genuine and kind woman who, as a child had a pet goat she couldn't kill. She had won the county spelling bee competition at fourteen, and had more blue ribbons for prize chickens and blueberry jam than had ever been seen around rural Fulton, Kentucky.

When her two brothers went off to work in the General Motors factories in Detroit, she packed her bobby socks and went off to lectures on Shakespeare and Donne on the quad at Ole Miss, and her fresh innocent beauty turned more than a few heads.

That's how I always saw Carolyn and the nasty drunkenness on occasion had never altered the picture. She was flawed and frightened and didn't know what she was capable of doing to herself and to her daughters.

Her husband understood I think, though he was powerless to help rid her of those awful recurrent demons. He had his own demons to grapple with, and they lasted a lifetime. They were children from this bleeding South, and they were good and caring people.

Alfred wasn't a racist, or unchristian either. To him, everyone occupied a certain place they had been given, or earned, in life and that is where they would remain. Carolyn thought she deserved more, or maybe in truth, she believed that she didn't even deserve what she had been given. That's what I think happened to her. She was harboring guilt that she was a horrible fraud. It troubled her for her entire life, even from her first success at that one room Kentucky school. Or, perhaps, it was taught to her by her own mother.

By the time Martha became of school age, they could afford to send her to a prestigious private academy in the city. She rubbed shoulders with the other privileged girls from families who had also prospered. It was almost as if it had always been that way and few ever suggested otherwise.

They might never become a part of Lee Garrett's tight little society because you had to be born into it. Apparently even marriage wasn't good enough as Lee's sister Sharon had demonstrated with a line of completely unsuitable husbands. Lee's mother could hardly welcome a battered Argentine boxer who had been imprisoned for twenty years for beating another man to death for accidentally spilling a beer on his coat sleeve. What could she say or do if she didn't even speak Spanish?

Martha, horses, clubs, and second homes came with all the veneer her family sought in order to legitimize themselves, and that they had never really been those people who did without. The French have a word for those, they call them parvenus, albeit with some typical Gallic disdain.

It's ironic, as I remember, that Alfred had his law firm's only black clients. They were three or four men who had achieved prominence in their community through a chain of funeral homes, barbecue restaurants, or used car lots. They were the generation that trusted only whites to know whatever essential truth was needed to be known. They instinctively believed that an honest white man would save them from grave danger with other white men, and they were right. His integrity was unquestioned by them and these men led the black community on the most fundamental levels in this river city. Those black firebrands had the attention of the young and restless with promises of change. These other older men understood what must be done to live in this unreconstructed South, and the best among them had turned to Alfred.

They didn't eat with him at his club nor have cocktails with Carolyn on the terrace of a summer's evening, yet they sat in his office laughing and doing business together in his conference room like the moneyed white men. They trusted him with their lives.

The racial divide was a mystery to me since I had grown up in a coal town where none of this black and white past existed, and since infancy I had never seen a single black person's face except for television. It was a mining town of mostly Slavic working class people, many of whom had immigrated there to mine before the Twenties.

After Vietnam I had followed a friend farther South who had been a tight end for Tennessee in the years of its championship teams. In those university years, I had a few black casual student friends from classes, and I don't think we did anything together beyond coffee at the student commons café. But I liked the South though, and afterward had drifted to New Orleans which offered more opportunity and had less of a restrictive Bible Belt atmosphere.

Race didn't mean much to me, really. And there was one light-skinned black woman, an art major, who would talk with me at length about writing and the arts, and sometimes draw psychedelic figures on my blue jeans while we would laugh about it. We were mostly friends. Gretchen was a fine figurative painter and she'd lived in this small studio apartment above the windy Tennessee River about fifteen minutes from the lawns and Georgian-style buildings of the older section of the campus people called Rocky Top.

I do remember an afternoon at the café where she had left the table with only the two of us sitting there. She had gone to the restroom while her drawing supplies were spread everywhere across the table. She returned sobbing uncontrollably then sat down and buried her head inside her folded arms. I waited for a moment raising her head with my extended hand and asked her what had happened.

At length she stopped the crying, and told me when she was washing her hands at the bathroom sink, two other black girls had accosted her calling her, "A honky-loving bitch." Both had started to viciously slap her face, and as she collapsed on the floor they had stormed out of the bathroom door.

I had been shocked at the brutal attack, and in my ignorance I had assumed that every black loved each other, which of course was absurd, and honestly it probably wasn't what I really thought. That single unpleasant incident was the sum total of exposure on any personal level that I had with blacks beyond the military where the two races tended to separate from each other by choice. They would behave in this rather tribal manner before being summoned to the common fight against the enemy which naturally changed everything quickly.

The young black woman and I became more as we shared intimacy but we kept it hidden, at least, I did. I think she preferred that too, although she hadn't actually said anything. For both of us, this was the first time we had ever crossed the color line. Although she had claimed some obscure strain of Native American blood, I knew that was a line she made up, perhaps trying to become something more exotic than she already was. We never talked about race in those few months when I would steal to her studio apartment some dark nights. It became a forbidden secret, and we worked hard even to keep it away from the liberals who usually surrounded us. Gretchen, perhaps, enjoyed the otherness this affair with a white man gave her. During the two years I had known her well, I never saw her around other blacks, not once, and perhaps by choice.

If she had any siblings she never brought them up in conversation, and I only knew that she had her mother and stepfather living somewhere outside of Knoxville. She said this unasked after sharing a cigarette, or the occasional joint. I never pressed her for more, because I simply didn't want to know. I wanted the distance.

Only once did she ever ask about my own past and about the coal town where I grew up. I told her bits and pieces of that ordinary working class existence. She showed little interest.

Gretchen drew me nude several times, and said that when she touched my skin it was the color and texture of silk, and often stroked my drowsing brow. It became a bizarre game with the two of us, and we embraced what we saw as a looming danger, although, this was a hundred-year-old university town in the end of the 1960s, not some southern backwater. Knowing this furtive romance, or maybe momentary liaison wouldn't be accepted, this edginess pushed me to continue with her.

She asked little of me beyond those nights together, and I offered her nothing more. Was being with a white man enough excitement for this pleasant and attractive young caramel colored woman? Maybe. We existed in a self-imposed racial-tinged dilemma, and hardly questioned the manner and deceit we practiced. What would happen if she became pregnant? I sometimes worried though dismissed that particular fear with the thought that we would do the obvious as others had inside some Knoxville clinic. She took the pill anyway. At the end, I believed Gretchen belonged with someone with the same skin color and black culture. She might have disagreed with that conclusion, I don't know, though she never let on. We never talked about it, ever, instead we existed within our own bubble.

I never repeated this crossing of the racial barrier again, even in New Orleans where it had become rather commonplace, at least throughout the French Quarter. It had always been a bohemian sort of place, with two hundred years of what the more critical among its citizens had referred to as matter of fact, wanton race mixing or miscegenation making any such marriage illegal.

No one knew of those nights that I had spent with Gretchen. I kept that part of my past from even the closest friends I had in those years, and maybe mistakenly I assumed Gretchen had done the same. A few years later, someone had told me in passing that she had gotten a master's in painting at RISD, and started to teach at Emory in Atlanta. Whether or not she had acquired a black or white companion or husband I never learned.

By the time I had joined the Memphis city government these thoughts were lost in the distant past, and there would be no point in revisiting them. With Martha, I had become part of an entirely different and somewhat more gentile world compared to my own working class upbringing, though it still had the taste and feel of the earlier segregated south.

The first return of Martha's sister from England, ostensibly to see her toddler son, had her mother, Carolyn, near apoplectic with shame and a thinly veiled anger resulting in increased sarcasm whenever she spoke of it.

29

Her drinking escalated. Before long, she had started in the mornings after Alfred had left for his downtown law office. By noon, or certainly during the afternoon, she wasn't a pretty sight, and she'd already had two fender benders in shopping center parking lots three days in a row.

Initially, Martha's sister, Carrie, had wanted to stay with her parents in the large midtown home, and her mother had grudgingly agreed. By the second evening there had been ugly arguing at the dinner table and Carrie went to stay with high school friends who had remained in the city after college.

Carrie's ex-husband had demanded that she surrender her passport to him if she wished to see their son. He said he would return it to her the day she planned to leave. Everything about the visit was acrimonious, and there had already been a claim that he had pushed her down inside her house for some unknown reason.

Alfred took it all in his stride and had arranged to lunch with Carrie at the Summit Club on the days she hadn't driven out to her ex-husband's farm to be with her child. Their first meeting was obviously cold, mostly on Carrie's part. She tried to explain to her father exactly what the circumstances were that had forced her to desert her husband and child. He had listened quietly with his usual lawyerly rapt attention. When she had finished speaking, he simply added, "I think I understand why you did what you did," clearing his throat and taking a deep drink from his water glass.

"He controlled everything in our lives. Everything," she went on almost breathlessly, "and I came to loathe him."

Her father shook his head for her to continue, indicating he understood.

"After a time, I wouldn't let him touch me, for any reason," Carrie said.

"Couldn't you talk to him about this?" Alfred asked.

With that remark, she answered him with a raised deepened voice and he lifted his hand into the air for her to calm down, after all, they were surrounded by men and women they both knew.

She leaned over the table now and started to talk in a whisper, "He turned my stomach so much I wanted to throw up. I came to hate everything he did, his footsteps, his voice, and most of all his fucking dog smell. He wasn't the handsome man people here think he is, from some fine family. He was a fucking monster."

"You could have separated from him, taken the child, and then in time, divorced. That's what would've been the rational step. Yet you didn't see it that way."

Both of them had hardly touched their lunches, and a concerned waiter came to the table and asked Alfred if something was wrong with the food. Alfred only smiled and shook his head to dismiss that concern, and the waiter left them alone again.

Carrie's finger had nervously started to circle the rim of her water glass, and she didn't speak for what seemed like several very painful moments.

"This man Ian was my way out of that awful marriage and this damn place, and I took it," she said angrily. "I never wanted to see that fucking house trailer again, or that half-built log house I never wanted anyway."

Her father kept his demeanor and offered his daughter the weakest of smiles, saying, "Well, I would have done it differently had it been me."

"But it wasn't you," she hissed back.

Alfred sighed softly and told her, "You're quite right, it's not my place to live your life, or judge you. It's been more difficult for your mother. She finds what you did hard to understand, and accept. But she'll come around, you must give her more time, that's all."

"She's a drunk, daddy, and she's got no right to criticize me."

The waiter returned to the table and Alfred took a cursory bite from the scallops on his plate, and the waiter disappeared.

Carrie's father added that if she now divorced, it would be thorny to sue for custody of her son in court. The opposition would readily charge her with abandonment.

"He can have Charles as far as I'm concerned," she said without rancor.

"Honey, you don't mean that," Alfred responded, incredulous.

"You still don't get it, do you?" she said, "I knew what I was doing when I walked out that screen door, and I wasn't going to look back."

"But as a mother you'll want to watch Charles grow, to guide him, teach him the values he'll need to find his way through life," Alfred pleaded.

"You already have your answer, father, whether you like it, or not."

Alfred couldn't accept his daughter's hastiness and he reached across to touch her hand, but everything he'd said had fallen on deaf ears, his point by point logic had already been refuted even before he'd opened his mouth.

Removing his hand, Carrie stood and told him she must leave though they would meet again before she'd return to England.

"Please come and see your mother," he beseeched her, "anytime, alright?"

Carrie said, "I don't think I can," and with this she left the high rise office restaurant dining room to a few tables of lowered eyes.

The waiter was now near Alfred, and he leaned down toward him, asking if he might bring him something from the bar. The question seemed to come from his genuine concern for Alfred and what he had witnessed at the table.

"Why yes, Harold, I think I'd like a small whiskey if you don't mind," Alfred said with a pained smile, knowing this situation with his daughter would seek its own level as these things often do.

During the next few days, no one saw Carrie, and on the fourth day Martha called me and asked me to join her and her sister for dinner. Carrie had wanted to eat at Justine's, the town's best restaurant, and we all met in their courtyard garden where she already had a table.

"Oh, the mystery man," she said to me extending her small hand, and laughed loudly as her sister did, honest and unconcerned.

"Well, I imagine you've already heard the worst, and most of it's true, I'm sure," she said with a smile. She favored Martha in the face but she had inherited more of Carolyn's youthful beauty with higher cheekbones, and although short in stature, had more of a model's chiseled features.

"You already know I had an unpleasant lunch with Alfred, and only now can I bring myself to sit down with mother and listen to her drunken sobbing."

Martha added, "The sooner, the better. Get it over with, and do what you're going to do."

"Let's order first, I want the escargot," Carrie said, and snickered.

"Oh right," her sister immediately chimed in, "you're so European."

In another instant, a man had come to the table to greet Carrie and kissed her on the cheek and asked her to come over to say hello to those near the courtyard wall, but she refused and waved to everybody instead.

She was coquettish, and it was comfortable for her, unlike Martha who was far too serious and perhaps uncomfortable in the shadow of her prettier sister.

Carrie was a decent dinner conversationalist. She had the acumen to ask me some friendly questions about myself as we talked, and toward the end of the dinner I came away liking her. She was a good pianist, I had heard, though she admitted herself that to strive for concert performance quality was beyond her abilities. Carrie was content to play well, and teach with those natural talents.

At some point during the dinner, she had tried to explain her abrupt departure from the marriage and of course leaving the child in the hands of a black maid and her husband. Her argument was that it was impossible for me to understand the dominance men in the South exerted over women: wives, mothers and sisters. You had to be a woman to understand what they routinely took from you, without quarter, or your consent, she explained. Carrie painted this particular husband as a man no worse than many of his own contemporaries, wealthy or impoverished, who had an inbred misogynist character.

"He refused to allow me to even have a credit card, and gave me a ridiculous handful of cash each week, doling it out to me as if I were the child and he knew better. That's the great tragedy in all of this," she lamented to me.

The farm and the rural life had been a lark at first, she added, but she was stuck there, day after day in that tin trailer, supposedly cooking these elaborate meals, and watching television at night while darning his socks.

That seemed an exaggeration at the time to me, and it probably had been. Her husband had attended private schools all his life, and had a university education in mathematics. Playing the so-called roughshod farmer role seemed ludicrous as she described it under the candlelight.

My takeaway from the evening's conversation was simply that the marriage had failed as many before it had, and many afterward would, nothing more. What was the point of demonizing this man whom I had never met, and I came to believe that Carrie's expectations perhaps were to blame, planted unwillingly long ago in her mind by her mother's fantasy?

The dinner wasn't acrimonious in any way, really, nor was it boring. I found the blond and blue-eyed woman across the table from me both attractive and engaging and couldn't picture her as malicious. Naturally I wasn't married to her nor had anything to judge her against save my own intuition.

Martha would forever interrupt her stories, and they would laugh about people and places I had no knowledge of as sisters might, and you could sense that they were close. They saw their parents as flawed people, particularly Carolyn, even before her alcoholism had surfaced. They accepted it all while loving those two people greatly.

Toward the end of the evening, Carrie announced that she had filed for divorce. Although there might be a rather harsh courtroom drama, she expected it to occur within the next year. When it did happen, she planned to move ahead and marry the British hunter as quickly as possible.

I asked her to tell me more about Ian, the British professional hunter, and the estate where he had a cottage and served as gamekeeper and marketing director for an ancient firearms manufacturer. He had spent some years leading safaris in Kenya, Uganda, and even inside socialist Tanzania. Ian had grown up on a British farm where his father had led shooting parties for the landed gentry around them, and he had simply followed in his father's footsteps.

Within the next few days, there were confrontations between Carrie and her husband and he threatened to never let her see the boy again. It was a predictable reaction from a man who had felt deceived. He had angrily informed her that she could only see the child if she left the paramour across the Atlantic. She had agreed since the hunter didn't want to be caught up in the awful recriminations. He himself had two children from an earlier marriage, and saw little of them though they were nearby. It was a common enough outcome I supposed.

I would see Carrie once more before she returned to the Surrey dales, and the three of us met again at the university club where the daughters were still junior members. We drank lemonades watching some friends of the two play doubles on the red clay courts.

Carrie continued to explain to me in more detail than I wanted as to why she had left her husband and her son. What could I do but listen patiently? I figured that she needed some sort of ally outside of her incestuous circle in Memphis who might possibly exonerate her, and perhaps I did.

In the middle of a prolonged silence while watching the players on the court, she turned to me and said, "Maybe I just tired of him."

"It happens," was all I could think of to say to her.

"I was engaged to someone before, and he broke it off," she continued. "For half a year, I staggered around the campus in the daze and music was the only pleasure in my miserable life. But no one in this fucking place would understand that."

I smiled at her reassuringly. "People are too quick to judge. They project things that's all, and time heals."

"They can get vile. My mother's one."

The only thing that had cast this lasting veil of shame over Carrie was the abandonment of her son. That's what stuck in people's craws and made them quick to condemn her, particularly women. Later, a woman I came to know whose husband was wealthy had said to me at some holiday buffet table, "She didn't think it through."

By that remark, I had assumed that if she had simply moved out with the child, or asked the husband to leave, then the whole thing would've been more acceptable to the polite society surrounding them.

No one that I ever talked to about the failed marriage suggested that she fell in love so deeply with this British hunter that her heart allowed her no other choice but to leave. There was a crying baby boy in the black maid's arms as she left with her small suitcase, clutching a plane ticket to Heathrow. That alone damned her in many eyes, and the expected viciousness of tongues would certainly follow. Carolyn, herself, would never recover from her daughter's untoward behavior. Her drinking escalated until her husband had finally come to realize there was little or nothing he could do to stop it. His solution was to pretend it didn't exist, a task at which he was singularly unsuccessful. So he, himself, drank more.

For years they had drunk socially as most upper middle class families did during the prosperous Fifties. Throughout the Middle South every holiday buffet had an even larger bar attached. Almost everyone that I had known was a frequent whiskey drinker as it was the times.

I learned almost nothing more about the hunter except that his appearance and manner were 'dashing,' and that the attraction had been immediate for the two. During this whole time, Martha was usually silent and if she hadn't approved of her sister's actions, she didn't let on to me or even to Carrie, though her sarcasm sometimes found its ugly way into the conversations. It was subtle yet the stinging remark was clearly meant to hurt.

Carrie left us courtside to visit someone else she knew in a different part of the city. When she was out of earshot, Martha said in her flat lawyer voice, "I can't wait until she's on the plane and I can finally breathe."

She asked the waitress to bring us another pitcher of lemonade, and continued to discuss how embarrassing and truly exhausting Carrie's first visit had been for the family.

"It's this scarlet letter thing with her here. Wherever she goes, as soon as she's out of the room people start shaking their heads and talking about her."

I responded: "Look, it's the newness of it, that's all. Give it another year, and nobody's going to care. They'll forget the whole thing."

Martha told me I really didn't understand Memphis. These people were tribal, clan-oriented, and though they might be 'cocktail Catholics'. They would never forgive abandoning a child. That went too deep and flew in the face of their beliefs.

In another day Carrie was at the Atlanta airport on the evening flight to England, and the subject was closed for the moment.

She did visit Carolyn the evening before she left. She sat there listening to a conversation that completely ignored what she had done, and was purposely steered carefully by Alfred's able charm. Predictably her mother had been drunk, and maybe she had forgotten some of the sordid details of the abandonment because she talked about the upcoming cotton carnival and mentioned Martha's legal successes. Carrie always knew she was the prettier of the two sisters and that was enough for her.

Chapter 4
Wyeth

The mayor called a staff meeting and the three assistants sat around the conference table as he assigned duties for the next quarter. He particularly desired to avoid any additional friction with Federal authorities and wanted one of his staff to be part of the internal police investigation on the recent shooting.

Two of the assistants were lawyers, but he named me as the police conduit, mostly because of my recent military experience. He believed I could better understand the cop mentality than the others and that they would come to trust me quicker. I joked with him that during college I had been a security guard at a Target department store and after a week they had asked me to leave because I let the teenage shoplifters escape. I threatened to call their parents if they continued this unsavory life. The story evoked a round of polite laughter from the lawyerly staff.

"This last shooting was worse than the earlier one. The motive for the police response was damn pathetic," Wyeth said, "and no one saw a gun until the guy was already dead on the floor."

The mayor reached inside his suit coat pocket and pulled out a pack of cigarettes, lighting one, blowing the smoke into the air as he reached across the shiny table for an ashtray. Immediately one of the two lawyers started to cough, and the mayor looked across at him with furrowed brow, saying, "You're going to start that again?"

The lawyer gave him a false smile and moved the sheets of paper in front of him once or twice with suppressed annoyance.

"Maybe we could add a few more black cops. That way it looks less like the whites are targeting Negroes," I offered to the room.

"Blacks, they want to be called blacks," the lawyer with the cigarette smoke aversion suggested in his pedantic manner.

"OK, we add more black cops. That's got to show the Feds we're with them on this," I said, believing it offered the appearance of an example of better civic control. "Maybe it's enough to keep them out of our hair."

Wyeth cleared his throat and spoke, "Not the solution."

"How many black cops do we have?" the other less smarmy lawyer asked.

The mayor took another long drag on his cigarette and blew the smoke in small circles above his head.

"I don't know exactly, but I'm guessing four out of two thousand officers or in that range, low," the mayor concluded.

"Hire more then," I said, confident it might show commitment to balance in the city.

"Not so easy." Wyeth continued, "The police union puts up too many obstacles and the captains running the police academy don't want black faces."

"It's time to force them to comply," the confident lawyer announced with a knowing grin.

"Let me tell you something, Percy," the mayor warned, his lips tightening. "If the mayor of any city loses the confidence of the police force, they're screwed."

He shook his head twice at what he considered a route of absolute suicide for a politician. The consternation forced him to light another cigarette.

"Look, if I lose the confidence of these cops, and they tell the newspapers and TV stations that I won't let them protect people from crime, I might as well go home because I'm finished as mayor."

He leaned over now with an extended arm and pointed his finger at the assistant who made the suggestion.

"This is a divided town, but the whites run it, and if I look like I'm giving away the store to the coloreds to keep them quiet that'll sink me even faster," Wyeth concluded.

"I understand," the young lawyer said, though unconvincingly.

"Maybe if you had stayed in Hartford..." Wyeth noted, and was corrected by Percy who said with some irony, "New Haven."

40

The mayor's voice deepened, "Wherever the hell it was, I don't care, but I've lived here my entire life, and I know what happens in Memphis."

The upshot from the discussion was that the mayor's office would do the paperwork to formally request the addition of more black officers to remain in compliance with Federal statues from the Johnson Administration. We wouldn't try to force their hand and demand specific quotas in the police ranks. My responsibility would be to work closer with the city police department, and through negotiation and trust, move them toward more racial openness.

The mayor had used the word 'openness' in the meeting and none of the three of us in the room had any earthly idea of how conclusive it might become. We finished and the mayor asked me to remain for some reason.

"I hear you and Martha are getting married," he added smilingly. "That's wonderful. Her father and I started at the same time, and sometimes on the opposite sides of the issue, but he's such a fine man. Carolyn, well, she's Carolyn."

I thanked him for his well wishes, and asked him how he saw the rift with the police department being repaired, his gut-feelings on moving forward.

"I know one police lieutenant that frightens me," he said quietly examining his hand as he spoke. "He's the worst kind of racist, violent, and would probably shoot some black in cold blood who'd accidentally stepped on his shoes."

"Are many cops like him?" I asked unsure of what he'd tell me.

He let out a prolonged sigh. "You know; it's been the curse of history. There are probably more like him than I'd want to admit."

Martha had told me about the separate water fountains in the city parks, and of course the public schools had been segregated until only a few years ago. Busing school children seemed like a pervasive reason for hate and violence. They were

41

the maids and gardeners and the demarcation of the 'haves and have-nots' was racially inscribed as it had been for many years.

Men, such as Alfred and Wyeth, had never feared any encroachment of blacks in their privileged lives. They had been insulated by their wealth, education, and the institutions of forced separation which had been erected long before they were born.

With that, we started to walk down the long hall toward his office and he changed the subject for a moment.

"I heard Carrie was back in town. How is she? She was in my daughter's class at St. Mary's and was always over at the house. I hope she knows what she's doing." After that, he disappeared into his office and I could hear him laughing with his secretary in the anteroom.

Later that week I met with the director of internal affairs for the city police department. He must've been the showpiece for the face of the modern cops. The man appeared overly affable and immaculately groomed in his tailored police blues and shining lieutenant bars. He had completed a degree at the state university in criminal justice, or was about to. He continually used the prefix mister, or sir, with me during the brief interview.

His answers about the last two police shootings were minutely detailed and seemed aimed to please from a public perspective. Under his smiling façade, there lay a reservoir of utter seriousness.

He produced a diagram of the crime scene of the last South Memphis shooting and took me slowly through the police response, pointing to various areas in the convenience store parking lot and the calculated movement of the officers involved.

Finally, we had gotten to the initial black man who had been shot in the convenience store doorway. The lieutenant stated that when the police had fired they had noticed the man behind him was in the process of passing the assailant a pistol. These were the circumstances causing the police to react with equal force: a preemptive move before their own lives would be placed in jeopardy.

I looked closely at the diagrams and listened carefully to his description of that afternoon before speaking.

"Did the police officers speak at all to this man, provide him some opportunity to surrender, hand over this weapon, and turn himself over to them?" I asked him gauging the emotionless look on his institutional face.

He was a confident police official and well prepared to thwart an attack on the department integrity and nodded knowingly expecting that question.

The lieutenant put both his palms flat on his desk, and began his explanation of the shooting events. "That was not possible. The man had already turned with the transferred gun in his hand. He had begun to swing his torso around to fire. There was no other choice given the officers but to do what they did and offer offensive fire to the obvious attack."

Listening to what he was telling me, I began to open my briefcase and removed a manila file with the other surviving assailant's statement.

I told the lieutenant the other black man claimed that he had a gun on him. That was true, but only for defense in his neighborhood from gangs. He had never handed it to the man who was shot. The man claimed the handgun had remained tucked in his pants when the officers had shot his friend, then they threw him to the ground. An officer had removed that pistol and said later that it had been pulled by his friend when it hadn't been. This was the essence of his statement.

The lieutenant remained unflustered and smiled at me. "Forensics disputes that conclusion. Both men's fingerprints covered the weapon. As I said, the first officer who fired saw the man clearly bring the gun upward into a firing position when he discharged his own weapon. It was an obvious case of self-defense."

There was an instant of silence, and I further questioned some of this explanation, but not with anger or with the benefit of knowledge that might refute his explanation, though I did question the certainty of this incident report.

His answer to me was painfully terse: "This city's streets would be strewn with the bodies of officers if every patrol man waited for an assailant to fire first."

I did finally cross the line with him and asked, "Do you think the shootings, the deaths of the alleged assailants, are racially-motivated? White policemen are shooting black men."

Holding his demeanor closely in check, the lieutenant looked at me with an unforgiving gaze, though, his face remained unchanged.

"You'll forgive me, but you're not from this city, are you?"

I shook my head, no, and he took a deep breath before continuing.

"You have a mistaken opinion about race in this city. There are several black officers on our city force, and I number them among my colleagues and friends as do others. We have community outreach programs, and the black-and-white respect in this city rivals New York, or Chicago, and certainly Los Angeles. I suggest you visit Atlanta, and come back to talk with me about racial unrest."

I let his opinion stand, since it made little sense to press him further. I informed him that the mayor wished to have a closer working relationship between his administration and the city police and welcomed any recommendations he might have.

The speech I gave him earlier was useless. The lieutenant referred me to the department public relations office that was headed by a middle-aged woman who had formerly written obituaries, or maybe wedding announcements, for the afternoon newspaper and couldn't break through the blue brotherhood.

The only possible route to make any real progress in closing this racial violence chasm was for Wyeth to exert pressure with the top police officials. To do that, he needed well thought out initiatives before making those calls.

There was something ominous about that police lieutenant that troubled me afterward. I had mentioned this strange feeling to Martha who had dismissed it as not understanding the people in this town.

"Look, you didn't grow up in the South, and you don't get the subtleties," she told me after coming back to the apartment following an exhausting day.

"Did your office get any fallout from the police shootings?" I pressed.

"No. Why would we?" she responded by putting her briefcase on the table by the door. She was wearing a white linen jacket and green skirt with her medium heels.

"I hate this uniform," she yelled from the bedroom. "Why don't they let us wear fucking pants like the men? It's not fair, dammit."

She went into the small kitchen and started mixing drinks for us. She asked me what I said, but I told her it wasn't important, though perhaps it was.

In another week, both the officers involved in the last shooting were exonerated by the department and they resumed their regular duties.

The assailant who had been shot had an unrecognized funeral at a storefront black Southside church. Things continued in the city as before.

In bed that night, I had started to ask Martha about the shootings again and she snapped at me that she had enough of these awful things during the day and told me to please 'hush' which was a favorite word of hers that seemed so archaic. It was Carolyn speaking actually, and you could hear it when Martha was calmed.

Carolyn remained almost the same in this constant stupor, or had gotten worse, it was difficult to fathom. Carrie's husband had filed for divorce which remained uncontested and he had been awarded custody of their son with limited visitation rights granted Carrie. There was no financial settlement for her since whatever her husband had inherited from his heiress mother had been always shielded in irrevocable trusts from the day of their marriage. Also, the cause of divorce had been legally declared as abandonment, and she was vilified in the courts. But it seemed Carrie didn't care, she was happy to be rid of the whole saga.

The wedding with Martha had been set for the middle of June, and even after the premature party at the Garrett farm, Martha's family had waited until Carrie's controversy had subsided.

Chapter 5
Amanda

Martha and I were married on a Saturday morning in Holy Communion Episcopal Church by the Right Reverend Howard Green who had made me attend some absurd classes on Christian matrimony in the church commons room since I had been raised a Baptist. They were half hour sessions of harmless conversations about scripture and the nurturing of children. Frankly, I think he did it for the company during mid-week.

It was a large wedding, which was Carolyn's doing, and the headcount was two hundred people, of whom I knew maybe three: my mother and sister, and one university friend from Chattanooga who was in medical school in Memphis.

Tradition called for a formal black tie dinner beforehand at either some club, or at Justine's. We selected, or rather Carolyn did, actually, Justine's where I first met Carrie.

There were fifty or sixty people at the dinner, none of which were Carolyn's or Alfred's working class family from rural Kentucky or Mississippi. They consisted mostly of their more acceptable society friends from Memphis and a surrounding plantation or two.

It was a genteel rehearsal dinner by those exacting standards, and a few rousing toasts were made by Alfred's contemporaries. The ladies dressed in summer fashion. There were no outrageous drunks there, except perhaps for Carolyn, though Alfred kept a close watch on her liquor consumption.

In truth, I was the one who had far too much to drink and found myself embracing or being embraced by Martha's cousin, Amanda, who drove into town from Ole Miss for the ceremony. Fortunately, that spontaneous coupling had only lasted ten minutes in the foyer of her parent's home. It was empty at the time, as Carolyn and Alfred had decamped to their lake house. I had been asked to drop her off for the night as everyone went on to another house.

Well, the ten minutes was a lie. It had lasted much longer. Amanda had taken me to the guest bedroom and disrobed. She was a wonderful tall dark-haired woman with the whitest skin, and she begged me to make love to her. And I did, with or without regret, I can't remember now. It was almost a flash, and so vague.

I remember standing at the window looking out on the street while she was talking to me from the bed, and then finally joined me at the window.

"I think people only want the people they're meant to have, and I knew immediately that we'd be together," she said, and I remained silent as the vestiges of sobriety began to return.

"Amanda, I'm marrying your cousin this Saturday for god's sakes," I exclaimed. "What the hell are we doing?"

"We're doing what we're meant to do," she said.

"Martha can't know this," I blurted, now fully conscious of what had occurred.

"It will destroy everything, my God."

Amanda kissed me hard on the mouth, moved toward her clothes and started dressing slowly. Putting her bra on, she remarked, "Relax, Martha will never know this, ever. Trust me."

"Oh Jesus," I said, distracted and numb with my behavior.

"C'mon, get dressed quickly. They'll be expecting you before long," and she handed me the white dinner jacket. "Now go."

This wasn't the last I would see of Amanda but it wouldn't be for a while. She did, however, come into our lives later under other strange circumstances.

Martha and I took a two-day trip to the Homestead in Hot Springs after the wedding ceremony and were back at work that following Wednesday. We thought nothing of month long European trips and preferred to continue as we had been.

The next time I saw Amanda, she was staying with us with her doctor fiancé on a summer night, and everyone got roaring drunk. She wanted all of us to go swimming nude at midnight in the duck pond at Audubon Park. She said we could easily elude the watchman who sat inside a building watching television.

All of us, three couples, crept into the sanctuary and stripped naked then dove into the pond of water lilies and white scum. We kept our voices low yet splashed around like raucous children, except for the somber Martha. She wouldn't be seen nude in public. "It's childish," she pronounced, and sat on the bank with her folded arms.

As we were drying off, Amanda came over to me and whispered, "I only did this to see you again, like that night," and she started giggling.

"What's the big joke? Me, the prude, right?" Martha cried out in the sultry Delta night air. You could see her pouty lips in the moonlight.

They left the next morning after breakfast, and Amanda told me we would see more of each other. She promised me this, though the next time I saw her was at her wedding to the doctor in Nashville.

The mayor won a second term based on his promises of coalition building. He did attempt to bring more blacks into city government despite the resistance from the city council. His promise had attracted the most vocal and radical of the black leaders, and the polarity seemed to worsen.

Carrie made a second visit to Memphis. This time she was mostly ignored as cannon fodder by the self-righteous matrons who had spurned her the previous year, and honestly, she had become old news to many.

I don't think she was welcome at the summer garden parties we attended, except for her closest school friends like Wyeth's daughter, Angela. Angela had gotten married the year before, two months behind us at Holy Communion.

Carrie didn't care. Her life was now in Great Britain and there were no children involved either. She had married the British hunter that past winter and only Alfred attended the small country wedding. Carolyn was supposedly too ill to attempt overseas travel, and she was sick, of course. She had become a bad drunk.

Carolyn had completely regressed since the abandonment and divorce, lost in her own alcoholism. She had Buster's Liquors delivered to her door during the week, so she would be unobserved with the clanging whiskey bottles. Twice a week a black man in his green and white van would pull into the house driveway with a cardboard box full of Dewar's and bad-tasting gin.

Carrie was almost a memory. Earlier, there had been a shouting match between Carrie and her ex-husband at the University club dining room and he had uttered some truly ugly things.

She had walked over to his table and passed it making some insulting remark that had him knocking his chair over and shouting across the room at her. I'm told the whole incident was rather sordid and was relieved that I had missed it.

By this juncture, Carrie's former husband had been seeing someone else, a divorced woman whose father was a Navy doctor at the nearby Millington naval base. Though she wasn't really plain looking, she clearly wasn't the beauty Carrie was, and a little overweight. That may have been the upshot of the comment Carrie made as she strolled by him.

Carrie was entirely capable of being cruel without much encouragement. The woman her ex-husband had been seeing had a small child herself as well, and they had discussed combining the two families should they marry.

The friends Carrie had been meeting there decided to forgo the dinner at the club and went elsewhere for drinks and some cheap bar food. Martha was always rather defensive about her sister, and honestly even the most ridiculous and self-serving behavior was immediately forgiven, attributed to family. But she wasn't quite as generous toward her mother Carolyn.

It was around this time Amanda came back to town. Her doctor husband had relocated to Methodist Hospital and wanted to base his pediatric practice there.

They became regular dinner guests, and we all began to spend weekends at the lake house in the West Tennessee countryside. He was engaging and kind, and loved to barbecue in the summer so I turned the grill over to him with pleasure.

Amanda had been thinking about law school, and she would talk to Martha about it almost incessantly. It got to be a too-familiar subject.

"God Dammit," Martha said incensed one afternoon at the lake house, "either she goes or she doesn't. I don't want to hear about it anymore."

Although Amanda could be coquettish with me, we seemed to let that alone. Instead, she claimed she wanted to fish all the time and no one would take her, so she would regularly join me in the evening at the lake front motoring the bass boat around the perimeter. I had set her up with a rod and we shared the bait, or I would give her lures from the tackle box that everyone used. We went out maybe four times, and she made no mention of that earlier intimacy until the last.

One August afternoon as we were fishing, she brought it up. It came as a surprise, and she wouldn't let it go easily.

"The two of us should have an affair, while we're young and have the passion. Don't you agree?" Amanda whispered from the front of the boat as she cast her bait toward the lake spillway.

"You can't be serious, Amanda," I responded shocked. "That would be a recipe for disaster. It would ruin both of our marriages in a heartbeat."

"When you're ready," she said, her voice soft in the gentle breeze, "we'll do it then. I'm a patient woman, but I'm tired of fishing. Let's go back, alright?"

I bowed my head toward her, and added, "As you wish, madam," laughing and pushed the throttle full tilt toward the opposite shore.

Two weekends later when Martha and Randy, the doctor husband, had gone antiquing for two hours, she took her bikini bottom off behind the large wooden float in the middle of the lake. While hidden from view, we coupled like two mating sea

51

snakes. She had a venom I was certain would kill me quicker than a water moccasin, though for now I was the willing victim.

Amanda naturally had her own set of problems which had manifested themselves earlier and had come to a head during her early university years. She had gone to Auburn as a freshman. Toward the end of the first semester, she moved off campus to a community house of Jesus freaks and had become erratic in her class attendance. They made her witness for Christ on street corners and collect donations for the cause, which she had done willingly. Then at some point, perhaps fueled by drugs, she had this dream that she was the Virgin Mary pregnant with the Christ child. On one chilly afternoon, she got into her car, which had about half a tank of gas and started driving in a trance from Auburn toward Birmingham, which had become Bethlehem to her. She was dressed in shorts, flip flops, and a college t-shirt with no suitcase or overnight bag.

Amanda was driving on the Interstate nearing the outskirts of Birmingham when the car ran out of gas and she pulled onto the highway shoulder. Leaving the car on the grassy roadside, she started walking along the busy highway. By this time, the temperature had dropped and there were snow flurries in the air.

After maybe a half hour, a man noticed her walking and pulled over onto the shoulder, and asked her if he might help: call Triple A, or take her to a filling station where she could get roadside assistance. Amanda said no, she just wanted to get to Bethlehem. The man thought she had been mistaken, and corrected her, saying you mean Birmingham.

He was the grandfather of four and a Baptist deacon. He had no untoward thoughts except to help this young woman who was now in obvious distress.

"I'll take you to Birmingham," he said, and tried to have a pleasant conversation and started to tell her about his granddaughters who were in elementary school. Amanda made little conversation, adding nothing about her mission, and answered his questions with simple one or two word responses.

In twenty minutes they approached the first highway exits to Birmingham and the man asked her where she wanted him to stop in the city. She said the next exit would be fine, and as they approached the turn off, he continued to talk about his family.

Exiting the Interstate, he asked her where he should turn, and she told him to go left for a while, which he did. They had come to the outlying suburbs of Birmingham and streets of ranch-style homes could be seen from the access road and boulevard they had entered.

"Where should I stop?" he asked Amanda and she told him to turn right down a street named Dogwood Lane she had noticed.

In several moments, he inquired which house did she want to go to, and she pointed to a house with a brick and stucco front. The man pulled his car into the driveway and wished her a Merry and Blessed Christmas, and was soon gone, returning to the highway.

By now, it had started to snow hard and a cold wind was blowing as Amanda walked up to the front door of a house she had never seen before. She tried to open the front door that was locked so she walked around to the side kitchen door. She picked up a Welcome Mat and found a single silver house key. The key easily opened the side door and she entered a pretty blue tiled kitchen with a stainless steel refrigerator covered with photo magnets and Post-It notes.

She walked through the kitchen past the living room and down a narrow hallway where there were three bedrooms. She stopped at the first bedroom, which was decorated like a teenage girl's room with music posters and psychedelic art. She walked over to the double bed, pulled back the covers, kicked off her flip flops, then got into the bed and fell asleep within several minutes.

She slept soundly for almost three straight hours and had a deep fulfilling dream. In this hypnotic dream, Amanda was Mary, the ancient virgin mother, and was married to a bearded carpenter. However, it wasn't in the biblical Judah, but rather on the western side of Jackson in a rundown neighborhood. They had come to settle in the backroom of an abandoned gas station that she had remembered driving past with her father.

It had probably been built in the late Forties after the war and still had this large Mobil oil neon sign of a winged horse charging through the heavens. Even the four or five gas pumps at the station had these circular smoky glass tops with the marvelous steed, which she knew was the mythical Pegasus from Olympus. It had a stucco front which had reminded her of the Alamo in San Antonio where her parents had once taken her on a family vacation through the Southwest. Her engineer father had driven them to Los Alamos where he had been an apprentice engineer straight out of Mississippi State. He worked on the Manhattan Project and the atomic bomb. He had hoped to show them the rugged New Mexico sandstone landscape and wanted them to see the Alamo, so they spent a day and a night there before driving northwest.

It was in the back of a garage that Amanda rested on a makeshift bed of oil rags, a sort of service station manger, and had gone through awful labor pains. In the midst of it all, a bright light had come from the heavens, and the pain ceased, then within the next minute a new baby boy came into the world.

There were several men and a few women who surrounded her and the swaddling newborn, which she had called Jesus because she liked the name. Someone had suggested it to her on that long journey to this modern Bethlehem.

The people that were admiring the child Jesus had come from Memphis and Little Rock and even as far away as Amman, a city she once studied in a survey course on contemporary world history in high school. They brought gifts of clothes, toys, and essential oil with which to anoint the child, and kneeled in front of the manger with adoration. They were dressed in long robes of fine silks and satins with gold piping on the sleeves.

The dream was so vivid that Amanda could hear the street traffic outside and even noticed a fried chicken restaurant directly across the street. When she awoke, there was a well-dressed woman standing in the bedroom doorway staring at her. She was a middle aged woman with dark hair like Amanda's, and was dressed in a skirt and blouse with a small tailored jacket which matched the color of the skirt. She had kind eyes, and was holding a soft leather briefcase in her arms while she stood rigid in the bedroom doorway.

Realizing that Amanda had awoken, the woman asked, "Who are you, and why are you here in my daughter's bedroom?"

The woman asked the questions in a calm voice, waiting for Amanda's answer to explain all this as she leaned casually against the wooden door jam.

The woman offered to bring Amanda a hot cup of tea and asked, "What's your name?"

Amanda answered her as she would anyone. The woman slowly directed the conversation to where Amanda had been earlier that day and where she lived before she came here to Birmingham. The woman was a psychologist and knew this young girl in her house was troubled, maybe even delusional, but didn't represent any sort of threat. Perhaps she had taken drugs, and had wandered aimlessly around the suburban neighborhood, completely disoriented to her whereabouts.

Amanda told her about her classes at Auburn, her friends on campus, and also about her boyfriend who had been almost a saint in her eyes. She explained how he had introduced her to his wonderful spiritual friends, and the holy sanctuary they had created in this rundown house a mile from the campus.

The psychologist encouraged her to talk, and said she liked conversation herself, really, and so Amanda became more garrulous.

Sitting up in bed, Amanda had looked intently at the woman, and said, "I'm here in Bethlehem to have the baby Jesus. He'll come on Christmas Eve. What's the date today?"

The first reaction of this woman had been surprise, rather than shock, at the strange story, and she paused for a moment looking closely at the girl's face to determine if she were perhaps dangerous in some odd way.

Not seeing that sign of aggression in Amanda's eyes, she moved from the doorway and sat on the bed.

"Amanda, tell me about where you grew up?" the woman pressed forward, hoping to learn more.

Almost with suppressed glee, Amanda told the psychologist about her large stone house that was quite lovely, and down the block from Millsaps College where her mother had been a student once. She said that when she was a small girl, they would take walks across that leafy campus surrounded by magnolia trees and elms. Her mother would tell her what it was like when she was twenty and would rush to class in bobby socks and saddle shoes.

The woman asked more about Amanda's parents, and Amanda told her everything about them, including the fact that her father had an engineering company that built roads.

In the rambling conversation, Amanda didn't make the connection between that former Jackson, Mississippi life and the Immaculate Conception. Yet the woman continued to engage her in this friendly and innocuous banter, moving closer to the head of her daughter's bed where she now calmly sat.

Fortunately for Amanda, this woman was a Birmingham therapist with a large family practice and had long experience working with troubled adolescents, so there was no need to involve the police. She took the necessary steps to defuse the seemingly unhealthy situation, and began by listening closely to everything Amanda told her, without interrupting which was a skill she had mastered many years before as an adolescent psychologist.

"The baby should be born in a manger," Amanda told the woman, but added, "I don't know where to find one, do you?"

The psychologist told her to just relax in bed, she was going to make them both some hot tea, and she would return in a few minutes. Amanda had passively agreed, and laid back with her head on the fluffy lace pillow, closing her eyes for a moment.

Inside the kitchen, the woman dialed Jackson telephone information and called her father's office that was luckily in his

56

name. A secretary answered his line, and the psychologist explained that this was an emergency concerning his daughter. In an instant, he was on the other end in near panic.

"Don't worry," the woman told him, "she's alright. She's in no immediate danger, and I'll be with her until you arrive. There's no point in involving anyone else."

The psychologist identified herself as a professional and said that Amanda was safe in her home where she would remain. She briefly explained what she had learned about the strange presence. He said that he would immediately drive to Birmingham, and if she could keep Amanda there at the house he would be at the front door in maybe four hours at most. He thanked her profusely for her concern and kindness.

After that incident, Amanda began to see several psychiatrists and was diagnosed as having a mild narcissistic neurosis that had been exaggerated by the same recreation drug usage that plagued many college-age adults. After six months' outpatient care at home in Jackson, she transferred to Ole Miss, and finished her degree in liberal arts with the promise of law school in the future.

That hidden side of Amanda was dangerous, and that innate wildness, or irrational behavior, mercifully had been dormant. Everyone considered her as an intelligent and charming young woman who would fit easily into polite southern society as a doctor's wife, or a mother who may even enter the law.

I don't remember who told me about the eerie Bethlehem incident, though the whole tale had left me absolutely speechless at the time. Abortions, drunkenness, or even unruly behavior, I could obliquely understand, but giving birth to the Christ child in Birmingham was too other worldly.

Amanda was statuesque with a classic Hellenic face, and in a summer print dress at cotton carnival parties, she could turn most men's heads, even those few decrepit grandfathers. I never met anyone who didn't like Amanda the moment they saw her, as she had this uncanny ability to light up an entire room with her wide smile.

Maybe I should mention that the men were the ones who universally liked her. The women were divided, particularly the younger ones who seemed to harbor some unspoken resentment or even slight envy at her fresh siren beauty and the insouciance she demonstrated with most people.

All this past behavior somehow explained what she had done on the wedding rehearsal night where we been alone for an hour and a half. But it didn't excuse my complicity.

Chapter 6
Born again

This last police shooting inquiry didn't end with my conversation with the lieutenant at Internal Affairs. There was something else that had kept the investigation alive requiring further study.

The convenience store owner was an older white man who had come to Memphis some thirty years ago from rural Mississippi. During the past few years, he had become a born-again evangelical. He called the precinct desk sergeant three weeks after the event, and said he wanted to come in to add more to the statement that he had given the investigating officers since it troubled his conscience. When he had finally met with several investigators, he gave them a story slightly different from what had been officially reported.

The man said that the two black men had been in the store for ten minutes looking around and not buying anything. It worried him and he called the police. Although they made him uncomfortable loitering, they had not threatened him. He was cautious and watched their every movement in the store. He happened to notice a pistol tucked into the one man's pants through a loose sport coat vent that allowed him to catch a quick glimpse of the gunmetal shine.

The same man bought a six pack of beer as well as a quart of milk and the store owner put them into a large plastic shopping bag with handles. The man then gave the bag to the other black man to carry. Both men had then started towards the door to leave. As they saw the two police officers exit their cruiser while unfastening the leather straps on their side holsters, the black man with the gun handed it to the other. He looked like he was about to put it into the shopping bag to possibly hide it. As the second black man was about to turn around in the open glass doorway to drop the gun in the bag, the first officer opened fire. The man dropped to the sidewalk in front of the store.

The convenience store owner claimed to have seen it all. The man with the gun had not turned around but was shot with his back half-turned about to drop the pistol into the bag with the beer and milk. It was a confusing testimony, though it suggested that the police officer perhaps had acted in undue haste. The killing might have been avoided with an arrest for carrying an illegal firearm and no one dead.

The police investigation now had entered another dimension and the store owner's testimony would need to be further examined, this time by another set of officers who would treat it as new evidence. When the word of the store owner's appearance at the precinct and his additional testimony reached the mayor's office, Wyeth was the first to know.

When he walked into his office, Wyeth had swung his leather chair around and gazed at the view of the Mississippi River and the grey metal Arkansas bridge from his window. I entered and as I spoke to him he remained with his back to me.

"This shooting is a helluva mess," he stated then quickly spun around to face me poker-faced.

"You need to go revisit your lieutenant friend at Internal Affairs, and tell him point blank that the mayor's concerned." he ordered. "I want a copy of the store owner's last statement on my desk today. Let's see exactly what he said and not someone else's interpretation."

I let out a deep breath, and nodded that it would be done forthwith. Wyeth lit a cigarette from the pack on his desk, and quickly inhaled the tobacco smoke deep within his lungs before a loud exhale.

"This is serious shit. Now the blacks have something to really scream about, and they'll get some outside radicals in, stirring up trouble."

I sat down in the chair facing his desk, sorting out my thoughts before speaking, "Wyeth, it may be that the store owner was wrong. Maybe the guy with the gun was passing it on for the other to shoot the cops. Maybe he was this known gang executioner."

He answered with anger in his voice: "Even if that's true, there's going to be trouble. The Feds are looking for something so they can send fifty marshals down here, and take over this goddamn town."

That evening, as Martha and I relaxed on the balcony at Kimbrough Towers overlooking the green park and the zoo, I asked her if her office had heard anything about the police shooting. With her feet up on the porch railing sipping a gin and tonic, she said: "That clown Ralph Warren called the office. He thunders into the telephone to Jim that's he's the voice of blacks and they want justice. He ranted on and on about police brutality. Jim sat there unmoved on the telephone and listened patiently until he finished, assuring him that the district attorney would conduct its own investigation into the shooting. So that needs to be done, starting tomorrow."

"Will you do it?" I asked, and moved some of her dirty blond hair from in front of her wire-rimmed glasses.

"I doubt it. I'm the last one hired in that office, the token woman," she matter-of-factly stated. "Jim is smart. He'll do it himself, at least to determine if it needs to go further."

"So they'll do something now?"

"Well, duh, naturally," she said spinning around with wide eyes, and playfully punching my extended arm. She stood to lean against the wrought iron railing.

"Jim will get someone else to do the grunt work, to see if it holds water."

Apparently the conversation was over because she quickly changed the subject. "I'm sick of this apartment. Let's get some bungalow in Midtown cheap and fix it up. We can keep it for a few years until we see some decent place we like."

"With three white columns like your parent's, right?"

"Maybe later, darling."

Shaking my head, I remarked, "I'm not the handiest guy around, you know. But I'll try. Good idea, counselor."

"I could ask Daddy to lend us the down payment, maybe five or eight grand. He would be happy to help. It would give him satisfaction after the Carrie stuff."

I kissed her forehead gently and we moved into the living room for the evening.

The shooting had all the twists and turns that you would expect, and Warren appeared on television claiming the Memphis police were whitewashing the investigation. In a moment of absolute hubris, he claimed both men were unarmed but corrected himself to say that an unused gun had been found at the crime scene.

Television reporters had found the store owner, and he made the TV news with his country drawl and sincerity as he sought to be a good Christian man. He began and ended each interview by declaring his faith, and told the ABC affiliate anchor that God came to him in dreams, leading him on the righteous path.

For a month, it became a media circus until it gradually died down and was relegated to the back pages of the newspapers or sometimes into a column.

The simple fact that a gun had been in someone's hand at the time of the shooting obviously made it advantageous to the police account. These men were not unarmed, and they both had prior convictions for petty theft and a string of other minor offenses. Their records suggested that they weren't model Memphians.

The assailant's handgun found at the crime scene had been loaded. Both of these men were known black gang members who were suspected of other violent acts probably including narcotics trafficking.

As Martha had explained to me several times, the illegal pistol was in someone's hand at the time of the shooting. Legally it would have been assumed that one of these men intended to use it to injure, or kill those officers.

The second set of Internal Affairs officers who investigated the case after the store owner's subsequent testimony had been added, and found that the officers had acted responsibly. It was a case of self-defense against an armed assailant who would do them great bodily harm with that gun.

Any local firestorm that had been started by the more vocal leaders in the black community had been quelled by the careful examination of this case by two groups of investigating police officers, and the district attorney's office. There were no charges leveled against these officers and no bill of indictment would be issued. Therefore, the case would be closed.

When the maelstrom had disappeared, Wyeth breathed a sigh of relief, and then lunched with the police commissioner who had agreed that they would add three or four black police officers to the force. They would recruit them for the next academy class within the next two-months. The mayor had dodged a silver bullet on this, and his administration had been left scandal-free, which was more than the beleaguered mayor of Atlanta might claim.

At the end of this term, Wyeth would be fifty-seven years old, and it might be the right time to throw his hat into the ring for governor. He had been chairman of the city council and a two-term mayor of Tennessee's largest city with enough national exposure to take the plunge. It wasn't easy running a southern city where blacks were half the population. He was a taciturn man and not overly ambitious, but he rather enjoyed being this big fish in an otherwise small pond.

There was a subsequent visit from one Justice department official to review the shooting, though there was little in the testimony that could lead him to intervene on the government's part. He was young and disappointed. He was one of Johnson's eager Justice staffers from Massachusetts, or maybe Vermont, who saw this region as an unreconstructed and evil domain.

Martha's boss, James Latham, took all of this chaos in his serene stride. He came from a prominent local legacy of state and federal judges. One of his late uncles had served as a cabinet lawyer for Truman until he tired of the capitol and the rampant hypocrisy. James was an old man in his seventies but had these clear blue eyes that looked through you if he caught a lie like some kind of laser beam. He had been married to the youngest sister of the last Memphis United States Senator, Randall McClure, though she had died young. They had a daughter (or was it a granddaughter?) who often rode with Martha on weekends.

For a time, things calmed down although Johnson's War on Poverty had targeted Memphis as one of the worst cities with widespread poverty and hunger. The best they could do was open two or three federal Community Action Agencies, and staff them with the more politicized blacks. They, in turn, would direct federal grant monies to these community groups, some of which were the neighborhood street gangs. It was a purely political endeavor to sustain the Democratic black vote throughout the south, and there seemed to be little succor that came out of it.

These gangs weren't as large or as well-armed and violent as Detroit, or Chicago's Blackstone Rangers. Yet they terrorized small black business owners for protection money, or simply sold drugs out of their vehicles in school parking lots. Every week there would be at least three or four fatalities from gunfire in some beleaguered South Memphis projects. Except for the occasional burglary or carjacking along Central Avenue, most of the violent crimes were black on black, and despite this problem, there were only six black cops out of a force of two thousand.

Martha and I found a small house on Overton Place, on what one of her friends called the poor man's side of the country club. True to form, Alfred lent her the five thousand dollars for a down payment. We moved in with a new golden retriever puppy.

As I calculated, Martha made about the same as I did in salary, although we were always broke because she funneled anything disposable that we had to boarding the horse she bought five years ago, and naturally, the veterinarian's large bills. A seeming healthy animal when she bought it, the horse now had developed arthritis in its knees that required cortisone shots in its legs if she attempted to ride it more than once a week for an hour.

Thinking it would help our togetherness as a couple, she arranged for me to take riding lessons. So on Saturday mornings, for maybe six months, I rode an older school horse round and round an indoor ring to the hushed snickers of ten year-old girls who were experienced enough to jump bareback.

At the end of those riding lessons in the fall, Martha had arranged to have me follow the mounted fox hunt she rejoined with a friend who put me on one of his Tennessee Walkers that had a comfortable rocking chair gait. It was a marvelous feeling to be outside in the frosty countryside cantering slowly after ten galloping horses chasing that wily Reynard. By late morning, the hunt was over and everyone had dismounted at the small clubhouse for coffee and a light breakfast.

It was doubtful that I would ever master a gallop quite enough to be invited to join the hunt, though the few times I followed the jumpers and the small pack of hounds, I enjoyed myself. It was a glorious side of life that I obviously missed as a child.

Martha would continue to ride each fall with the club until she became pregnant. All the money that we spent on horses and their paraphernalia could have purchased a rather nice new automobile. But it kept her balanced and underneath all that supposed aplomb, there was a lot of Carolyn's madness that percolated near the surface.

Like Carolyn, she could never be wrong in the smallest thing. Then, if she were found out, she denied it vehemently. That behavior came to her unfettered from her mother, as well as the same alcohol gene, as she would abuse the bottle given half a chance. Martha was intelligent and a damn good lawyer, but it wouldn't last, the career. I could already see that. In her southern women's deepest soul, she had wanted to quit work, and have the identical life that was her mother's, though, without the consternation. That was what Martha really wanted.

Carrie had planned a third visit back to Memphis, though this time she would show off the handsome international big game hunter that she had married, much to the envy of her women friends and schoolmates. Ian would have lunch at the university club and possibly show his manly physique on the tennis court where he could clearly hold his own against any decent opponents. Carolyn no doubt would be mortified, and start drinking even more than she usually did, which was the case, and Alfred would smile his disingenuous smile as always, making his empty compliments to the ladies.

When Carrie arrived in town, they had the good sense to stay at the Peabody Hotel. They met the family later, us included, for a brunch at the tennis club on a sunny spring day. Ian was continentally cordial, and he deferred to Carolyn which was a nice gesture, and in a word, kind.

After Carrie had taken the time to introduce the couple to Ian, who rose and showed some gentility, people started to visit the table. Soon afterward, her ex-husband walked into the dining room with the chunky doctor's daughter who was now his wife, and ignored us. Her former husband chose instead to have his brunch courtside, and they turned their backs to the large picture windows fronting the inside diners.

Martha had been the first one to see them enter the room, and she had leaned over squeezing my hand, saying, "Good God, look at this."

Carrie had already seen him and had simply shrugged her shoulders then quickly turned to Martha sitting on her left. "Maybe he'd be happy to see our old house guest again. What do you think, Sis?"

I could see Martha's face blanch, and she lowered her head. I heard her say to Carrie, "Please, that's cruel, why make this thing any worse than it is?"

Carrie let out a loud guffaw, and Ian turned toward her momentarily moving his attention away from Alfred who had been telling him an inhumanly long story of some uninteresting subject.

"Don't worry, little miss perfect, I won't do anything to embarrass you," Carrie spit out like a spoiled teenager and the so-called pleasant table conversation continued as before.

Several couples in the club dining room familiar with this family history seemed to trade furtive glances from the court back to our table and Carrie. It was the price I imagined of being part of this incestuous southern society. Just as we were about to exit the dining room, Carrie ran back to the nearest picture window to the courtside dining and started to bang on it with her fist until her ex-husband turned around. She waved at his scowling face and scampered toward us as we waited in the club foyer.

Perhaps there was something diabolical about Carrie, I don't know. It seemed that it was so easy for her to be hurtful, almost like it was second nature. I began to wonder how much a part her ex-husband's supposed excess control had played in the marriage failure.

The rest of the visit mercifully had less drama, and Carrie drove out to the country to spend an hour with her son, bringing him gifts that British male children might like. The new wife had seen a reason to spend the afternoon in town with her own little girl at the zoo. Carrie's ex-husband stayed outside busying himself with his dogs in the kennel until the hour was up, and later trudged back to send this woman on her way. Only the barest of conversation was ever made, however, nothing concerning the child's welfare, or his needs were discussed.

For a brief evening, the two couples sat in Carolyn and Alfred's living room and spoke mostly about Ian's birthplace and the English countryside. He had brought Carolyn a cardigan sweater that the smart set among British landed gentry tended to wear, and she appeared thrilled with the gift.

I asked him several questions about hunting in Africa. He had answered them cheerfully, painting a rich picture of the flora and fauna he'd experienced that he longed to return to. Alfred brought him the shotguns that had been passed down by his Mississippi civil war grandfather, and Ian examined them carefully praising the craftsmanship of the barrel and stock.

"It's a dying art," he offered in summary, the life of a gamekeeper and professional hunter, given way to television shows with none of the romance.

"Honestly, I think the only place that I want to live now might be the outback of Australia." Ian added, "There are places half the size of Tennessee where only a handful of farms exist, and you're pretty much on your own."

"That'll be our next move," Carrie chirped and put her head on his shoulder, and that terminated the evening.

On the short drive home, Martha was silent except for saying, "I'm so relieved she's leaving tomorrow."

The whole controversy that Carrie had created by leaving her husband and son for another man became of almost no import to anyone who had known her. Her absence on another continent made it even more foreign. It was not dissimilar from having some relative in a distant state you hadn't seen but twice in ten or twenty years. Then they suddenly die and only on rare occasions when family members might remember does it ever get discussed.

Carrie's ex-husband abandoned his dog training business not long after the tennis club debacle, and entered real estate sales in the city. His mother, who had the family money, had died and he inherited a princely sum from her. Eventually he opened a handful of his own sales offices that all ended up doing quite well. The man gradually softened his approach in dealing with Carrie. When his son had reached his sixteenth birthday, he at last allowed him to travel alone to England to see his mother, and it happened without incident.

Carolyn continued to carry the burden of shame from the way the marriage ended, and increased her drinking. It was sad to watch her. I remember one week when she had the flu and had stayed in bed except to steal down to the kitchen to drink several bottles of vanilla extract for the briefest of alcohol rushes. The addiction had probably been part of her family history and I think her father was an excessive drinker prone to rages with the mother and children. But who's to recognize where these things come from? There are many roads to Rome, and most likely as many or more paths to alcoholism. This would be an ugly end for an otherwise elegant woman.

Amanda and Randy were frequent guests at the small Overland Place bungalow because they had moved nearby to the other side of the country club golf course. We were neighbors of a sort. The other side of the green was known as the rich man's side because the houses were generally three times as large with a long driveway from the street. They had settled into a pleasant brick five-bedroom home on Cherry, financed by both Randy's impressive medical paycheck and financial help from his comfortable father.

Friday evenings, we would entertain them which was basically returning the favor since Amanda had seemed to initiate dinners and backyard barbecues. After the third one, Martha though it would be a good idea to invite others beyond her cousin so we would have eight people over for most of these festive evenings. When Amanda invited us to dinner, it was always only the four of us.

As this moved into the summer months, we extended it to the lake house that Carolyn and Alfred were visiting less and less as her drinking escalated. She also had trouble walking some days. Typically, Amanda and Randy would stay for a Friday night and sometimes on Saturdays but his hospital schedule often changed that plan. Sometimes Amanda would drive the hour to the lake house herself.

That didn't seem to bother Martha who had always liked her female first cousin as 'goofy' as she might be, as Martha sometimes bluntly put it. They were bucolic days and nights. We'd do our requisite fishing spin around the lake at dusk without Martha who hated to fish, or even eat the fried creatures as she called them. One of those evenings when Amanda and I were in the boat, Amanda returned to her long ago comment about us again, and I had only laughed.

"Forget that," I scolded her, "those are things in the distant past, let's keep that hidden, OK?"

"No," I won't," she responded, "because it's not over, mister."

"Amanda, you're scaring me now," I volunteered.

It was her turn to laugh, and she did so loudly as she moved her hand through the placid lake water floating off the far bank.

In a moment, I started the engine and swung the boat to the eastern corner of the lake and slowly moved it in a small brush covered bayou.

"Look, it's silly to talk like this," I said to her exasperated, "You've got a doctor husband and a lovely home, and no worries. Are you crazy? Why on earth would you risk that, that…?" and thought escaped me.

She crossed her arms and turned around in the bow and moved her head from side to side and touched the water with her hand again, putting some of the liquid on her flush face under the straw hat she wore.

"I do what I want, and that's what I want, for now," she said, announcing we ought to go back to the house because she had tired of fishing.

As we left the bayou, I told her this craziness had to stop because it would blow up in both our faces. What I had done before with her I didn't regret, though things were different for the present, for both of us. We weren't children anymore.

"You watch what happens," she turned around saying and threw a fish rag at me as we moved quickly across the middle of the lake toward home.

In another hour, I started the grill and we barbecued hamburgers that we brought. Martha had prepared a simple lettuce salad as well as a potato salad to go with the summer meal. I had caught some fish earlier but put them in the refrigerator to gut later in the evening on the dock where I had a night light.

We had the meal on the side porch and Martha talked about horses and the law, both topics that didn't interest me much. Amanda rambled on about Randy's younger brother who had left Trinity University in San Antonio after he'd been caught with amphetamines in the residential hall. Randy's parents were torn about whether to send him to some halfway house program for a possible addiction, or attempt to treat him at home. Randy's father had contacted several of his psychiatrist friends and they in turn recommended that he first try to reincorporate him into family life at home. Randy himself wanted his brother in an outside rehabilitation program, away from his parents, and that had been his initial response when his father consulted him.

Amanda offered no real solution to her brother-in-law's emotional problem considering her own history, and there certainly was no mention of her pilgrimage to Bethlehem. She was merely reporting something that was going on in their lives.

We had been sitting outside at a picnic table. The sky had started to darken as we continued to talk, and at one point I could feel Amanda's bare toes touch me under the table, rubbing up and down my leg. I jumped up from the table, and announced that I'd better clean the fish before it was too late, and we could freeze them for later.

It was dark now so I turned on the dock light and started to cut open the bass and fillet them. Since there were only two, it would take a matter of minutes, and I gave myself over to the task. After I had filleted one, and was washing off the flesh from a spigot at the dock, I noticed red painted toenails next to my hand as a bent down to turn off the water under the dock. As I looked up, I noticed Amanda smiling in the moonlight holding the fishing knife in her hand. She said with a girlish snicker, "I'm going to use this on you if you don't behave," and with that remark, dropped the knife on the dock and ran quickly to the house.

"Amanda, you can clean them next time, "I yelled at her as she disappeared through the basement door.

Chapter 7
Another Shooting

Wyeth called me at the lake place and said that he would like to see me if I could this weekend. Would I be able to come by his house in Chickasaw Gardens late on Sunday? We would all be back in Memphis by the late afternoon so I had agreed since it wouldn't inconvenience anyone. Martha always had legal briefs to look over from the office, a sort of never-ending string of investigations.

When I drove around the half-moon drive that faced Wyeth's Georgian southern colonial, his border collie greeted me as I stepped onto the porch with an unconvincing bark, and as I scratched her head, she began to move her tail in a clockwise sweep.

"Relax Sam," Wyeth called to the black and white dog from the doorway. I followed both of them into the sunroom on the eastside of the spacious house.

"The Justice department lawyer from Atlanta called me, and he said that they hadn't quite closed the police shooting case yet. It seems that there was some video footage taken in the store."

"What?" I answered, incredulous. "In a joint like that?"

Wyeth stretched his long legs and gave me a pained smile, saying, "It's a small franchise operation, with maybe twenty of these convenience marts in three southern states, and the franchise package includes a single camera aimed at the door."

"What you're telling me is that they have video footage of the shooting," I ventured to assume, barely hiding my shock.

"I don't know," he offered. "The footage goes electronically back to Biloxi, Mississippi, where the franchiser is headquartered and they archive it, or probably destroy it. The Justice agent I talked with wasn't sure. He'll talk with them tomorrow."

"Then we have the guy pulling the gun, or not, right there on tape," I said.

Wyeth nodded his head, and added, "And we'll know if the cop shot a man for probable cause. It'll be there for all to see. That could be a good thing, or not."

By the end of Monday, Wyeth was on the telephone with the Justice man in Atlanta, and he learned that they had some footage of the day in question. He had no idea of the quality, or what it demonstrated.

That night the Justice lawyer called again and said he had reviewed the film footage and the quality of the store and franchise surveillance system was so low quality and that all the figures appeared as dark unrecognizable shadows. They would need a closer forensic examination. Washington had hired a motion picture laboratory on a sub-contract basis in Chicago, the most advanced cinematic and video examination capabilities for this purpose. The company, Editel, also had film offices in New York and Los Angeles.

Wyeth said he and I would meet the Justice agent in Chicago at the film house offices to review the store video footage, and that the Memphis Police Commissioner would most probably want to join us.

We boarded a plane the next morning for Chicago and took a taxi from O'Hare to a warehouse office on West Madison in an industrial area where the company was located. Once inside, we were escorted to this small posh projection room with stuffed chairs resembling a private movie theatre. The Atlanta justice lawyer was already there, but the Police Commissioner had cancelled because of an emergency.

Once initial greetings were over, the Justice official asked the projectionist to run the tape. We would instruct him when to start and stop or go back over the frames. There were maybe two minutes of the deserted door scene which I could see before we noticed the two black men approaching it. But then the next action was so blurred and fast that nothing was recognizable until a police officer was in the open doorway with gun in hand.

We rewound the tape and stopped it as the men approached the store door and isolated a frame we wanted the projectionist to enlarge. That took him a minute or two and the three of us sat silently waiting for the isolated frame on the screen to be grossly enlarged. It now filled the entire screen and you could see the man at the door turn to the man behind him and receive what looked clearly like a handgun.

The projectionist enlarged the next three frames one by one and in the last frame shown the man had his hand wrapped around the pistol stock. The alleged assailant didn't signal that he planned to drop it into the bag he was holding. Rather the video frame which wasn't entirely in focus instead suggested that he was about to turn and fire the weapon.

In the dark I could see Wyeth drop his head backward in this demonstration of sheer relief, though in another second or two he was sitting erect and he appeared rather stoic. The Justice agent asked the projectionist to bring up the lights, and he turned to Wyeth with an unemotional face.

"It appears he intended to use the weapon in some fashion," the Atlanta lawyer said in interpretation of the frozen video frame, "and the argument could be made based on this footage that he would shoot those two police officers. Was it a robbery gone bad? Who knows?"

Wyeth was circumspect for a long moment, and he added, "For me at least, this footage shows enough cause to initiate a preemptive police response."

The agent laughed, and said, "Wyeth, I agree there was a weapon, though he never actually pointed it at the officer who fired."

Immediately the mayor made a half turn in the movie seat and turned to the Justice official, "This would get nowhere in any criminal court, and you can name the city yourself. Obviously that policeman didn't know for certain if the gun was loaded, or that the man planned to hide this gun in a shopping bag because he and his accomplice were fearful to have possession of an illegal firearm in violation of the Tennessee law. Maybe in truth, he handed this gun to the guy who was a better shooter. These men had long gang histories, for heaven's sake."

"You've made your point, and my recommendation will be that the incriminating footage shows a firearm with possible intent to use it."

As we left the warehouse film office, Wyeth asked me to walk the few blocks to Michigan Avenue where he wanted to get his wife a fancy silk scarf at Saks.

He was walking hurriedly toward the boulevard a few steps in front of me, and called back, "You can't imagine what favors this gift will buy me," and he howled at his own audacity.

Once in the cab on the way to the airport, he confessed, "That bastard wanted to hang us over the shooting. He was so goddamn anxious from the beginning. That prick kept this thing alive, not Washington."

For some strange reason, the eight months that I spent in Chu Lai had qualified me as Wyeth's eyes and ears of the city police department. He was incessant in assigning me as the liaison for the adversarial relationship he had come to have with them.

Wyeth loathed Frank Holston, the police commissioner who was a career officer, and would make unkind remarks about him in front of the mayoral staff. He simply didn't trust the man he claimed, and believed he'd been promoted to the highest level of incompetence.

Earlier that week, Holston had met alone with Wyeth. He told him that over the past month, there had been six burglaries of gun stores in the city and more than a hundred pistols and high-powered sporting rifles had been stolen. From the six robberies, they found one suspect, a young Southside black man, who had appeared to have been involved. After they had heard damning words from a police informer, they issued a warrant and searched his ramshackle cottage in a black neighborhood. The police had found six high powered rifles, two pistols and two hundred rounds of live ammunition without any evidence of legal ownership. There were no bills of sale nor did the man have a state license for any of the unregistered guns required by law. Upon closer examination, the firearm's serial numbers didn't match any of the Memphis burglaries, but instead were traced to three different Arkansas small towns which had reported sporting store break-ins the month before.

Holston became concerned this movement of firearms into Memphis was part of a larger conspiracy of a possible violent uprising by blacks against the whole white establishment. The guilty black man had been arrested on unlawful possession charges, and he was currently being held in the city detention center for further questioning. The commissioner had wanted the mayor present for the questioning hidden behind a false mirror, and Holston scheduled the interrogation for tomorrow afternoon.

Agreeing to attend, Wyeth had asked me to join him, and next afternoon we drove to the police detention center ten minutes away from city hall bordering on the Mississippi. We were seated in comfortable chairs facing the interrogation room, and we could see a small table and chairs through the two-way glass.

The police commissioner himself, and one detective entered the room and sat down. The door opened and two uniformed officers brought the suspect into the bleak room. He was physically seated by one of the officers, and his handcuffs were removed. The officer moved to the wall next to the door and maintained a position of observance facing the prisoner.

The first thing that was said came from the black man himself, and he denied that he had done anything wrong. Some guys that he had met in town had given him the guns to sell to his friends. He had a lot of friends who hunted, he claimed, and he was about to do that when the police broke into his home.

The detective corrected him, using his first name: "Lamar, we didn't break into your house, we had a warrant."

"Shit, that's the same thing, man," Lamar responded and started scratching the top of his head with one of his newly freed hands.

The detective ignored his remark, and opened a manila file he had on his desk, looking down momentarily at the pages before he spoke.

"The guns you had in your house were stolen from three sporting goods stores in Arkansas, Lamar," he said with a sinister smile. "How do you explain that?"

During this very early part of the conversation, the police commissioner looked blankly at the black suspect and said nothing.

The suspect started shaking his head back and forth, and let forth with a few expletives before he answered the question, saying, "Look man, I didn't know them guys, only met them one night on the street, and they lied to me, get it."

"OK, so you meet these men on the street some night, and they know right away that you're this wheeler-dealer who can sell the weapons to hunters you know. Is that your story?"

Lamar nodded his head, yeah.

The detective had started to laugh out loud, and slapped his hand on the table top. "Wait, wait," he interrupted. "Answer me this first. Do you have a license from anywhere since you know so much about deer hunting, huh?"

"No, man. I used to hunt a while ago, not anymore, I work too much," Lamar said unconvincingly to the detective.

"It's easy enough to check the records to see if you ever had any license. You must think we're stupid to believe this nonsense."

His voice changed in an instant, "Listen, you asshole, who gave you those guns? And who were you planning to shoot with them? The police?"

"Man, I wouldn't do that shit, are you crazy?" Lama said excitedly. "I'm stand-up, and go to work, that's all."

The commissioner spoke for the first time and his voice became sinister. "Lamar, we think you're lying. You're part of some bunch of radical niggers who want to kill people in this city, whites, and you got those weapons to arm your friends. You want to be cop killers, all of you, isn't that right?"

Holston had leaned forward in the chair as he said that, putting his hands on the table. Now he reclined in the chair and folded his arms to wait for the suspect's answer.

When the commissioner had said the word nigger, I flinched for an instant. It was the only time that I had heard some high public official use the demeaning term. Wyeth remained unmoved next to me as far as I could determine, and he had lit his ever present cigarette blowing smoke out of the side of his mouth in my direction probably without thinking.

"No sir. I'm law abiding." Lamar almost yelled now convinced that he might be beaten up by these officers for the associations, "I don't want to hurt nobody."

The detective again snickered, and looked at the second page of the dossier he had in front of him, and commented, "Well, it seems you have several convictions for assault, Lamar, and one of them involves a Memphis police officer. How do you explain that? It seems you got a violent nature, I'd say. You like to hurt people, huh?"

"No, no," he insisted. "Yeah, I got in some fights when I drank too much wine, now I don't drink none. I stay home and mind my own business."

Continuing the detective, added, "We're ready to do a deal with you, Lamar, so you don't spend the next ten years in jail, but you need to tell us who gave you those guns, then we can help you."

The black man let out a nervous laugh and then started to speak.

"I don't know their names, they wanted me to sell the rifles, and take my cut, that's it. They said come back to this bar with the money, they'd find me."

"That's a bullshit story," the commissioner interjected, and he told the officer leaning against the wall to take the suspect back to his jail cell.

Standing handcuffed, Lamar said, "That's what came down. I was just selling the stuff," and he was led away by the officer before he could add anything else.

Coming into the observation room alone, the commissioner greeted the mayor and me. "Well, you saw for yourself this man was lying. He knows more than he's told us. But this is the beginning of the interrogations, and we'll find out what he's up to. We may have a serious conspiracy to deal with and some black radicals. We should be prepared for that."

Wyeth thanked the commissioner for his vigilance and involving us in the investigation process, and asked Holston to keep him closely informed of what they might learn from this suspect and others.

Outside of the detention center on the way to my car, Wyeth shared that he feared Holston might be right about the threat of escalated racial violence. He said that from this moment on, I was assigned to this investigation on a full time basis. "It's you and the police. This has become a damn pressure-cooker."

Wyeth avoided using the word, conspiracy, though that's exactly what he meant, and from the brief police interrogation, I believed it might indeed be true.

Turning the circumstances of the questioning over and over in my mind, it had become a conundrum. This suspect was probably lying about how he had received these guns. It made no sense for street criminals to have this need for high velocity rifles, which could be used for possible assassinations with the assailants hidden three hundred yards away from his victim, or victims.

The Arkansas police had reported no arrests from these burglaries. Their only suspect had been released with a solid alibi, and the subsequent investigations had uncovered no new evidence. None of the guns had been recovered, except for those we had, and fifty or sixty other weapons were still missing.

I read over the Arkansas police report a half dozen times. The reluctant conclusion was that there were similarities with each of the burglaries. The detectives on the case said they believed these break-ins had been committed by the same individual. It suggested the possibility of a larger conspiracy theory. The whole thought that a black radical group had targeted Memphis for widespread random killings was unnerving.

Over the past week, I had discussed what I learned with Martha. Her response had been that the police were overreacting. It was probably rowdy blacks involved in larger scale gun sales, trying to make some big money. Blacks bought guns to rob and kill other blacks, and that constituted easily ninety percent of the violent crime in the city. The balance was these rednecks from Arkansas or Mississippi that got drunk and shot their uncle dead on the front porch, and that particular category of incestuous crime was rather common.

"Look," she explained as if I were a child, "I've lived here all my life, and I can assure you there's not going to be a black guerilla army taking to the streets, shooting bankers coming home from work downtown. That's paranoia. Holston is a racist idiot anyway."

"I wouldn't be so sure, Martha," I offered, "you didn't sit behind the mirror and hear the lies about getting those guns. What the suspect said was pure bullshit."

She laughed, "Honey, that's the way blacks talk. You get used to it. They're like children half the time."

"Right, some kid who carefully picks you off as you climb the courthouse steps. That kind of child."

She finished her drink and reached out for my empty glass. "You don't understand this place. The cops get anxious with the blacks. It happens sometimes, almost in cycles. One violent thing, and another right after then everyone worries about race riots, and a week later things return to normal."

"Martha, do you really think it's any different from Detroit, or Chicago?"

By this time, she was inside the kitchen and had opened the backdoor to the yard and called back, "Yes, I do, because it is. We understand each other here. It's not perfect but everybody's okay with it."

I couldn't entirely believe her explanation and didn't persist with the conversation, instead walking out into the yard up into the small gazebo we had erected for summer nights.

Within a week, the police commissioner had directed his white officers to increase patrols in the more notorious and violent black neighborhood in the city. One of the officers had noticed several cars parked in front of a bungalow with Illinois plates of which he had kept track. As he entered the plate numbers through the Illinois DMV database accessible to all US police departments, he had found that one of the license plates had come from a car reported as stolen two months earlier. The other had a registration canceled with the supposed destruction of the vehicle following an accident.

The Illinois car was stolen from a tree-lined residential street in the university Hyde Park neighborhood in Chicago late at night during a rainstorm. It was a burgundy two-door 1967 Oldsmobile hardtop sedan with a single owner and the subsequent complaint and cursory police investigation had turned up nothing.

Based on that reported information and concern about the transport of stolen vehicles across state lines, the Memphis police commissioner directed two police cruisers of armed officers to plan a subsequent assault on the house where the vehicles had been parked and where the suspects may be hidden. This police raid had been organized under the guise of probable illegal activities in their jurisdiction.

In reality, Holston had suspected this as the first real evidence of what he believed were outside militants entering the city to plan and execute an agenda of racially-motivated white slaughter, supplied with arms and black guerilla soldiers from other locations, all with prior agitator and revolutionary violence experience.

During the early hours of nightfall, Holston's officers surrounded the small home in which the living room was illuminated from a picture window fronting the quiet street. Standing on the dusty porch, the police officers could see four black men seated in the parlor and could hear voices and laughter coming from within. With a signal from the sergeant in charge of the operation, an officer kicked the front door open followed by the first group of three cops who entered the frame house with guns drawn, immediately shouting and confronting the men in the living room.

The cops in the first attack wave had pointed their weapons at the blacks, and the sergeant ordered these suspects to drop to their knees and put their hands on their heads. It was an order quickly followed, backed up by the threat of shooting them if they resisted. It was convincing to all the seated men in the room. The second wave of three more officers then entered and cuffed each man that was on the floor. They were then forced to stand and hastily questioned by the sergeant in charge to identify themselves as another officer removed their wallets.

One of the men's wallets contained an Illinois driver's license and listed the man's name as Bobby J. Rawlins. The other man was believed to be his associate and had no identification.

The sergeant spoke rapidly to Rawlins, and told him they would be charged with transporting and receiving stolen goods and taken to the main detention center for booking. Two blacks started to curse the officers, and complain about being framed when almost instantaneously, a nearby white policeman slapped his face hard telling him to shut his mouth. Rawlins didn't speak but stared hard at the sergeant with a look of menace on his face, his mouth frozen in rage as he was led out the front door.

Inside the detention center, the suspects were fingerprinted and photographed and finally locked together in a single large holding cell. Within the hour, Holston had arrived at the facility and after talking to the arresting sergeant, he had Rawlins brought alone to the interrogation room.

After a telephone call was made to the Chicago Police, it was discovered that this man, one Bobby J. Rawlins, was a known black separatist. He had been arrested on numerous occasions for inciting to possible riot, disorderly conduct, possessing illegal firearms, and perhaps just as many other unlisted misdemeanors. No charge, however, except for illegal firearms possession, had involved any jail time.

His Black Panther organization had also been politically affiliated with the massive Negro street gang, P. Blackstone Rangers. They themselves were responsible for frequent murders on the Chicago streets in the mostly black neighborhoods. The gang was largely funded through its narcotics trade, small business extortion money, and prostitution. There had been several violent crimes including the assassination of a police officer believed to have been committed by these Black Panthers, and a police assault on the suspects had left two of them dead in a recent city shootout.

To the Chicago police, the so-called neighborhood initiatives of the Black Panthers to supplement school lunches and open community centers for disadvantaged youths was a subterfuge for their true intent.

The real motive was to engage in a widespread American racial war pitting millions of urban Negroes first against white police and then to attack the general populace once the police were subdued. It was a frightening war in the making, despite their support by pacifist leftist organizations and even some church denominations who willingly donated money to this cause. The Episcopal Church was one.

The Panther headquarters in Oakland was a third world armed camp of hundreds of militants who had increasingly been involved in violent confrontations with local police, resulting in several shooting deaths. The Chicago branch of these so-called revolutionary Negroes was even more violent than California, considering their incestuous ties to the notorious street gangs which controlled large sections of that sprawling metropolis.

Holston filled the mayor in on the arrests after the fact, and surprisingly, he had invited Wyeth (that would also mean me) to the Rawlings questioning. We got there mid-morning and continued the same protocol as the last suspect. We stood behind the hidden mirror this time, and sipped coffees delivered by some staff cadet, who was passing through his two-month rotation during the probationary period until he became a full-fledged officer.

Rawlins was a towering handsome black man with a full Afro haircut and an attitude. He had silently taken his seat across from Holston and two other officers of whom one was a uniformed lieutenant and the other most probably a detective.

"Mister Rawlins," the detective began, "would you please tell us what you were doing with that stolen car, and why you were at that particular house?"

Rawlins simply guffawed, and he took a deep breath before saying, "You're holding me here illegally. I want to talk with a lawyer now."

"That may be possible, this conference with an attorney, but first we need you to answer some rather pressing questions we have," the detective continued. Holston remained silent, his stare focused upon the black man across the table.

"This is stupid harassment," Rawlins said with curled lips, "my lawyer will have me out of here today. It's my right in this stinking country as you should know, if you don't."

"Mister Rawlins, please answer the few questions we have, and we'll see what the next step is," offered the detective, and again Holston was mute.

"You're a resident of the city of Chicago, isn't that true?"

Rawlins gave this sarcastic laugh, saying, "Yeah."

"Also you were in the possession of a car stolen from that city, driving it we presume from Chicago to the Memphis address where it was found," the stocky detective stated. "You drove that stolen car from Chicago, didn't you?"

"Yeah," Rawlins hissed, "Someone sold it to me, but he had to get the title from his cousin. I didn't know it was stolen."

"You deny receiving stolen property?"

"Yeah."

The detective turned to the police commissioner and whispered something to him while opening a manila folder in his squat hand and pointing to the pages inside. The commissioner didn't answer, though he nodded for the officer to continue.

After the arrest of Rawlins and the others, two of the officers had remained at the crime scene, and thoroughly searched the bungalow finding no weapons. They had also checked the two Illinois cars, and forced open both trunks which contained spare tires and car jacks for repair.

"What was the purpose of your visit to Memphis, Mister Rawlins?" the detective continued, "Can you tell us that?"

"I was visiting some friends, old friends, when you kicked down the door," the suspect said. "You don't give a shit what you do to blacks, do you?"

"That's not true, Mister Rawlins. We treat all the citizens in this city the same," the detective threw back, his mouth slightly twisted. "In this particular situation, you were in possession of stolen property and perhaps you were the one who took that car off the Chicago street."

Rawlins erupted in loud laughter and shook his head back and forth. "I bought the car from a man I'd met, like ten thousand other cars are sold each damn day. This is an unlawful arrest, and false charges. It won't work, pigs," he threw out at the police sitting at the table, looking from one to the other.

"Who are you calling a pig, you thieving black bastard?" Holston said to Rawlins. "Watch your mouth."

"I don't have to talk with you crackers, so ask your stupid fucking questions all day. I have nothing to say," he added, and crossed his arms, leaning back in the chair.

"Rawlins, we'd like to work with you to clear up this misunderstanding," the calm detective continued pursuing his question strategy.

"If you're innocent of the charge of receiving stolen merchandise, of course you'll be released," he explained in a lowered more conciliatory tone.

Holston put his hand up to stop the detective from continuing and spoke: "We think you're part of a conspiracy to kill police officers in this and other cities, as does the Chicago police. You were down here to arrange for weapons to be shipped to Memphis from Chicago. Part of your Black Panther plan for revolution."

"You're crazy," Rawlins said directly to Holston, "Who told you that shit?"

He took a really deep breath and puts his hands on the table, leaning with a menace toward the police commissioner and

Rawlins spoke slowly, "Lemme spell it out for you, man. I don't give a shit what happens in this place. I've got enough to do in Chicago to keep innocent kids from getting shot by people like you."

"Your criminal record suggests otherwise, Rawlins," the suited detective contended, dropping the Mister permanently from his speech. "You been charged and convicted with the possession of illegal firearms."

"That's so I wouldn't be killed by you people," Rawlins suggested to his inquisitors. "Self-defense. You follow me down the street every damn day and night, and what you have found out? Nothing, nada. It's your white man's paranoia after two hundred years of oppression."

"You deny you came here for the purpose to arm and incite blacks to commit crimes against their fellow citizens?" the detective laid out, ending his interrogation.

"Hell yes. I came down here to drink beer and eat barbecue with some friends," Rawlins said. "This is harassment for being black, nothing more. Another nigger to push around, and that's bullshit."

Holston offered nothing to Rawlins last remark, rising from his seat. He spoke rapidly to the suited detective to conclude the interrogation. He would be returned to the holding cell where they would subsequently decide the next step after talking further with the Chicago police. It had all become a dead-end with no weapons cache found to incriminate the men.

As it ended, Wyeth whispered to me, "What do you think?"

I told him that I thought Rawlins was a thug capable of shooting policemen in cold blood. His manner had made my skin crawl. Although the testimony had suggested he hadn't done anything beyond stealing a car, or having someone do it for him. According the Chicago police, he had dozens of illegally armed black revolutionaries ready to do his bidding.

* * * * * *

Martha wanted to spend most hot weekends at the lake house since her parents had pretty much given up their usual visits. It had become her get-away since her sister remained in Britain and showed no interest in returning, except for the annual pilgrimage to see her son.

The lake had been the brainchild of Alfred who knew of several farms in the locale which had been offered for sale at reduced prices. The lake property was a small valley which had been cut by a spring-fed stream. After consulting with his civil engineer friend and fellow churchman, Alfred calculated that the pastures could be made into a twenty or thirty-acre lake, created from the spring water. His vision was correct, and within eighteen months a dam had been constructed and in another year it held a twenty-three-acre lake. The three Episcopal parish friends built their rustic homes on the eastern side of the lake where there was a wide bluff and planted a surrounding perimeter of pine saplings. By the time Martha and I spent our weekends there, the forest growth embraced the lake.

It was mostly her school friends with their small children who were weekend guests. Once her boss, Jim Latham with his new wife, who happened to be his third, and twenty-two years his junior, stayed the weekend. He was irascible, and quick-witted and drank nearly as much as Carolyn the two evenings I saw him, though held it well. He was always ready with an anecdote about some thorny case, or Harvard Law School, which he attended.

The man had a cadre of former classmates high up in the federal government and throughout Wall Street firms. The president of Lehman Brothers had been his roommate for a time in Cambridge, and they talked often on the telephone.

I remember him calling the present police commissioner a diehard racist. He believed Holston ran the department like some small town Mississippi sheriff who looked the other way when there was the occasional lynching in his county. Obviously, they occupied two different worlds. Holston had been a small town Mississippi kid that had come to the big town for better opportunities. He had joined the Memphis police department after a stint in the Marines. He served as a lance corporal, and had been in the last armed conflict in Korea. He had been at Inchon.

Although a rather visible public official, Jim had a pervasive patrician demeanor which ruled his personal and professional lives. He let everyone know that fact, although with subtlety. His vocabulary and speech patterns reinforced this with a supposed superiority in every conversation he had.

I liked him as a man, and Martha adored him since he had singlehandedly broken the glass ceiling in his office. He took her under his own wing, mostly as a favor to Alfred. She was thorough, terribly competitive, and her performance was never an issue after she joined the district attorney's office.

The second evening with Latham, he had gone on rather long about Holston and the suspected brutality among his officers toward blacks. He called it open season against basic human rights. I thought that might be rather high handed, yet he did cite one case after another of excessive force. Finally, his young wife changed the subject to something more innocuous, which I welcomed. In his presence during those dinner remarks, Martha had become entirely too much of a criminal lawyer again and that weighed too heavily on the conviviality of a summer weekend.

Jim didn't like fishing, swimming, or walking in the woods, instead preferred the town gossip which Martha was well versed in, the frequent bad marriages and subsequent adulteries among their friends and acquaintances. I listened to the banter between them, as did Jim's wife, who sat on the couch next to him with this Miss America indelible smile on her face.

The conversation returned to the current case. Latham obviously knew all that had happened between the mayor and Holston, including the recent white police shootings of blacks. He was aware that Rawlins had been detained as a possible criminal suspect. There was little that went on in the mayor's conference room or the police precincts that he wasn't aware of. The man's finger was in every pie in the city.

"Maybe Rawlins was planning to move guns here" Latham said, "I don't believe he drove a stolen car down here on vacation."

I laughed when he said that.

"He was probably arranging how to move the guns under the radar, and making certain that the local blacks could get the job done, checking them out," he suggested over a scotch on the porch as the sun began to set.

"The Chicago gangs could bring hundreds of guns into Memphis. That wouldn't be tough to do," he added. "How they would want the locals to use them, that's what Holston needs to find out. Is it to kill cops, or cause havoc?"

"You think Rawlins was here for a reason, other than passing time?" I asked Latham.

"Oh yes, my friend, he was in town for a purpose alright," Latham said. "Now, exactly why is what we need to know."

Martha added, "Jim, you don't think that these Panthers could direct violence here, not from Chicago? Blacks in Memphis aren't going to kill cops because somebody blows into town and tells them it's time for a revolution."

It wasn't that simple he reminded an interested Martha who had finished her second bourbon. He said that they could possibly get someone or maybe a handful of local blacks to shoot at least someone, someone white. That could happen.

Chapter 8
Deeper water

It was a pleasant weekend with Latham and his wife, and on Sunday afternoon, Amanda and her doctor husband had driven out for the day. She, of course, was her coquettish self, at least concerning me when no one was around. She would incessantly tease me about things which made me uncomfortable.

Instead of going home as they had planned, she wanted to stay the night at the lake. She had cajoled her reluctant husband into it. We put them in the third bedroom, and after a catfish dinner we continued with the conversation well into the night on the porch.

Amanda wanted a night swim, and she tried to enlist Martha who was too busy talking with Latham, and her husband didn't want to, so it fell to me to make certain she didn't drown. We both swam out to the dock, and no one had bothered to come to the window to watch us, so she had come against me in the dark on the far side of the barrels out of sight from the shore.

"I want you to at least pet my fur," she giggled. "Wait a minute, I'll get the bottom off."

"Dammit, no," I said irritated at this dangerous game, and jumped into the black water from the float and begun to swim back to the house with a fast crawl while she had called out, "Chicken," and started back herself.

The week began routinely with the mayor. There was one day in the office we were discussing federal grants. The next day was the opening of a new addition to East High School which had been completed and offered the possibility of a larger student body for one of the city's best public schools.

That Wednesday Alfred met Martha for lunch downtown to discuss some mysterious surprise he had conjured, or was about ready to do so. In the evening she told me about a friend of his, who was mostly retired and wanted to sell his ante-bellum home in La Grange. He had thought of Alfred who had admired it for years. It was one of the smaller gracious homes in the civil war

90

village which had escaped the slaughter at Shiloh intact, and it had become a distant bedroom community for some former Memphians.

He thought this would be perfect for Martha and myself and our family. What family? I asked, and she said the one which would be here in about nine more months. That led me to become speechless, and when the words finally came, they didn't make much sense in the telling.

She had decided on her own to stop taking the pill, and since she turned twenty-eight that June, she, like so many southern women I knew, decided she had wanted to have at least her first child by thirty. Between excitement and sheer nervousness, we talked about what we would do with the child, and what a life-changing experience it would be for us.

As for the house, we looked at it the following weekend. It was lovely indeed with four bedrooms, a sunroom, and large living room on a corner lot in the picturesque village of maybe twenty-five homes and a boarded-up general store that had been shuttered in 1954.

The white clapboard and brick house had been built by a Mississippi steamboat captain in 1857 and it was far more modest than the surrounding homes. The issue, other than money, was the distance from Memphis, and Alfred had downplayed that. As for the upfront payment, he said that he would lend it to us through an interest free loan, or make it an outright gift, it didn't matter. Still, the commute to the city was difficult, and it was made on secondary roads where a pick-up truck in front of you could add fifteen minutes for at least half of the trek before the roads widened and you were able to access the interstate around the city neighborhoods to downtown.

We told Alfred we would live at the lake house for a trial week as it was twenty more minutes driving time to downtown. We would know then whether the drive was doable, or simply too exhausting and lastly, dangerous at the end of a tough day.

We did precisely that. Martha loved the La Grange house, and it was so magnificent as it sat against the skyline with its sleeping porch above and its gazebo azalea garden behind. But after a week driving back and forth, we both knew it would become far too rigorous, yet we went ahead and told Alfred we loved the house and wanted it.

He took over and said it was easier for him to buy it after a few negotiations with his friend, and that he would hold the mortgage and we could buy it at some below market interest. Alfred arranged for the first meeting with the owner which, unfortunately became complicated less than a week after we'd agreed to buy the house. On that following Tuesday, this man's wife had suffered a debilitating heart attack at the tender age of sixty-two which had left her seriously compromised. After the first cardiac incident, she lingered another two weeks and then finally died in her sleep.

Since it had been her childhood home, their grown son now became involved as it would be passed down to him in her will, and he might decide to occupy the home himself. With this obstacle in our path, Martha and I simply put it all behind us, concentrating on the prospect of children in our lives.

Her plan was to continue to work for the District Attorney until two months before she was due to deliver the child calculated by her doctor to be in early Spring of 1968. The excitement we felt about the birth was infectious, and Alfred was overjoyed with the idea of another grandchild. Perhaps Carolyn was too, in her subdued and distant way. Because of the unusual circumstances of their younger daughter's abandonment of her son, they had no real visitation rights with their grandson. They were hungry for that connection. The still angry father and ex son-in-law prevented them from seeing the child out of this suppressed vengeance. It was as if the boy didn't exist to them, and that was hurtful.

During this maelstrom over the house in La Grange and the news of Martha's pregnancy, the days at the office seemed to slow, and little happened of any import. We returned to a routine of having dinner out once or twice a week, and weekends with friends, which were usually Martha's.

Her friend Lynn came over one evening and over a cold chicken dinner, she confessed that her lawyer husband had been arrested, booked and then released on his own recognizance over a fraud accusation. She explained to us while holding back her tears, that he'd been unlawfully using his real estate client's escrow money to play the commodities market. With the sudden downturn in pork bellies or soybeans, he had lost several hundred thousand dollars, which he didn't have, on margin calls. His downfall came when a recent storm had hit Memphis and had blown down hundreds of trees in the city's residential neighborhoods and damaged quite a few homes. Conan had been holding escrow monies for these homes, and when the sales were aborted because of the storm damage, he was obligated to return the escrow monies he had already squandered in the market. Several buyers had finally turned to the police as he had been avoiding them.

It was a rather messy situation. Martha told her that from a legal standpoint, she feared that he would be prosecuted and there would be a trial. The District Attorney's office would charge him with criminal action: there was no way out of that. They would want to send a message to others on white collar crime, yet she felt it would be more of a hand slap. Conan might serve the smallest of terms in the county jail, which can be as little as a month. There probably would be a plea bargain made before the trial, and he would plead guilty to a lesser charge. Since his record was otherwise clean, the judge would be lenient and give him the minimum time in jail. Alas, he wouldn't be able to escape the embarrassment of incarceration, however minimal it might be. But he wouldn't be locked up for years.

Lynn, who she'd known her entire life, had started to cry and Martha went over to her and hugged her as Lynn rocked back and forth in her arms with anguish and fear.

It happened as Martha had predicted and Conan spent a month at the Shelby County penal farm where he trimmed lawns. His law license was suspended, or revoked, and their marriage disintegrated within a year. After that, they both disappeared from our sight.

I had liked Conan. He was one of the first people in Memphis who had been a real friend, and in the Fall he'd take me to his father's Brownsville farm to hunt birds. We'd do that for a week each fall, and I had looked forward to it.

Conan obviously had a dark side too. Because Lynn was such a sound sleeper, he was able to creep out of their house at night and drive across the bridge to West Memphis, Arkansas. He had a sinister purpose. He'd pick up teenage girls at drive-through restaurants for quick sex. It seemed rather odd to me: Conan came from an upright family. His father was a Harvard-trained lawyer and his uncle was a prominent neurologist. His grandfather served as the dean of the large Presbyterian church and its prestigious boy's school. Conan had played football as a defensive end at Washington and Lee then attended Vanderbilt law school, and otherwise could be confused with the most conventional of young men in the city.

I only know about the West Memphis nighttime visits because he had confessed them to me as we talked over drinks alone one evening. He felt since I hadn't grown up in the same incestuous circle, I was the only person he could reach out to with the sordid story and therefore had become his priest and confessor. He hadn't invited me to join him in these hidden journeys across the bridge. Although in telling me what he did, it offered the opportunity to accompany him if I wanted. I had no way of knowing how long he had been making those trips. Yet I don't think he developed any kind of relationship with a single girl that he met. His behavior seemed to be opportunistic and random in the so-called liaisons with the women he met. I thought it was for the excitement of a new sex partner.

At the time, his wife, Lynn, was in last year of law school. I imagine her being sound asleep at night may have been fueled by mental and physical exhaustion. She had been encouraged by Martha's example. Since they had been close friends for years, Martha tutored her along this career path as a mentor friend.

When they left our lives I did miss him. Conan was the only friend I had in Memphis who wasn't associated with the Mayor or a husband of one of Martha's friends who we saw socially in town, or for weekends at the lake house. I called him once or twice after his release from jail to meet for lunch or for a drink downtown, but he never returned my calls. I decided that he wanted to forget everything concerning his past. Later, I heard that he had married a woman with two small children. They had moved to Nashville where she had a decent position with state government, and he was working consulting. Lynn got her law degree, and was working in private practice, and often met Martha for lunch. She was friendly and soft-spoken.

Martha had a troublesome first trimester of the pregnancy and suffered a miscarriage. Her mother contended it had come from her continuing to ride horses on an occasional weekend. Her doctor claimed that particular conclusion was nonsense, and attributed the tragedy to what happens to some women with a first pregnancy.

Naturally, she had gone into this deep depression though she was a strong-willed woman, and before too long she would come to terms with the loss. After discussing the awful loss that it was and my feeble attempts at trying to console her, it became a subject she left alone. She threw herself into her work with an increased fervor.

Chapter 9
Holston

Holston had uncovered a new lead in this conspiracy: a black man who had claimed, under questioning, that Rawlins and his other Chicago friend had provided him with another contact who had guns. These particular guns had been found during a routine traffic stop for a broken taillight. The suspect had a trunk filled with hunting rifles he was holding for a friend who would then sell them. Of course, this friend who had given him the guns couldn't be located. He didn't live in Memphis but rather "somewhere" in Arkansas, a location that was unnamed to police.

The police had found ten high-velocity hunting rifles and a box of long-distance scopes to be fitted onto the weapons. The man had the flimsiest of excuses for his possession of the weapons. It was clear that he had been lying to police at the traffic stop and later during an interrogation at police headquarters where he was being held without bail.

Investigation of the weapon's serial numbers suggested that they had come from a wide area in the Midwest. Five of the ten came from sporting goods stores in Wisconsin, and the others from stores in Dubuque along the Iowa border. Half of these weapons were taken from stores reporting earlier burglaries. One had come from a home break-in reported to police and the two rifles had serial numbers removed from the barrel with a metal file.

This information had sent Holston into a frenzy. He had become convinced that the city was under attack by the Panthers, and before too long, his white officers would be shot down in the street by snipers. Any possibility that this was a gun running business for street crime, organized or otherwise, escaped him completely.

These conclusions of a wide racial revolution couldn't be easily dismissed, especially in a majority black southern city with a history of racial unrest. Armed violence led by blacks against white police forces in Detroit and Los Angeles in the past year had

96

strengthened his resolve to prevent it from happening in Memphis.

His department was put on high alert. He instructed his precinct captains to warn their officers about this eventuality and to do everything in their power to undermine this black armament. The consequence was that the number of arrests of blacks for routine infractions skyrocketed in the city. Many of the more zealous white officers created this environment of unspoken martial law. These violent responses to rather minor offenses had another purpose: to ferret out and stop the arming of black vigilantes.

To the city as a whole, nothing appeared changed. The white citizens on their way to and from work who pulled into his tree-lined neighborhood driveway saw nothing untoward happening in this sprawling riverfront town. Beale Street continued with its raucous black saloons, and the Southside had a life of its own with the same amount of shootings of blacks by blacks that had occurred before.

The police had a different mission. It wasn't to answer domestic abuse calls, or a knifing at a black neighborhood barbecue, or the continual liquor store break-ins. These crimes played second fiddle to the greater need: to find these black revolutionaries and the arms caches before it was too late.

The police were urged on by the commissioner to do just that, with whatever it took: a beating or adding some incriminating evidence. This was a culture of street criminals, most of them Negro and savages.

Wyeth's response to the Wisconsin guns and their scopes was to be cautious though vigilant. The weapons which were flowing into this city in unknown numbers had him uneasy. He was sophisticated enough to know that there was a historical black resentment against the white police. Wyeth was certainly aware of this escalating violence that had plagued other major cities pitting blacks against whites, which was generally the police. In his defense, he had talked with other city mayors where this had happened and tried to learn from their experience of what they'd done right and wrong. However, there was no consensus. What had worked in Los Angeles hadn't worked in Chicago, or even New York.

It became impossible to develop any cohesive strategy from these cities to protect citizens against the black unrest and subsequent violent acts. It had seemed as if the damage had already been done and it was simply too late to quell it completely. What he could do is try to meet with black community leaders, and appeal to their humanity as well as their fear that their wives and children could be in danger if the racial violence became organized, or even institutional.

In a single year, this national racial polarity would spawn black guerilla armies in each American city who set their sights on first murdering those obvious symbols of white authority and oppression, namely the police, and then killing innocent whites.

I could see the change on Wyeth's face each day. His mouth became unmoved or downturned and his blue eyes had this premonition of apocalypse to them.

In the interim, Holston had an ace up his sleeve that he was feverishly working at: his mole. He had found a young black man who was finishing at LeMoyne Owen, the small Memphis black college, with an associate degree in criminal justice, which was a rather new program funded by Federal grants.

The young man had been a good basketball forward on their varsity team until he tore a ligament and was sidelined. He had thrown himself into his studies, and saw himself as a muckraking black police detective. Out of some shithole in the Orange Mount section, from a single or no parent home, he played basketball in the police athletic league during the summers. He was known to the officers who ran the program as a decent kid. He was mannerly and well-spoken, different from the rest of delinquents they usually watched over. They encouraged him to look for more.

Holston had sent him through a special tactical class at the police academy. Now the twenty-year-old black man was poised for his initial undercover assignment. No one knew he'd become a cop, part of the deal with the department. Holston made him a regular officer in anonymity operating within his own impoverished black neighborhood. They found him some half-assed counter job at a white-owned liquor store. It had been arranged for him to steal from the inventory and resell the whiskey on the street. They supplied him with cheap narcotics too, to peddle on the corner, and gradually he got a reputation as a tough guy with connections, and ready money.

Jackson Wright became the spy who would infiltrate the Black Panther initiatives to supply guns to would-be local radicals. Against all police regulations, and in secret, Holston supplied him with confiscated handguns to sell on the street. Wright spent weeks making deals for pistols in the backseat of cars, and in alleys. He became a 'go to' dude in that criminal world, all the time a conduit to the highest levels in the Memphis police department.

It might take weeks or even months, but Holston had positioned Wright as the eyes and ears of this arming of blacks. He became dedicated to do exactly that. He had two white police lieutenant handlers who he reported to, and they gave him the specific undercover assignments that came directly from Holston.

Once, when he was picked up for suspicion, he had been taken to the department and had agreed to let the officers slap him around, bruising his face somewhat before he was released, unencumbered. Wright was dedicated to this department, and his view of bringing these radicals to justice. They had been successful in bending his intellect and will to that end.

He had caught wind of some trafficking in weapons, and though it was gang-related, Wright insinuated himself into the transaction, taking handguns and a few rifles then supposedly selling them. In truth, he'd turned them over to the department for investigation, and was given cash to buy them as part of this covert arms deals.

These were small steps which needed to be taken. This positioning of Wright as a born-again revolutionary would begin to establish him with the more radical cells in the city that he found. They were mostly small groups of out of town blacks from St. Louis and Chicago, and they were few. The militants he talked to, or supplied a few handguns, had no leadership. They consisted of a handful of street criminals who spent their time stealing, or drunk, with no discernable politics of racial revolution.

To these reports, Holston reacted with outward anger, and he insisted Wright keep looking. The department would supply him the illegal guns to distribute and laundered money to buy those guns trafficked from the outside agitators. No arrests would be made until Holston had clearly determined how, and if, these several radical cells fit together at all, which looked doubtful.

The street activity Wright found was little more than a few black gangs who sold guns for random crimes to those desperate hoods who wanted the firearms. There was no national Black Panther strategy to arm urban blacks, at least not in Memphis. All Holston had uncovered thus far was the familiar raft of violence in the same black neighborhoods where it had always existed, perhaps with a few more new faces behind the gun triggers. Yet, the commissioner was convinced that there was a national conspiracy and that Rawlins and others like him were the advance party.

He was in constant communication with terrorism officers in the Chicago Police department. He had flown there for two days to be briefed at what they found after the Panther shoot-outs, which was nothing more than an overreaction by police. That was the opinion of the Chicago newspapers, and others of a more progressive bent, although Mayor Daley had contended it was a city under siege.

Chicago had forty-five officers assigned to monitor radical black organizations there, and it held a tactical SWAT team in reserve should a preemptive action be required. They were the same officers who had fired thirteen hundred rounds during the recent Black Panther attack which killed three young black men.

There had been an outrage among many in Chicago that the police had slaughtered peaceful, unarmed men in an ambush, but unused weapons supposedly had been recovered from the apartment. It was simply that the black inhabitants didn't have enough time to get the guns and were mowed down in the fusillade of police bullets.

The Chicago police commissioner was unapologetic about the incident, and claimed it was a fine case of police response: protecting its citizenry from dangerous radical elements. At a press conference, he had held up one of the weapons found in the apartment, a 357 magnum pistol, and showed the newspaper and television journalists that the gun was loaded, He dramatically emptied the large rounds into his hand as cameras clicked.

Holston was in in the audience, and he remarked later how closely allied the Chicago Mayor Daley and his police department had been. Both focused on the common goal of protection and finding these revolutionists before they created havoc and murder in the streets.

His work with Jackson Wright would continue, and hopefully it would produce the same result as it had in Chicago: the destruction of these black criminals before they had a chance to get better organized.

"That attack was an example of precision police work," he had said to the Chicago lieutenant who squired him around the city and had looked bored, yawning and anxious for a cigarette.

"You identify these radicals and surprise them before they can even think straight," Holston said to the officer, who simply smiled.

"They only understand force," Holston concluded to the back of the officer who was hurriedly heading out the door.

Frank Holston was not stupid. He could've never advanced to the head of the Memphis police department had he been. However, he was a man of singular purpose and sometimes that purpose overtook him.

Upon his return to Memphis, Holston met personally with the two lieutenants and Jackson Wright and then they laid out a new strategy for embedding this renegade black undercover cop into the Panther radical groups. Holston believed his recent visit to Chicago had been most productive, and he had a far better understanding of the mechanics of this present menace.

* * * * * *

Martha and I had some difficult days following the miscarriage and, understandably, she became distant and recoiled from any show of intimacy. This was something that only time could possibly heal, and we spent more time at Holy Communion, attending church most Sundays except when we were at the lake house alone, or with friends.

Amanda and her husband had been invited by Martha on two consecutive weekends in the same month. Amanda's craziness, that only I believed existed, had this quirky way of unnerving me, however it was invisible to the others.

Amanda became more brazen with her forward sexuality. Although she was careful of what she actually said or did with me that might have been misunderstood by Martha or her own husband, she did far too much conscious touching. I had certainly been guilty of what I had done with her in the past, at least admitting to myself those lapses in judgment, but I wanted it forgotten. Both Amanda and I had established seemingly successful marriages, and this flirty gamesmanship she wanted to practice became annoying.

That next week, after some of the most distraught days of our marriage, Martha announced that she was going to Puerto Rico for four or five days with a few close Memphis friends, which included several couples and some singles. She wanted to go to the island alone to have some time to think, and it was so little to ask, she had said. It seemed reasonable to me, so I told her to enjoy herself.

"I'm not going there for a good time," Martha reiterated to me. "It's because I need to recover emotionally from what happened. Certainly you can understand that much."

I told her I understood, and I did, that she would walk the beaches and work through the pain and loss of the miscarriage, and hopefully come out the other end, a stronger and happier woman.

We had a pleasant dinner together downtown the night before she left. I had told her that for a short time I was stationed on the island, attached to an engineering battalion preparing to soon deploy to Vietnam. We had spent weeks attacking Vieques island from the beach while tracking down a camouflaged enemy in this the deadliest of war games. She showed no interest in my wartime anecdotes, and said that her trip was necessary for her very sanity. I held her hand at the table and praised her in all the ways I hadn't in the past, kissing her forehead as we finished our dinner wines.

Martha was far more fragile than she led people to believe. She'd spent a lifetime trying to please a critical mother whose own madness had become unchecked. Out of the recurrent fears that perhaps troubled Martha, the most fearful was that she had become an out of control alcoholic like her mother. She abused alcohol enough to know that was a remote possibility. At the lake house, she was drunk far more than I ever had been, though usually when the two of us were there alone. When visitors arrived her alcohol consumption moderated, and she seemed this ordinary attractive and intelligent young southern woman who enjoyed people.

She had been half drunk her last year at Smith, and it had been a problem socially, though academically she excelled and coasted into law school. Once in the rigors of Vanderbilt, she'd concentrated on the prize, and had graduated cum laude with offers from several Nashville law firms.

She went off to Puerto Rico with this circle of friends, including a man that she had been involved with years ago in college. Everyone in Memphis had been involved with everyone else sometime, particularly in her circumspect group of friends. I drove her to the airport and gave her a gift of an expensive pair of sunglasses to wear around the hotel pool then waved as she disappeared though the Departures doors.

Honestly, I didn't care how she conducted herself in San Juan. I would come to believe that we do what we're meant to do, and the thought of her trip left me as I turned onto the Interstate highway toward home.

I had learned later that while in Puerto Rico, Martha stayed half-drunk for the entire vacation. She wanted to drive the rental car one night and her friends had physically thrown her into the backseat for her own good. Then there was the aggressive flirting with a waiter, which had needed reporting though I ignored the unsolicited account of the whole trip. She hadn't easily escaped that long shadow Carolyn cast, or maybe it was a result of her recent loss.

Amanda had invited herself to the lake house that weekend over the telephone, but with her husband, and I didn't protest. We could have a pleasant, uncomplicated visit, with the usual fishing and country evening air. She promised to bring a picnic feast that she prepared, and for the past week she had attended a cooking school for summer outdoor parties. Her husband had been freed of his usual hospital duties, and all he said he wanted to do was read John Le Carre spy novels in the hammock on the porch with a gin and tonic.

They were both decent company. The young doctor had few interests beyond medicine. I liked his forthright seriousness anyway. His conversation sometimes required slight interview techniques, though otherwise he had a hidden sense of humor that might erupt almost out of nowhere, laughing raucously at his own bad and inane jokes. He had these ever present brash puppy characteristics.

The Amanda weekend had been fine until her husband had been called back for an emergency surgery since he was a pediatric specialist on the Le Bonheur children's hospital staff. He didn't want to spoil her weekend and the many dishes she'd brought, so he asked me if I would drop her home on Sunday evening.

No sooner had he left the driveway that her neurotic side began to show its face, and she sat down on the great room couch with a cold Budweiser, and announced, "Guess who's going to have a nude swim tonight? I'll tell you. The two last people on Noah's Ark."

She wanted to work in the kitchen, and she'd brought fresh peach custard for ice cream. I went into the downstairs closet and found Carolyn's ancient Kentucky wooden crank ice cream maker and brought it upstairs.

Once we washed out the metal canister, she emptied in the custard. From a bag of ice in the freezer, she poured shaved iced around the cylinder and added Morton salt to the melting pieces.

"Your job, mister, is to keep cranking," she announced. "Take it out to the side porch and give me some room in the kitchen because I have a lot to do."

As I walked toward the door, Amanda smiled and blew me a kiss.

The old crank was a little rusty and I had a difficult time getting it started. Those first few circular turns were like tightening tire lugs until the crank had been primed enough. Finally, it worked, although still time consuming for a small dish of ice cream. Inside, Amanda had prepared a hot salad of chicken livers in a hazelnut sauce that was poured hot over wilted red bib lettuce. She then heated a baguette she baked fresh at home, and poured a Sancerre wine she'd brought along.

"Take it all out on the side porch and let's enjoy this course as the sun sets," she added laughingly as she removed the apron covering her white shorts.

Once seated outside, she toasted me with our clinking wine glasses and wished me "Bon Appetite." I admired her auburn highlights while she ate her salad with gusto. They were more noticeable in the orange dusk of the sunset.

"You lived in France," she said, "How was it? I mean the women."

It was a ridiculous question, and I gave her an answer that to me seemed equally ludicrous though true. I had been discharged from the military in Europe, and stayed for half a year, soaking up the otherness I thought I'd find in Paris.

105

"You know the two things I liked most about French women?"

"No, but I'm dying to find out," she said with a giggle.

"Number one: They all had these wonderful appetites and clean their plates, on the street, in a restaurant or even at home, with this fierce passion, almost like they were making love to the china."

"You don't say," she said, her smile broadening. "And the second?"

"Well, every French woman I got to know more intimately, and there weren't many, all peed with the bathroom door left open, and you could hear that tinkling sound in water. That was marvelous."

"Oh for god's sakes, you're not serious. You can't be," she sang out throwing back her head with laughter. "You wanted to hear a woman tinkling. You liked that, the sound?"

I said loudly with my wineglass in the air, "I didn't just like that sound, Amanda, I adored it. It was music to these wax-filled American ears."

"Would you like me to pee with the door open tonight? That'd make you happy if you could see me peeing and hear the…"

"That would be so wonderful if you'd just pull down your panties and pee for me, because that's what God wants you to do when your bladders full," I said with this near clinical severity her husband might have employed, not with the children, mind you, but perhaps talking with some parent.

"You think I won't do it, don't you?" she teased me, "But I promise you this, mister, when we're alone I'll always pee for you with the bathroom door wide open as wet as rain."

"Amanda, that would make this tired life worthwhile," I uttered with a tinge of playful sarcasm, "since I left France I've never heard that musical sound only women can make."

"Tonight your wish will be granted," and with that, she finished eating and headed into the kitchen to finish the next course of this gourmet picnic.

As strange and unbalanced as Amanda was, it was impossible not to find her seductive, and beautiful at the same time. I feared for what I'd do tonight, and to what she would become a willing collaborator.

Hearing her banging pans in the lake house kitchen for some uncanny reason, made me think of a passage from Matthew's gospel: "Learn from me…because I am humble of heart." I wondered why I allowed these awful things into my head and my heart, but yet these same thoughts were excited by Amanda's scent which had remained in the humid night. What have I learned? Nothing it seemed.

That night as the moonlight shone across the lake from the master bedroom window, Amanda was naked and leaning against my arm. She had closed her eyes and her short breaths signaled that sleep was near. I moved her arm gently and she looked at me leaning on her side when I asked her, "What are we going to do about this? It's just insanity."

"I think you and I married the wrong people, and that's the real problem, darling," she whispered. Her slender finger traced a line down my cheek.

"We could fix that by getting divorced, and this charade would be over. Then we could get on with our lives," Amanda said without emotion. "I think, and I don't know if you would agree or not, but we're the ones who should be married. Not what we've gone and done, honey. That's an unholy mess."

I let out a deep sigh, and told her I was confused. Maybe we had let this passion consume us. We needed to stop and think about what we had done, and what it'll mean to the people around us.

Amanda sat up in the bed and looked out the window at the bright moon: "You did what you wanted. I may have made it easier for you to do alright, but it was always your choice. No one gets the blame."

She was right, of course, and it occurred to me that she'd entered my consciousness so very deeply I wasn't certain that I'd ever get her out, or want to.

I got up from the bed and went in the kitchen to the refrigerator, and brought two cold cans of Busch back to the bed. I popped the tops and handed her one.

She said coyly: "Look, we can continue as we are. There's no hurry to make any kind of move. A decision is when you do nothing, that's a decision."

"Okay, that's tonight's decision. To do nothing," I told her and put my half-drunk can on the bedside table and moved closer to her.

She laughed, saying, "I hate to waste good beer. Oh well," and she swung her lithe body closer to mine in the hot sheets while the ceiling fan sung an unknown melody in the stale cabin air.

In the morning we acted as if we had already been together for years. We sat on the side porch under the ocean print umbrella and drank our coffees with great leisure while watching the Kingfishers eye the bayou for insects.

There was nothing to do on that summer day except to enjoy it. Within a half hour she had on her swimsuit and was paddling slowly out to the float in the lake's center. All of a sudden I heard a scream and saw her thrashing the water. She started screaming louder then started splashing around in a circle like a drowning man. She went under the water and surfaced about eight or ten feet from where she had been. By then, I'd jumped into the fishing boat and was speeding toward her, Once I reached her, I pulled her into the boat with some difficulty.

"What's wrong? What happened?" I asked in a panic and she pointed to marks on her calf. She told me that she had run into a water snake and that it had bitten her.

"My God, let's get you back to Memphis, or that county hospital, before the poison spreads," I spit out.

"It wasn't a water moccasin, thank the Lord," she said, calm but taking these erratic loud breaths, bordering on hyperventilation.

"I know what a water moccasin looks like. This was one of those thin green snakes but it scared the bejesus out of me," she confessed.

We had reached the shore and I helped her out of the boat and then up to the house. Once inside, I had her sit down and went to get the rubbing alcohol and antiseptic cream to cover the punctures.

"Should I telephone Randy?" I asked her, his name suddenly sounding strange on my tongue.

"No, no, let's get back into town like we planned. You go ahead and lock up. I want to calm down with a short nap."

I asked her if she wanted a whiskey and she laughed at me, "Honey, you're not going to amputate my leg. Please, let me have a little rest to get over the excitement."

On the ride back into Memphis, she appeared comfortable, and was talkative about things which had only marginal interest for either one of us, such as the cotton carnival and what a few mutual friends had done with new houses. Her leg looked alright except for this small bright red spot around the puncture wound, and the leg didn't appear swollen. I asked her if she had any pain from the snake bite and she said that there was this slightly numb feeling in the muscle of that leg that hindered movement, so she kept the leg rigid for most of the trip.

When we got to her house on Cherry Street, her husband's car wasn't in the driveway. She asked if I would help her into the house. As I lifted her from the seat, she let out a squeal of pain but found she could put pressure on the leg and gradually limped into the house. I told her I was going to call Randy at the hospital and tell him exactly what had happened so that he could give her proper medical attention in case of any infection, or possible allergic reaction to the snakebite.

After two prolonged holds on the phone, I managed to talk to him, and he said he was out of surgery and driving immediately to the house. I told him I would wait until he arrived to make certain she was comfortable. He thanked me and hung up.

"Well honey," she cooed from their couch, "We are regular drama queens, don't you think? And that's only part of the story." She started this suppressed giggle, and pointed me toward their liquor cabinet where she said I could pour her a tall straight half glass of Jack Daniels.

By the time she finished the drink, she looked at her watch and motioned me over to sit next to her. "He'll be here in a minute. You and I are an ill-fated pair," and kissed me gently on the cheek before reclining on the couch.

Randy was inside the door and at the couch with his medical bag in a single motion. He was examining the wound as I told him what had happened.

"It'll be fine. If it were poison the whole leg would have ballooned after two hours. But we're going to the emergency room anyway," She pleaded with him enough that he agreed to broach the same subject again in two more hours. If nothing became worse, she could stay at home. He gave her a quick antibiotic injection, and a mild sedative to calm her frayed nerves.

Amanda closed her eyes and Randy and I shook hands. He thanked me again for all my efforts. Turning toward the sleeping woman, I found my way out the half open front door.

Driving home, I couldn't help but think what might come of this suicidal behavior with Amanda and how at some point it would force me to act. I would let it simply find its own level as dangerous as those shoals might become. After the turmoil of that morning, I knew I was in trouble with this woman. It was going to career out of control, probably sooner than later.

There was the part of me that honestly didn't care: that part of me I rarely acknowledged existed inside, and sometimes let it guide my actions however foolhardy they were.

Pulling into the driveway on Overland Place, I could see the little girls from two doors down the street riding their tricycles furiously trying to beat me to the driveway. I waved to them over the car roof. I parked the car and went into the house.

Martha had left a note on the counter that she was riding out at Rachel Griffin's barn in Germantown, and might be late.

She liked to visit with old Rachel who was a gruff farmwoman who had come south with her journalist husband. Rachel's daughter, Melissa, was a world-class show jumper and a member of the United States Equestrian team that was training in Connecticut for the upcoming Montreal Olympics. Melissa would go on to win a gold medal.

Martha had gone to school with the eldest daughter, Samantha, who worked as a journalist with Newsweek in New York, and she adored the family. She would give any excuse to exercise some of the ten horses that Rachel boarded. Rachel would sit in her country kitchen and talk about colic and bad hooves for hours.

Martha probably wanted the narrow world Rachel had. Law was something her mother Carolyn thought Martha should do with her sharp intellect, and had pushed her in that direction. Alfred remained passive about the career, even as an attorney himself.

Martha did have the slightest tinge of Carolyn's pretense and tended to separate her own world into the haves and have-nots with inherited wealth at the top. She never particularly focused on the self-made, the opulence, or even the comfort they enjoyed as it was a means to an end, which was acceptance into the right society. Was it a lack of self-esteem? I don't think so. What bothered Martha most in life was that her sister had a prettier face and she couldn't forgive that. Her sister had all the dates and the attention from adolescent boys. Attractive mothers would constantly praise her younger sister's beauty queen looks, while admitting that Martha was the better scholar as she did so well at St. Mary's School, and won the coveted senior Latin Prize.

Maybe that's why Martha drank as much as she did later: that and the pressure of this obsessive personality of her constantly critical mother, and the whole DNA package she'd inherited.

On many nights before Carolyn had gotten chronic with her drinking, we'd have dinner with the two of them. Her mother never complimented Martha for anything: not an attractive blouse, a truly chic haircut, or even the prestige of being the first woman lawyer with the District Attorney. Evenings were all about Carolyn and her many trials and tribulations. When Carrie decamped to England with her lover, the dinners became morbid. Alfred would occasionally try to steer the table conversation to more palatable topics, but his success was limited, and Carolyn usually dominated the ultimate direction of the remarks.

When she had gotten too sloppy in her table behavior, maybe two years after Carrie's departure from Memphis, those family dinners ceased. We would only occasionally stop by their house for fifteen or twenty minutes of hurried desultory chatter.

Since he worked downtown, Alfred would sometimes meet Martha for lunch at the Summit Club. They generally did that about once every two weeks, so they were able to retain their closeness as father and daughter. I sometimes joined them, but that was rare. I had always felt that with her mother's distance, this time alone with her father was important to Martha.

Alfred was an agreeable man, and I never had harsh words with him as long as I knew him, even under difficult circumstances. I genuinely liked and respected the man, and in my way, I felt that there was much about Carolyn that was worth embracing as well. Perhaps, you could make the argument that Alfred's dysfunction in this family manifested itself in a subtle manner of manipulation: regardless of what he had done, his final exit was always that of the innocent or wronged party.

He was a self-made man and his strategies always seemed benign. What he had gotten in life, the money and those professional kudos, came naturally to him. Maybe he had created an entire façade as his way of outsmarting those who sought to hold him back, and he bettered them.

I remember that someone once tried criticizing him. He remembered Alfred and Carolyn lived next to a federal judge early in their marriage. Whenever the judge would go into his backyard, Alfred would sneak out to engage him in conversation making certain that as a young lawyer, he had a friend in a high place on the bench. I thought that accusation rather innocuous, and it didn't seem much of a criticism to me. I'd do the same, or any other ambitious young man.

When Martha had suffered the miscarriage, Carolyn wasn't much help in consoling her daughter. Carolyn had already leapt into her own dark and bottomless abyss which would consume her and destroy the wonderful parts of her left, making her last years vile and painful to all around her.

Four months after the miscarriage, Martha's drinking had begun to escalate: mostly at home, though sometimes at restaurants or garden parties. Few people noticed this subtle change, yet I began to see it affect her. It created an uncomfortable young woman who shrieked from any idea that she might be wrong. The most innocent comment would become a shouting match. Increasingly, I had to be wary of almost anything I said around Martha, or how I said it, as the tone was suspect.

You could accuse me of making her insecure as I had been carrying on this surreptitious sometimes romance with her first cousin. That alone would be a perfect excuse to behave like some lunatic. However, Martha wasn't a lunatic. She was a troubled young woman, and it hurt me to see her suffer so much. I tried to discourage drinking, though I hadn't stopped myself. Once or twice, I pleaded for moderation with cocktails, and she had stared at me as if I'd ask her to jump off the Mississippi River bridge.

I never stopped drinking as it was part of the time we lived in, and the South that I had come to embrace with its never ending garden parties and cocktails. It was much better than the ratty bars and coal miner drunks who beat their wives and kids on Saturday nights I'd known from my childhood.

At the age of twelve, my own father had put my mother's head through the kitchen wall as I stood by helpless to stop him. It was a horrible sound. I still hear the same sound in my own mind, that awful crunch and then the broken wall. For my entire adolescence, I had frequently dreamed of killing him, and even now at times, though he's been dead for more than a decade. His twisted cruel face still haunts my rest on many nights.

Amanda did recover from the snakebite, and within two days she was buzzing around town in the Buick convertible Randy had bought her for her last birthday. The incident gave her something to talk about at lunches. She held her hand on her heart and rolled her eyes as she entranced those other women who hadn't experienced snakebite. Venomous or not, Amanda had been bitten by this wild, writhing snake who clearly meant her harm and the story became more thrilling and embellished with each telling. I think she kept a square bandage on her shaved and oiled leg long after the wound had healed.

At the Memphis Country Club pool, she would summarily show mostly curious women who believed that all snakebites were indeed fatal, and the fact that Amanda had survived this awful ordeal was, well, a genuine miracle. She'd tell them it wasn't a water moccasin at all, but that didn't matter. She had been attacked in the water by this grotesque serpent that had intended to kill her if it could, and had certainly tried. The thought alone caused these older women at the club to shiver on those ninety-degree steamy summer afternoons, and the pain Amanda must have endured caused them to become weakened.

Her rescue was likewise part of these conversations. One version I heard mentioned was that I had selflessly batted the huge snake away from her throat with my bare-hand, perfectly willing to suffer the serpent's wrath to prevent Amanda's drowning. I then pulled her safely into the boat, kicking at the attacking snake with my bare foot. Maybe I had also resuscitated her, as one woman suggested, a skill that I obviously mastered with wounded comrades in the dense Vietnam jungles.

Despite the strict dress code for women at the country club dining room, Amanda violated it with her dime store flip flops for two solid weeks as news of the vicious serpent attack spread. The black barman and waiters had remarked to her and Randy that water moccasins were dangerous snakes indeed, and she was a very lucky woman to have survived. To these comments, Amanda dropped her eyes demurely and smiled as did her confused husband who didn't seek to correct this misunderstanding with snake species.

When people would mention anything to Martha about Amanda's snakebite trauma, she would shriek to me later, "Good Christ, when is this going to stop? I was bitten by a squirrel as a child and no one cared, not even my mother."

But in true Amanda fashion, she held on to the harrowing tale as long as it amused her, and when it didn't, it was immediately discarded.

Amanda wasn't afraid of the outdoors. She would fish with her father and his friends. She had hunted ducks in blinds several times when women would be invited to accompany the men on the Mississippi flyway. This was all for some little show of extra attention which Amanda had relished. Martha liked her cousin, though she believed Amanda often behaved like some spoiled child, and there were some who would agree.

It was an era when most upper middle class white families had black servants: maids, cooks, and gardeners who found their way each day in the back of the slow-moving city buses to these elegant and conservative white homes.

There wasn't a proliferation of enormous wealth like Newport or Greenwich, or even the North Shore of Chicago with its McCormick and Marshall Field mansions. It was a town filled with five bedroom Georgian brick and spacious ranch-style homes that rested firmly on the shoulders of a vast black underclass left over from the rural migrations.

Martha's parents and Amanda's in Jackson had risen with the post-war capitalism that found its way to the South, and all rose with that abundant tide. They weren't the scions of those white-suited planters of a hundred years before, or doctors who eschewed the family land for the city and whose perfumed wives played bridge. They were different: the sons and daughters of tradesmen made good.

There were exceptions like Amanda's Italian-American doctor husband whose mother's family had a beer distributorship for half the city. They were the sons of earlier successful immigrants who had come from Detroit, and Rome, New York. They quickly assimilated into the privilege that came as part of the white Deep South. In a single generation their voices would become truly southern, like Randy's who went to college at the University of Virginia and later to medical school in Memphis. He'd become a native to this region, and he belonged where he had found his tribe.

Chapter 10
The Strike

The Teamsters had pretty much dominated the city's labor unions over the past thirty years. As they had become almost totally black, the union management in Detroit and elsewhere, backed off some of the labor issues, such as contract renewals. They turned it over to the locals to negotiate themselves.

Wyeth and his top labor negotiator had talked with the city sanitation workers about a small hourly raise added to their upcoming contract renewal, and his adviser had suggested a few pension benefits to sweeten the deal.

When the city sat down to negotiate with the black labor unions, they had expected it all to go smoothly and there was no reason to suspect otherwise. The union president for the sanitation workers was a fifty-five-year-old black man that Wyeth had known for some years, and they had a cordial business relationship as well as mutual respect. But he had stepped down from the leadership at the eleventh hour. He was replaced by a new firebrand who had been a second vice president. The new leader was a boisterous and caustic thirty-five-year-old garbage truck driver originally from a small Arkansas town.

When they all had sat down and finished exchanging pleasantries, the man who was dressed in a tight-fitting sport jacket and chino pants, had tossed the ten-page contract renewal across the table at Wyeth's labor deputy.

"You need to do better than this," he told the man with an angry pinched face, "cause we're not working for nothing anymore."

The negotiator who had been trained in arbitration cleared his throat and said, "Mister Jones, we think these increases in hourly wages and the better pension package are fair additions to this new contract, and should be attractive to your membership."

"My ass, they are," Jones spit out, and he crossed his muscular arms across his barrel chest. "You need to sharpen your pencil, or we're striking."

Taken aback by the angry words, the labor deputy tried a more conciliatory tone of voice. "We understand you want the best for your union and the mayor has charged us with making this renewal better than anything we've done in the past. He's behind higher wages and increased benefits a hundred percent."

Wyeth shook his head affirmatively to the deputy's statement.

"That's all bullshit," came out of the mouth of the new sanitation union president.

"We're talking about a living wage, and you don't seem to get that," he said. "We need another dollar and fifty cents an hour, like Detroit has."

The deputy gave the man a false smile, and moved the papers in front of him while looking at the mayor once again before speaking.

With confidence in his logic, he said, "Mister Jones, Detroit is a much larger city than Memphis with very significant tax bases. It houses the American automobile industry. You can't compare the two." And with this last statement he started to shake his head vigorously to reiterate the disparity between the cities.

The black man stood up as well as the other union man alongside him at the conference table. Jones leaned over with his hands on the table.

"Look, this city has misused black people and paid us nothing to pick up your damn garbage every week. You either give us another dollar and a half an hour and more medical stuff, or we ain't gonna do it anymore."

"Please, let's not end this without some give and take," the deputy said to the backs of the black men as they walked toward the door.

Jones turned around as he had planned earlier as a strategy and he said to the white men at the table. "You give us that increase and we'll talk."

"But the city budget can't provide that…." the deputy almost stammered.

"Then we're out of here and you have no contract," Jones said, turning to slowly walk out the door.

The other man with him was silent for the whole meeting and looked back once more at the table of negotiators. He gave a wide smile that showed a shiny gold tooth in the front of his mouth.

"For Christ sake," said the mayor, "who was that guy anyway? I've never seen him before. Why he is suddenly here and not Sam?"

"Don't know," suggested the distraught labor negotiator, "Somebody in union headquarters in New Jersey must have wanted to change horses mid-stream. I don't get it. There's no way the city could afford that wage demand."

"That son-of-bitch knew that already," the mayor added, and took his cigarette pack off the table and started for the door himself.

"I'll call him, and see if we can't meet somewhere in the middle," the deputy added to an unconvinced Wyeth.

"Good luck. They're not going to settle. Someone's stirring up trouble," was Wyeth's answer and in a moment he was gone.

I heard about the meeting later from the Eastern lawyer on the staff who had sat in. He said that his feeling throughout was that these blacks had come to cause trouble, not to negotiate any labor contract.

By the next afternoon, three of the labor deputy's telephone calls had gone unanswered. He had his secretary type a letter with the points he'd hope to make on the telephone then had it messengered to the union office on Poplar. That letter went unanswered, and the existing contract would expire in the next twenty-eight days.

What would happen next was anybody's guess and Wyeth asked his labor deputy to go over the Memphis union president's head and talk to the headquarters out East to seek some kind of reconciliation and help with the contract negotiations. Instead they turned it right back to the local union autonomy and washed their hands of the whole matter suspecting some hidden racial discord.

It was one more headache of many that had faced Wyeth in this second term which was so different from the halcyon days of the first time around.

We had coffee together that next morning, early before the other staffers had appeared, and he told me he had a bad feeling about the garbage union. Wyeth believed that it had been influenced by outsiders, perhaps even people from its own headquarters. Labor wanted to flex its unused muscles once again and bring some mayor to his knees.

It was not necessarily underwritten by these radicals. Perhaps it was nothing more complicated than bringing back some of the Depression hard-nosed labor behavior, and the officials up North told them to go ahead, float the balloon and see what happens.

"If nobody picks up garbage for three weeks, we've got a health problem with rats running around East Memphis neighborhoods," Wyeth lamented. "This town is gonna stink to high heaven. Thank God it's not July."

Finally, by the end of the week, there was a return call from the union president; however, he told the mayor's office secretary he would only speak to Wyeth and no one else. He was finished with the mayor's mouthpiece, as he called the labor deputy.

When Wyeth got on the telephone, the man was cordial and, in a sense, respectful, though he reiterated to the mayor that the garbage worker's wage increase would be met, or they would strike. It was that simple.

"We don't have the money," Wyeth calmly told Jones, and the union president responded with, "Then find it somewhere," thus ending the brief conversation on that discordant note.

Not everyone had turned their backs on Wyeth. Hal Wolfson, the president of AFSCME, the national union of which the Memphis sanitation workers were a part, for a moment had been aggressive about striking though he had several calls with Wyeth, and reason had surfaced.

Wolfson was a Jew from Newark, and as a last ditch effort, he had boarded a plane from La Guardia to talk to the mayor personally. Wolfson had urged the mayor to reach out to these garbage workers with a compromise offer, or at least a plan for an arbitration which had everyone at the same table. Jones had no knowledge of that particular meeting, and Wolfson pleaded with Wyeth to grant the sanitation union a dollar an hour raise. The national officials would pressure Jones to accept the offer, he promised.

Regardless, Wyeth remained intransigent and unmoved. His strategy seemed to be to do nothing until the very last minute, and only then submit some token wage increase. This skewed approach appeared to be doomed to failure, and naturally, it was. The result would be a general strike called for by the AFSCME workers in Memphis, and possibly a similar response from the Teamsters who controlled the city bus service. This could all be followed by the airport baggage handlers who were overwhelmingly black, and the city would be effectively shut down.

Holston hadn't left his conspiracy theories, and through his handful of paid black criminal informers, he learned of two possible locations for illegal gun trafficking. The first was at a dogfight site in the small community of Rossville, due east of the city which had a large rural black population. It sponsored weekend dog fights where heavy drinking and betting took place. Rossville was a dusty one block long town with a single stoplight and dilapidated hardware and feed store. The village was surrounded by a perimeter of small cotton and soybean farms as well as four or five horse farms breeding quarter horses for show jumping, two of which were rather splendid with white picket fences.

At these primitively orchestrated dog fights, there may be as many as a hundred blacks. Thousands of dollars changed hands and most likely illegal weapons, without having a radical group sponsorship. In the past, it had been not much more than a drunken brawl, and there had always been fist fights, and the occasional shooting. The recent dog fights were a bit different, however, according to the supposed trusted informant. There may be outsiders involved now, so the police should be particularly vigilant.

The location was down a rutted dirt road inside a clump of pine forest belonging to a black farmer. The sport (if you could call the slaughter of these dogs, sport) drew crowds of blacks from the city and the entire county.

The police raid had been carefully planned by Holston, and he would place officers in strategic locations around the dogfight pit and the tin roof pavilion. When the time was right, they would spring into action. A total of ten armed officers had been deployed for the tactical attack on these suspect radicals and weapons traffickers.

At eight on a steamy Saturday night, a long string of cars began to move slowly down the Rossville dirt road, enveloping the narrow road in this mushroom cloud of dust looking like a brown fog moving toward the pavilion.

Inside the cars all the inhabitants were Negroes. There wasn't a white face among the slowly milling men who parked these late model cars in a fallow field outside the enclosed tin shack hidden amongst the pine trees.

A small footpath led to the clearing and a straight line of blacks in slacks and t-shirts. Given the lateness some even still sported dark sunglasses walking along, followed by several men who wore straw pork pie hats or sweat-encased baseball caps. Within the thick pines, this stream of men had begun to surround a corralled pit where one dog and his handler sat waiting for their opponents to arrive.

The dog held by a rope around its neck was rambunctious and pulled incessantly against the restraints. It was a muscular male pit bull that probably weighed eighty or ninety pounds, and its mouth had been fitted with a leather muzzle.

The makeshift corral was surrounded by a string of small light bulbs, and the whole arena had taken on an orange tone, lighting the many black faces. On a railing around the pit, cans of cold beer began to appear from a cart that one black man pushed, and whiskey bottles could be seen along the wood plank barrier. Cigarettes and cigars were lit and the smoke rose amidst the nighttime tumult.

No guns could be seen, though some of these men were armed with a handgun hidden in a loose pant pocket. There was camaraderie within the building crowd, and thus far, there was no obvious hint of gun running, though the night was young.

Hidden in the brush around the dog pavilion were five officers, strategically placed with twenty or thirty feet separating them in the darkness.

Within fifteen or twenty minutes the second dog and handler came out of the blackness and climbed into the pit. Another man, the organizer, stepped in front of the dogs, and he told everyone what the rules were for the fight. He said two men of his would survey the crowd and take down the bets for the competition.

Before he had finished talking, two young black men with pencils and pads began to survey the crowd around the corral for bets, writing down the name, the wager, and taking the cash. They had done this before and moved quickly and efficiently throughout the gathered garrulous men.

When they had finished, the taller of the two nodded to the organizer who sat nearby in an aluminum lawn chair. He rose and indicated that the fight would begin when he dropped a white handkerchief to the ground.

A sergeant hidden in a thicket who would give the signal for the raid had seen no brandishing of guns, thus far, or any men moving away from the wooden rails which surrounded the pit to possibly cluster elsewhere. But, it was early and he was an experienced officer that had learned patience during stake-outs. He wouldn't give the signal to move until the moment was right.

The fight began with the dogs tearing at one another. The crowd was alive with excitement, shouting and yelling for one or the other to finish its opponent with a bite to the jugular. Within six or eight minutes of the fighting, one dog had managed to bite through the muscles of the other's leg crippling him, and with an erratic limping motion, the injured dog went down and was slaughtered.

The crowd went wild, and shouts of joy and curses broke the stillness of the night. Men were laughing and patting each other on the back for their successes. Slowly then the promoter's two men made their rounds along the wooden planks paying off the winners according to the earlier tally. The dead animal was removed from the pit, and another would take its place to battle the winner. But there would be a ten or fifteen-minute lull in the violence, so some of the men moved from the railing, breaking into familiar groups of four and five friends.

Watching the movement closely with small binoculars, the police sergeant had noticed a handful of men who had trudged down the path toward a car parked in the field. His attention was focused on them as they approached the car. The man at the head of the line leaned forward and used a key to open the trunk. With a flashlight, he lit the trunk, and with the binoculars the sergeant could see weapons. Immediately, he sent one of his officers to the others with this information, and they moved quickly en mass through the darkness to intercept the black men who had surrounded the open vehicle in a small semicircle.

Within two minutes, four officers with drawn weapons were on the black men. They ordered them to drop to their knees with hands on their heads or they would be shot on the spot for resisting arrest.

The sergeant had caught up with the younger officers who had sprinted through the assault. The nighttime atmosphere had been relatively quiet other than the area behind them as the next dog fight had already started with raucous yelling and the animal growling from the pit.

Inside the trunk were three sawed-off shotguns, ten boxes of shells, and eight handguns of various calibers, all neatly laid out on a green felt cloth that you might see at a sporting goods conference. The five men on the ground who had been looking at the weapons, were cuffed and remained prone on the ground. The black man who had opened the trunk and presumably was the seller was brought to his feet and taken ten feet away where he was questioned by the sergeant.

His accent marked him from another place, and he acted unfamiliar with where he had driven. He told the sergeant he was from Oklahoma, and that he had been staying with friends in Memphis who asked him to sell the guns for them. They told him to come to this dog fight and maybe find a few customers. He had a driver's license which identified him as someone from Arkansas, but the man claimed he had left Little Rock about six or eight months earlier and had moved to Oklahoma City where he had a job with an oil company as a rigger at the nearby drilling sites.

There obviously was enough probable cause for arrests. The sergeant and one of the other officers took the man to their hidden cruiser to return him to Memphis while another officer loaded the weapons into the cruiser for transport to police headquarters downtown.

The suspects, these putative gun buyers, were also arrested and transported downtown in other police cars. The remaining officers left the site, after being pretty much undiscovered by the fight crowd, and the operation was deemed a success.

As the sergeant telephoned Holston about the raid, a smile began to cross the sun-wrinkled face of the commissioner. He whispered inaudibly to himself, "Well, I'm gonna get those black bastards now," and let out a chortle.

He hadn't been to bed yet, instead, he was sitting in his den in the midtown ranch style house waiting for the sergeant's report. The entire thing had pleased the veteran cop immensely. Now he knew this conspiracy to arm the city blacks for revolution was indeed happening, as it had been proved out by tonight's police vigilance.

It took him maybe a half hour to put on his casual clothes and drive downtown to the police detention center where the suspects were held. Once inside the building, he pulled the arresting sergeant aside, and was debriefed about everything that had been heard and seen during the night. Next he was taken into the evidence room to examine the weapons they'd confiscated.

"Well, well, those fuckers plan to use sawed-off shotguns and maybe rob a few banks while they're at it," the commissioner said to the sergeant who nodded.

"Five boxes of ten-gauge shotgun shells over there," the sergeant indicated, motioning with his head to another table across the room.

"Did the guy tell you anything?" the commissioner asked.

The sergeant laughed, "It's all the same lame bullshit, selling stuff for a friend," that they'd heard a hundred times when they arrested blacks possessing illegal weapons.

"Did you have someone dust them for fingerprints?" the commissioner continued in the conversation, and the sergeant informed him that he had the forensics expert on duty do that right away when they brought them in. They'd been here for over an hour and a half.

"Alright, let's see what our friend with the guns has to say for himself," the commissioner said and followed the sergeant down the corridor to the interrogation room where this Oklahoma suspect awaited them, neatly cuffed and guarded by a uniformed officer.

Two hours later, the commissioner left the suspect. They hadn't gotten what they wanted in order to follow the black conspiracy thread. This particular man had an aunt and uncle in Memphis, and he'd spent summers as a teenager with them. He did have some friends from those earlier associations who could have supplied him the illegal weapons. Tomorrow, the serial numbers would be checked, and they would know more.

The buyers were familiar faces to the police, and most of them had arrest records for misdemeanors and a few lesser felonies, like passing bad checks. Questions from those men produced nothing. They were street thugs who might buy a handgun or shotgun for their own violent purposes. They all denied that they were in any kind of racial revolutionary cadre, or know anyone who might be. They were who they appeared to be, petty criminals.

Holston booked and held the Oklahoma man, and would bring weapons charges against him later after additional questioning. This handful of purported gun buyers were released, though watched closely by neighborhood patrolmen.

The Oklahoma City police had no prior knowledge of the suspect, and the oil company verified his earlier employment as a rigger in its western state fields. They reported him as a decent roustabout. His aunt and uncle came downtown to seek his release. They told police that they had known him since he was a small boy, one who was always thoughtful and polite to adults, and a good Christian. They guessed he had been influenced by some bad crowd in the neighborhood, and innocently duped to sell these guns.

Holston and the investigating detective listened patiently as the elderly couple sang the boy's praises. The cops concluded the meeting when it became apparent that they had nothing to add to the conspiracy trail.

"Nice old couple," the detective pronounced, and Holston looked at his watch, with little interest in their good character.

Within a half hour, Holston and the detective brought the Oklahoma man back for further questioning, and he seemed overly agitated at the prospect.

Holston leaned over to the detective and whispered into his ear when he saw the man's face at the door, "Your boys been a little rough with their questions, maybe?" and gave the cop next to him this knowing smile.

The detective noted the smile. "No sir. Everything was done strictly by the book, as you ordered."

"Good," intoned the commissioner, "we don't want a bunch of lawyers saying we're hurting prisoners," and the sinister smile lingered.

The man who sat in front of the commissioner had a few new bruises on his coal black face, and his lip had been split. He had a look of terror on his face. Without wasting pleasantries, the detective started to question the man as the commissioner listened quietly; nothing new was said.

Finally, Holston touched the detectives arm, and said, "I have one or two questions for this gentleman."

"Yes sir," said the detective and introduced the commissioner to the suspect who became even more frightened to know he was sitting across from the top cop.

Holston spoke in a brittle voice: "Well, again, who told you to take these guns to Rossville? The same men who asked you to sell them, right?"

The suspect said, "Yes sir."

"But you haven't told us the names of these men, or where we can find them to verify your story."

"I don't remember them giving me names," the Oklahoma man answered with trembling words.

"But they knew your name, and they knew where you lived, right?"

"Yeah, I think so," the suspect uttered.

Holston curled his upper lip and spit out: "Think so?"

In a rage, he continued: "You'd better have those names for me tomorrow when I come back. If you don't, you'll spend thirty years in jail, you dumb bastard."

The next day the commissioner got the two names from the prisoner. The names Holston got were two thugs who had done time in jail for auto theft, burglary and felonious assault. They were street criminals, and bringing them in for interrogation to link them to a radical black conspiracy proved an entire waste of time.

They were in the racket of selling stolen and illegal goods on dark streets to the highest bidder, and illegal gun traffic had always been in high demand. It had been a question of simple opportunity and the hours of questioning didn't divulge any larger purpose beyond a pocketful of ready cash. The men were charged with trafficking in illegal firearms and disappeared into the court queue for later trial.

Because of this covert warfare against the unseen black revolutionary conspiracy the police commissioner had launched, Martha asked me why the District Attorney had been sent these consecutive cases, almost back to back, for illegal gun possession and sales. It struck her as rather strange. I told her as much as I knew, which had been limited as it was sifted through Wyeth's prism of how much he cared to share with me.

Jackson Wright, who had been undercover for almost five months, found no evidence of conspiracy cells among the worst Memphis gangs he moved with. The gun trade had become less lucrative to the largest two of these street gangs. Instead, they focused mainly on marijuana sales within their regular black neighborhoods. There was an increasing number of young white adults who would buy illegal drugs from dealers with no questions asked.

Wright informed Holston that he needed ten thousand dollars for drug purchases to get into these gang hierarchies and determine if they were supporting a conspiracy. He needed to put hard cash where his mouth was, and buy their trust. He would then know for certain if the black radicals were organized and posed the threat the police had assumed they did. Otherwise, all that the tactical police raids were accomplishing was the random collection of guns meant for criminals.

Initially, Holston balked at handing this rookie cop that much money from the department's disposable funds, and to buy drugs, no less. Even if the strategy for the purchase was legitimate, it would be impossible to defend publicly if it ever were to be discovered. But he went ahead and provided the cash for the operation, and within a week, Wright had bought the drugs for street distribution.

Marijuana had found its way into Memphis from East St. Louis, and before that, New Orleans, where mafia sources had gotten it from Mexican smugglers who flew it into rural airports in Louisiana.

By this time, Wright had become a high flier with the largest black gangs in the city, and the intelligence he provided the police became truly worthwhile. Now the department could closely monitor gang activity before it unfolded, and they were successful with more targeted preemptive tactics to control street crimes.

But as for penetrating those cells of black revolution, Wright never learned anything that could help Holston crack them, or if they even existed. The so-called black conspiracy remained a secret.

Even within the police department itself, there were a few seasoned captains and lieutenants who felt the commissioner was wrong. Unlike Detroit, Chicago, or even St. Louis, Memphis had been spared those violent black revolutionists in the streets. No white police officer had yet been targeted for assassination. There weren't any bank robberies to fund the armament of the more violent segments of blacks.

Nor was there any real evidence to indicate it might, and certainly not in the near future. This southern city appeared safe from institutional and targeted killings which came with the Black Panthers and the coterie of gunmen who followed them.

However, Holston continued to be recalcitrant. The man steadfastly refused to acknowledge defeat and continued his efforts to uncover conspiracies. It had completely consumed the commissioner. Many times well into the night, he could be seen pacing the floor in this stark war room he had created in the detention center basement, sometimes accompanied by two or three of his most trusted officers.

Lately, there had been a spate of arrests of black men who had been identified as persons-of-interest, and they were interrogated next to Holston's downstairs war room. The whole conspiracy thing had taken on a life of its own, unknown by many within city government and with no real accountability except to the commissioner himself.

Chapter 11
Guns

The criminal gun possession charges fell to Martha to prosecute for the District Attorney. The circumstances sounded similar to the other firearms litigation they'd encountered: illegal weapons for cash--and she dutifully began the trial process.

Holston persistently made calls to the District Attorney himself suggesting a deeper criminality, a black conspiracy theory, to overthrow the government and other ancillary felonies. The conspiracies disappeared the very moment Jim hung up the telephone. Finally, in a fit of overwrought anxiety on the direction of these cases, the commissioner made a personal visit to Jim's office. You could hear him raise his voice behind the closed door while Jim remained steadfast and calm, which he did with most out-of-control people.

You could hear Jim say, "Commissioner, the evidence doesn't support this conclusion. I'm sorry, our hands are tied."

When one of the staff attorneys passing Jim's office had recognized the commissioner's raspy voice, he made an angry face holding a closed fist in the air as if to deliver some knockout blow.

Martha sat in her small office across the narrow corridor unmoved, her eyes scanning the papers on the desk. The commissioner stormed out of the door, and said in a sarcastic manner, "Thank you for your valuable time."

After Holston had left, the District Attorney came to his door and called out, "Martha, can you come in for a few minutes?"

Inside his office, Jim let out this prolonged sigh, and said to her, "I imagine you heard everything that went on through the door," and he laughed.

"Everybody did," Martha answered, her smile demure.

Jim shook his close-clipped grey head. "That man's beyond exasperating. He's convinced the blacks are busy arming themselves for this Armageddon. If he tries to influence these gun cases, ignore him, and just refer him to me. I'll take care of it."

"I can handle it, Jim," Martha said, and seeing that there was little else to discuss she stood still, prepared to leave.

"Of course you can," Jim said with a wide grin, "I'll let you get back to work," and dropped his own eyes to the pile of folders on his desk.

It did worry Martha that the police department had become the antagonist in the whole trial process she faced. She needed to ignore that intrusion and concentrate on the successful prosecution of the charged men. These would be the first criminal cases she would try by herself, and she naturally had some pre-trial jitters about how she'd conduct herself in front of whatever criminal court judge she would face. Her only real experience in the courtroom process had been on two recent cases that the Attorney General himself had prepared and then turned over to her fellow staff lawyers. She had done all the background investigation and judicial paperwork for the trials, and both cases had been easily won.

On the drive home along Central Avenue, she kept pondering the ridiculous conspiracy theory that Holston held onto. Martha couldn't help but feel he had already become that seamy side of justice in the South: one of those corrupt racist sheriffs who blindly watched innocent men lynched. It was perhaps an over-exaggeration of the commissioner, but he had become unreconstructed to her with his fervor.

As we both made dinner, the conversation changed to the lake house. Her parents were going to deed it over to her as a birthday gift. To be fair to her sister, Alfred had put aside the value of the property in a trust available to her now British sister, Carrie, upon his death. We both loved the water and the solitude it brought apart from our city lives. After hearing the news, I went out for a pricey cabernet wine to celebrate with the light dinner.

The loss of that ante-bellum house in La Grange had disappointed Martha. She would just as soon leave Overland Place, which was chosen by her father because it was, well, nice enough, and available at a bargain price.

Both of our public service salaries didn't add up to much in those days, though we found the work meaningful, and stimulating. These weren't selfless acts on our parts, but rather a way we could be committed to a positive change in this world.

With the lake house becoming ours, we took a new interest in what we wanted it to become. Martha would draw out these sketches for an addition to the rustic house which gave us a sunroom where the side porch was, and later converted into a nursery and playroom for children. She had a childhood friend we often saw whose husband was an architect. Before I knew it the husband Mark stopped by one night to show us preliminary drawings on the lake house addition.

After he left, I looked at her and said, "Is there something I don't know? Are you pregnant?"

Martha laughed. "No, but it could happen any time, and I want us to have a house we really want and not Alfred's cottage."

Naturally, it made sense that this lake property could become the glue in our lives. I was prepared to throw myself into it whatever it took. We would devote that part of ourselves to making the rustic house a special home and an extension of these two separate people.

We had a weekend there alone, and we studied the renovations Mark had suggested. We made a few changes to his specifications, and later suggested to him that we add another bathroom off this sunroom and a semi-enclosed outdoor shower for swimmers to use.

The next weekend Amanda and Randy came and stayed for Friday night and half of Saturday. It was pleasant enough, and Amanda didn't say much about what usually remained unspoken though she did insist that we see more of each other as we trolled the lake for biting bass at dusk.

I could see Randy and Martha in conversation on the side porch, probably some subject concerning childhood diseases which was a favorite topic of Randy's. Recently he said he planned to specialize more in childhood cancer treatment. He was a stellar man in most ways, and probably had no clue as to what

Amanda was beyond the cloying behavior she'd shown him as a young wife. It was something unfortunately a little different from his mother Estelle, whom I'd met at cocktail parties over the years.

Estelle had this annoying habit of talking baby talk with adults, usually men. The more liquor she consumed, the more she practiced it. That inane babbling was accepted as normal dialogue at some summertime garden party because, after all, she was Estelle. She had been indulged as a young girl during a time when young debutants in Memphis could act silly. They were these ridiculous concoctions of infantile words, such as 'drinky-poo'. Though she was an accomplished portrait painter who had been trained at Moore in Philadelphia, she insisted on employing this continuous drunken childish banter.

At the beginning of the second year of her son's marriage, Estelle had asked Amanda if she wouldn't sit for a portrait. Amanda had sung out, "Nude? I've love to," to the narrowed eyes of Estelle's somber husband Jere.

"An odalisque, please," Amanda added to the reddened family faces, and then she shook her dark hair with this deep belly laugh.

"You're so serious," she'd reprimanded her father-in-law who had managed this weakest of smiles, and nervously took another sip of his bourbon and water whose ice had melted in the July heat.

Jere was a gangly, bent-over man of sixty something with thinning hair. He had done well in commercial real estate as northern factories relocated to Memphis for its cheaper labor costs. He favored blue pinstripe suits, or pink oxford cloth shirts and chino pants and was wearing the latter ensemble for this weekend.

In his favor however, Jere was no pushover. He had been a B-17 pilot as a young man during the Second World War flying fifty missions over Germany. Jere had been shot down in 1944 on a bombing mission, and basically carried his co-pilot, another boy from the South, on his back across miles of German soil until they were captured and imprisoned in a prison camp outside Dresden.

As a child, he had been interested in painting, and his own mother had a reputation then in Little Rock, and later Memphis, as a watercolorist of ornate flower arrangements. In fact, Jere had carried a mini-set of watercolors in his flight uniform with a tiny brush. For the nine months, he had been in the German prison camp, Stalag 64 he had carefully recorded the lives of these American and British flight crews. Jere had painted them on the backs of cardboard matchboxes that he had broken open flat.

Upon liberation, Jere had kept most of these tiny matchbook paintings in a box the Germans allowed him to keep once they saw that he was a serious artist. They were mostly figures of the men standing around, and miniature portraits.

When Jere returned home to Memphis and married Estelle, he had finally shown her his wartime watercolors. She marveled at his technical knowhow, and that may have been the very reason she finally married him.

About ten years after the war, Estelle had arranged with the Memphis Academy of Art where director Ted Johnson was a close friend to host an exhibit of the German prison camp watercolors. At the time, it had created a sensation and the Commercial Appeal had run two color pages in its Sunday magazine and later offered to print a monograph of the exhibit miniatures. The hardbound book now sat on Estelle's coffee table and was a source for continuous comment, particularly after several cocktails.

Looking at this man now, it was rather difficult to picture him inside the glass cockpit of a Flying Fortress dodging those German guns, yet he had. He had been awarded the Distinguished Flying Cross, a Bronze Star for bravery, and the Purple Heart medal for his wounds, though he never mentioned them to a soul.

He would bore you with his weekend golfing scores, or what the output of the new Panasonic factory he'd located to Memphis was, but he'd never comment on his wartime experiences. The young co-pilot he'd kept alive until the prison camp died in his arms of a fever from wound complications. To this day, the very mention of that young pilot brought tears to his old eyes.

Estelle hadn't wanted Randy to marry Amanda, even though it was obvious that she was a very beautiful young woman, and most men would jump at the chance. Estelle had called her 'high strung' and 'headstrong,' and worried that she would dominate her more passive son which was perhaps the case, as it had been in her own marriage.

Amanda had always done exactly what she wanted. The exquisite face and the slender figure let her get away with it, and often. When Amanda finally paid attention to Randy's advances, returning the smallest of affection, he became fatally smitten with this dark-haired belle, and the hospital resident quickly proposed marriage.

In her mid-twenties, Amanda thought it was time for marriage as did most of her southern contemporaries, and she accepted, perhaps not loving him, and they were married in the Episcopal cathedral downtown.

For some odd reason, Estelle had recruited the Bishop who had lived in Nashville to perform the wedding that June Saturday. No doubt her motivation was to have a remarkable ceremony for this marriage with a true prince of the church officiating, and the elderly man succumbed to her charms. Maybe she had painted his portrait in exchange for the arduous ecclesiastical journey to Memphis.

Even though Amanda and Randy weren't invited to the lake house as often as they appeared, it didn't matter to Martha. She embraced having her cousin around the cabin. Randy wasn't the most stimulating guest for a weekend, though he held his own in the wide range of subjects we discussed which often ended in hot and heavy alcohol-fueled debates.

Amanda and I hadn't been intimate since the snakebite episode, but it was still on her mind. If her words didn't encourage me, her body language did. Yet, it all escaped the notice of Randy and Martha, and from what they knew or had seen, we were simply a group of close friends who liked each other immensely.

Those warm weather lake visits continued, until I had asked Amanda to stop and she'd flown into a vicious rage. After that unpleasant weekend, she stayed close to home and she hadn't talked to Martha for weeks, which was unusual.

Eventually Amanda called me, and I met her for lunch downtown at an eatery she had chosen. Sitting around us with dress shirts and ties was a lunchtime crowd from the city offices and banks, and Amanda confessed that she wanted to continue what we clearly had found together. Her life with Randy wasn't anything that she wanted. He had been pressing her incessantly about starting a family, a thought she said had disgusted her. I admitted to her that I just didn't know, and it seemed suicidal to pursue this unhealthy relationship, although I had wanted it to continue. We finished our lunch with an unspoken agreement to continue. She kissed me gently on the mouth at the restaurant door, as any mother might do for a son, and ran around the corner to the city garage for her car.

Martha became wrought with the two criminal cases for the illegal guns, and for some reason, they were put at the head of the court docket. The first trial was scheduled for nine o'clock that following Tuesday morning, much to her chagrin. She believed she needed more time for preparation and had appealed to Jim who told her pointedly that she was ready.

The nights leading up to the trial, she would come home and lock herself in the bedroom with pretrial papers, picking dinner out of the refrigerator and working until bedtime. By the end of the second night of this, I simply went along with whatever her schedule needed to be, and silently read a novel in the den.

At breakfast on the morning of the trial, she was already nervous and had spilled coffee on her skirt, then had to hurriedly put on another outfit. By the end of the afternoon, I was anxious to call her and see how it went, though I restrained myself until I would see her at home.

Being the first home, I made myself a drink and sat in our makeshift den when I heard the side door open. I called out to her, "How did it go?"

"Well, "she said and paused, "I need a drink first, "and I quickly made her one from the small bar we'd set up in a sideboard.

She took a deep drink from the whiskey glass, and turned to me with a smile, "Actually, it went quite well. The suspect was found guilty on all charges. The sentence will be read tomorrow afternoon, and I imagine he'll get five years."

I gave her a thumbs up sign, and laughed.

"When I started to present the opening remarks to the court, my throat closed up, but then the first words came out of my mouth, the sound of them calmed me down, and after that, I was fine for the whole trial."

"Congratulations darling," I said to her and gave her this huge bear hug until she said she couldn't breathe. "I'm so proud of you."

Martha was almost breathless: "Well, this particular criminal court judge is known as a 'law and order' type. Generally, if the evidence doesn't fall apart before his very eyes, he usually finds against these defendants."

"The black defendant pleaded: Not Guilty. His defense lawyer claimed unknown men had duped his client and he had no knowledge that the guns were illegal. The judge looked more bored than angry with the whole thing."

I marched around the small living room with pride. "I can't believe you won your first case so decisively. You're one tough lady lawyer."

The other trial followed ten days later with the same outcome. The Oklahoma black man was found guilty and his sentencing would follow.

Martha had been victorious in her first two criminal court appearances with solid convictions, and the results blossomed on her face. Her eyes brightened and her skin seemed to glow with her lakeside tan. She was confident of the future. When she was around people, there seemed to be more openhandedness from her than before. It was almost as if she had become unshackled from Carolyn's damning influence, reminding her that she could be even smarter, or more accomplished, if she really tried. Because she wasn't prettier than her sister, life would be more difficult for her. All these awful things had weighed her down for years, and she'd come to loathe herself, though now that might disappear. Martha had a new lease on life.

Jim Latham had praised her strategies and tactics in the courtroom to her fellow staff lawyers. The men surrounding her at the District Attorney's office grudgingly took the first steps toward respect for her considerable talents.

Martha had proven herself under fire in front of rather strict jurists. These two prosecutions would be the beginning of her many courtroom successes.

For the next two weeks Martha walked those steps of euphoria. She was aggressive in what she demanded for her caseload, and she had her way. She had proven herself, and teamed up with one of the more experienced staffers to prosecute a rape charge.

The assault had been on a white woman that Martha had known, but hadn't recognized from her years at St. Mary's School. This woman was four or five grades behind her, though she had an older brother. Martha had known him among her circle. He had played polo briefly and she'd lost track of him when he went to college on the East Coast and had stayed. Martha thought he lived in New York, or New Haven. She wasn't quite sure, just 'New' something.

This alleged rape had been during daylight hours in the parking lot of a state building for social services. Missy Connelly, the young woman attacked, had been a caseworker for the Tennessee Department of Human Services, more commonly known as the Welfare Department.

The social workers came and went from the Department headquarters as their field worked determined. That afternoon Missy had finished filing applications for renewals for several of her women clients with small children. She had spent the entire day at the office, and had opened her car door when a black man grabbed her from behind and forced her back onto the front seat. He pinned her flat on her back with her arms at her sides. The man was over six feet tall and muscular. He held a sharpened screwdriver at Missy's throat and told her he would kill her if she made a sound. Terrified she nodded her head and whispered, "Please don't hurt me."

The man warned her again to be quiet, and he pulled up her short skirt and tore off her bikini underpants with his strong fingers. Then shoved two squat fingers inside her vagina and turned them round and round to lubricate the opening. And in that next fearful moment, he raped her on a sunny Thursday afternoon in the state office complex parking lot.

After he finished, the black slapped her face, and told her never to talk about this to anyone and ran into the shadows. Twenty minutes later, she had enough strength to get out of the car and walk into the state building.

Hysterical, she explained to the uniformed security guard what had occurred. This older white man immediately called the police, and a cruiser with two officers came to the scene.

The officers were sensitive to what had happened, and when they learned it was a black, they became enraged but kept their emotions in check. They immediately got on the department radio and called for a female officer to meet them at the Methodist Hospital emergency room. The standard police procedure for rape victims was followed. The subsequent medical examination she underwent and the following police questions horrified Missy yet somehow she had the strength to get through it.

A month after the assault, again through some paid police informer who had heard another black man brag about 'screwing some white woman' in the state office parking lot, an arrest was made.

Her clothes from the assault had been retained as evidence, and sample of semen had been found on her skirt. The semen matched this black man's DNA, and the fingerprints taken off the door handle were identical to the alleged suspect. DNA examination was a new forensics test that had just been approved for the police. It wasn't well-known, but had found increased usage.

The man had no police record, and the informant's tip gave the police probable cause to detain him for questioning. He worked as a day laborer for the local Manpower office, and did mostly landscaping tasks. He lived with his elderly mother on a small Southside street where he'd been his entire life. When the officers knocked on his front door, he had run out the back and was climbing a fence to escape when he was subdued and arrested.

After booking at the downtown center, he was presented to the victim for identification as part of a line up at police headquarters. Missy identified him as her assailant. This was the rapist she told the two detectives working on the case who then took her written statement.

The suspect denied he had committed the rape. He claimed he had never seen this woman before, and he hadn't been near the State parking lot on that particular day or any other day that week or the one before it. He couldn't prove his whereabouts.

For the District Attorney's office, the suspect's semen DNA samples on the victim's clothes substantiated his guilt, and, they had his fingerprints too. What was uncertain was exactly how the court-appointed defense attorney might try the case.

Undoubtedly, Missy would be called to testify and identify the defendant as her rapist in open court. But the defense cross examination surely would be ugly and publicly humiliating for her, as they usually were.

Martha was the lead attorney in the case, and she arranged a meeting with Missy out of the DA's office at some anonymous downtown café. They talked about the trial for maybe an hour. She warned Missy that at best, these trials were vile.

She wasn't certain what the defense courtroom tactics might be, though Martha was certain that hurtful things would be said. This case was different from many rape trials since they had conclusive forensic evidence from the scene that matches this man as the assailant. What Martha had hoped for, was to approach the defense attorney and suggest that if this defendant pleaded guilty, there could be some plea arrangement. An agreement would be made which involves substantial prison time: eight to ten instead of the maximum twenty-year incarceration.

If this occurred, Missy wouldn't be subjected to this painful trial, and justice would be done. The man would definitely go to prison, most likely for ten years.

Upon hearing that, the only thing Missy could do was weep into her hands. Martha reached across the booth and pulled Missy's head to her shoulder and let her cry as long as she wished.

This was a rape case Martha said to herself as she drove home that evening. This was not some black being railroaded. The evidence against him was too conclusive and he should go to prison for this horrendous crime. "I'll put him there for ten long years. I promise you that much." Martha whispered to herself as she turned off the car ignition.

Several meetings with the defense attorney produced no clear path to bargaining. He claimed it was a case of mistaken identity in the police line-up and suggested that the forensic results may have been tampered with to get an easy conviction in court. It was a back-and-forth conversation that appeared to go nowhere, and finally Jim Latham talked to the defense attorney himself.

In the DA's office, he had pointedly told Martha, "This clown is going to be hung out to dry along with his rapist client, and I'm going to be sitting in the goddamn courtroom alongside you. I'll tell Percy that I'm replacing him on the prosecution."

The trial day soon came, and Jim Latham was true to his word. He tore apart the clumsy defendant when he took the stand to testify, catching him out in his own sad lies. Latham had the jury eating out of his hand as he talked them through the entire case, point by point.

When Missy finally took the stand, the defense attorney started to get particularly ugly suggesting she spent most of her off-hours haunting bars with numerous affairs. The defense said that she had seen a psychotherapist at some point during her late adolescence, and perhaps had suffered from misplaced desires and invited random men to have sex with her. It was nonsense, though it clearly hurt Missy as she wept openly on the stand.

At last, the judge had shut down the defense comments, striking them from the court record. Then with a brilliant cross-examination strategy, Latham smoothed the way for the jury to convict the rape suspect, disputing everything the defense had presented.

In less than an afternoon, the jury returned its verdict: They found the defendant guilty of all charges and returned him to the city detention center without bail before sentencing. The sentence returned was thirty years in prison without the possibility of parole, and since the man was fifty, it may well have been his death sentence.

Unfortunately, Martha had little part in the trial, but she'd seen a consummate and experienced prosecutor systematically and with great finesse convince the judge and jury as to the defendant's obvious guilt.

Leaving the courtroom, Latham refused to shake the defense attorney's hand and stormed past him out the door, muttering under his breath that the man was a grandstander trying to build his reputation on the backs of ignoramuses.

Martha did all the paperwork for the trial, and Latham had reviewed it and prepared his courtroom strategy praising her for her attention to detail.

She liked working with Jim and knew he respected her. The whole experience of being a part of his courtroom expertise had invigorated her. He trusted her in the trenches of court. She knew that if there came a difficult case to win, that he would hand it to her and she became euphoric again.

Despite the court victory, the city newspapers had sensationalized the entire proceedings. The two dailies and the local TV stations had dragged poor Missy into the continuing racial polarity. A white woman had been raped in broad daylight at the state office complex, which was supposed to be safe by some crazed black man who may have wanted her murdered. He had been armed with a weapon.

How safe were the city streets? The biting newspaper editorials challenged the police commissioner. Why can't a young woman walk without fear of her life to her car after a day's work at a state office complex? Was this the same as a deserted back alley or late night saloon? Tell us where there's a safe place in the city of Memphis? The critics continued to bombard the mayor and his police commissioner. Why can't we walk the streets? This never-ending barrage went on and on unabated.

Finally, Wyeth met with Holston and told his police commissioner who was still wrought up with black radical conspiracies that they had to do something about this lack of confidence they faced.

Maybe the city should put more policemen on the neighborhood beats, and increase the visibility of uniformed officers in the white enclaves midtown and out in East Memphis. The mayor contended it wasn't a matter of community relations with an expansion of community service officers and more police athletic camps for disadvantaged youths. They needed an offensive, and right now, to stop the spread of violent crimes. There was no other alternative available to them.

"You need to double the car and foot patrols, and if it costs more in overtime, we'll find the money," Wyeth urged Holston who remained mute.

"We can try that, yes," Holston added with this disingenuous look.

Wyeth became more excited. "Look, I want to create some kind of crime prevention task force, with prominent people, white and black, some preachers and whatever, to get that confidence back."

"Wyeth, that's not enough," Holston warned. "You're talking about rapists, murderers, and radicals. You need to get them where they live. We're talking blacks now. That's where almost all of the violent crimes come from."

"What do you suggest?" Wyeth asked, his hands nervously turning a ball point pen around and around.

"You go into those black shitholes, and you put the fear of God in them. That's how you get it done: break a few fucking noses, some arms and legs. Then they get the cops mean business."

Wyeth looked at Holston incredulously, unconvinced that these rough vigilante tactics could do anything. Yet he told the commissioner to try anyway.

"Just keep the goddamn District Attorney off my back, alright?" Holston added, rising from the chair and starting out of the mayor's office.

The city newspapers continued to criticize Wyeth's administration as soft on crime, and the battle for safer streets began in Memphis.

Chapter 12
Cracks in the Sidewalk

Amanda started to behave more neurotically, although any intimacy we chanced was mostly infrequent, but still, it was a wholly dangerous game to play. She kept pestering me about finally leaving Martha, and then the two of us could escape to Miami, Atlanta, or even Jackson where she'd grown up.

"We could be courageous and just stay in Memphis," she said once at an impromptu lunch downtown. "I don't give a damn what Estelle thinks, or even my own cousin. Not when it's my life we're talking about."

Honestly, I don't know why I continued with her, except that she was the most beautiful woman I'd ever known, and one who returned my affection at least. In a sense, I became the unwilling prisoner of my own emotions. Did I love her? I had convinced myself that maybe I did, otherwise how could I continue this madness. Nobody would understand, or forgive what we were doing. But I couldn't take that last step somehow, to give up on Martha and finish our short marriage, and change my life. Yet, I did think about it long and hard, 'Stop this while there's time. Don't wait until you have two kids, and walk away. Do it now. That's what Amanda wants, and she's ready to do the same.'

Amanda didn't harangue me too often about leaving Martha. It sort of came and went in this tango we danced. I think she savored the gravest danger. It somehow fulfilled an out of balance void she had for conflict. She was often far too headstrong, and her attractiveness had allowed it to continue. She orchestrated the intimacy she and I enjoyed and wrote the rules for the game.

Randy was going on a five-day medical conference to New Orleans and he had wanted her to accompany him. She made those few excuses she needed to make, so he left disappointed that he had to sit alone beside other doctors and their wives poolside in the French Quarter. She would've been elegant in her floral print sundresses; he had mused looking out the aircraft window at the Crescent City skyline.

At this point, thornier court cases had come Martha's way that took more of her time. Jim Latham included her in more litigation than some of the other staff lawyers, but he had made certain there wasn't bad blood. Latham had given all his lawyers courtroom opportunities, and made certain everyone had important cases.

More weekends were spent at the lake house, even into the winter, which was mostly rainy. The week that Randy was in New Orleans, Amanda had invited herself to the lake after calling Martha. Because Martha was involved in a prison deposition taken that evening at Brushy Mountain, I went out with Amanda.

Why Martha never thought about Amanda and I being thrown together away from prying eyes, I'll never know. Maybe it was her naivety, or she didn't care. Every one of our friends and acquaintances could see how Amanda behaved. Though perhaps, if you act like that all the time, it somehow neutralizes any danger.

We spent that Friday night at the lake house, and slept together in the master bedroom. It was the first time in several months, and we both liked it.

In the morning Amanda brought me coffee, and had already lit a small fire in the living room fireplace. She had been up for hours, and we sat close together on the couch looking at the morning mist on the lake surface.

"Alfred was the smartest in the family, you know, like Martha is," she said without purpose. "My nutty mother Louise was the middle child, and pretty conventional for her time. My father was an engineer and provider."

I moved closer to her and put my arm tighter around her slender shoulders.

"The youngest child Elkington, or Elk, as he was called, went off to the Pacific war and came back to Columbus. But being ambitious afterward he went off to Bucknell on the G.I. Bill. He had met this pushy Irish Catholic girl somewhere, that's Marlene, and she talked him into going to law school at Cornell, which he did. She was from Buffalo where it snows all the time, and her priest uncle married them in St. Something or Other right there."

"I see," I said in answer to her storytelling.

"Uncle Elk got this job in Louisville with Procter and Gamble. They stayed there supposedly happy for ten years and he didn't come back much. But, she was this staunch Irish Catholic alright, and they had five kids in maybe eight years. Is that possible? Eight years?"

She started to count pregnancies on her fingers.

"Yeah, I guess you could do that," she figured, and got up to go in the kitchen to refill her coffee cup and mine.

"He was whip smart, and I'm told they loved him at Proctor and Gamble, but he wanted to live somewhere else other than dull Louisville, and for some strange reason, they went back to Buffalo."

She took a long drink of the warm coffee and smiled at me, continuing: "Well, she had that priest uncle there, maybe that's why. Anyway, Elk couldn't find a decent job as a lawyer, and he started to behave irrationally. Not like some man who was at the top of his law class at Cornell. He saw things at night that no one else saw, and he had these nightmares."

I had listened carefully to what she said, and offered, "Maybe he was having a nervous breakdown, it happens to intelligent people too."

"Oh, I know that," Amanda said. "But he couldn't work at all, and they had these five young kids. All one right after the other. I guess that's what Irish Catholic girls like to do, have a lot of children. Very old country."

"Maybe they wanted them," I ventured.

"Well, he didn't because Elk had called Alfred from Buffalo late one night, and he said, 'this is too much for me, I can't go on living like this, it's insane.' and two days later he killed himself. I think he hanged himself in the basement."

"My god, how horrible. I'm so sorry," I confessed at the sadness of the story.

Amanda said she wasn't sure why she had thought of this morbid tale. Maybe it was the frost on the outside of the lake house windows that made her think of frigid Buffalo.

Despite all these disconnects with Amanda and her often neurotic behavior, when we were together it was such complete serenity. With Martha, everything was obsessive control she desperately wanted: Where were you were sitting and did you have the right coaster under the coffee cup? When was the car insurance payment due? Did you write a thank you note to the Hopkinson's yet? It was incessant, that compulsion to know everything you did, or even thought, and right now, this very minute. It exhausted me.

What else could it be but this lifetime of her mother monitoring her every waking moment from the crib through elementary school and onward to now. This awful mold remained unbroken. I found myself waiting for her to direct every move we would make in our miserable lives, and I had come to thoroughly resent it. Maybe that alone was enough reason for Amanda. I don't know.

Amanda was spontaneous. I think she was painfully honest with her own emotions. Whatever manipulation she employed to get what she wanted was always easily transparent. She had an honesty with herself that Martha lacked, and perhaps I did too.

Martha could be affectionate and she often was. She would do wonderful things for people she liked or loved, and for me often. However, she was beyond any disagreement or reproach, no matter how small. She'd couldn't admit when she was wrong, ever. Her position was always intractable, and in the end, she defended it with rage. It killed the innocence of a husband and wife dialogue because you were always on your guard. Whatever beliefs she held, religious or political, or even otherwise, they were all unassailable. It tired me each day. What you do in a situation, such as mine with Martha, is that you don't push back any more. Instead, you go around and circumvent that person. You find a way to avoid those subjects which might invite discord then you distance yourself, and that's precisely what I did. Maybe Amanda was my ticket out of the swamp.

If Martha moved a book, she denied it, and if she'd left the car keys on the living room coffee table, she hadn't done it. There was no incident where she could be the one held responsible, no matter how insignificant. You watched what you said when you made even simple conversation with her and learned the pitfalls of suggesting a complicity where she might be a willing partner to it. To get along with Martha, you handed her back what you thought she wanted, or wanted to hear. It was no more complicated than that, and sometimes, it was unbearable.

We're all broken in some profound manner. That terrible despondency was carried to me from my mother's depression. The total avoidance of any conflict, which came out of living in a domestic war zone in that tortuous coal town house, all added up to this unbalance that I had pretended not to possess. It was an act.

Martha's quick intelligence allowed people to accept her awful obsessive control as Amanda's beauty let her do the unthinkable. They had an almost automatic forgiveness on the other end. Martha's desire for this absolute simply wore you down. You were sentenced to Chinese water torture for all time in the purgatory marriage while drip after drip came down on your forehead. Then she would fool you one day by bringing home some thoughtful gift, and shock you with her warm generosity.

Because Martha was smart, she would do nice things for people that registered with quick thanks. It made you think perhaps you were always on her mind, when you weren't, or not often. Instead, Martha wanted you to be where she expected you to be, and there were never any surprises with her.

After a time, watching Carolyn fussing over how many cigarettes were in her pack at 4pm, or counting her Crane's thank you note cards when she hadn't planned to write one, you began to see those similarities between mother and her eldest daughter. The first thought was that it was alcoholic behavior and the ever present desire to plan for your next drink.

When Martha came to the lake house on Saturday, Amanda had dutifully made a cold lunch, and we ate it on the side porch. We let Martha unwind from the earlier deposition, and the pressure of her most recent court case.

"I've never seen a man with more tattoos," she said of the black prisoner she had deposed. "He's doing fifteen years for manslaughter and has had a long history with gangs in New Orleans and Memphis," she went on.

"What were the tattoos like?" Amanda asked as she munched on a baked chicken breast, pulling off the white meat in strips and dropping it into her mouth from several inches away as if she were a trained seal.

"Some of them were of voodoo stuff, and he had these blue and green vines that wrapped around his neck that went up to his mouth."

"Disgusting," offered Amanda and she laughed wiping her small greasy hands with a napkin.

"He was articulate, and that kind of threw me, for some guy that beat another man to death with a lead pipe," Martha explained. "Hit him so many times his skull had flattened."

"Like those crows on the road?" piped in Amanda.

I've often wondered, if people, particularly women, can sense the emotion for a lover on someone's face, or maybe in the voice. If they've ever been intimate, then it's a dead giveaway. They know the infidelity. That's what I'd heard anyway, though Martha rattled on with her cousin, laughing and describing the catcalls from the tiers of cells when she'd strolled by the inmates with the warden.

We moved inside after a while and Martha went to change. Amanda just shrugged her shoulders with her gentle smile.

"Guess I sleep alone tonight. Oh well," she sang in a soft whisper.

The whole thing was inexplicable to me, and it defied understanding that this subterfuge with Amanda could continue undetected.

I had started to make a fire and had gone outside to get more logs from the woodpile when I heard Martha's laughter with Amanda. In the firelight Martha and Amanda discussed mutual women friends, some of whom were starting families, or a new marriage, and others who had divorced. They had assigned blame to the divorced women, except in one instance. The husband had left her. He never came back from his real estate office out East at the end of the workday. It had been going on for six months and there had been no word from him. His local family was mortified at what he'd done, particularly his father who was a law school colleague of Alfred's.

They also talked about Lee Garrett, at whose guesthouse I'd stayed years ago with Rusty when I met Martha, and how strange he'd become lately. Martha said that he's turned into this ultra conservative. She thought he had become involved with people on the Far Right. Not those ridiculous redneck militiamen who flew Confederate flags from their pick-ups. No, he was involved with men with money and influence who flew their own corporate jets into Memphis for a dinner meeting and owned hundred million dollar companies. They threw their money around where they wanted, and often covertly.

"I'd heard slave labor with Lee," Amanda added to the conversation.

"What?" I exclaimed looking at her in amazement.

She leaned forward in the chair. "Well, I'd heard he bought that Madison Chicken operation in Arkansas with two other guys. Jack Steffin and somebody, and they run these four or five plants, and pay people that do the plucking fifty cents an hour."

"Oh c'mon, Amanda, that's against the law. It's not close to minimum wage," I said.

"Anyway, that's what I heard," she crooned, "and from a really good source, his ex-wife."

That brought a roar of laughter from Martha and me, then the three of us laughed so hard until we were almost in tears.

How could we all be this close? I thought to myself, and do what we're doing, as if it's almost normal to be sleeping with each other. Was that right, and with whom, and where? Isn't it betrayal of someone? Yet, as I stared at Amanda's full red lips, then to her sparkling brown eyes, I suddenly didn't care what happened, or certainly who might judge me for what had occurred. This was a horrible betrayal of the so-called sacraments, for that was what we were doing to each other.

Martha had Monday off, and she wanted to stay an extra evening at the lake house. If I joined her, that meant driving into town at the crack of dawn. But we decided to do it, and Amanda left that afternoon as she planned.

In the evening, we sat in front of a roaring fire as there was a chill outside in the winter air. Martha asked me, "What do you really think of her, Amanda? The truth."

The question took me off guard, and for a moment I felt that it had dangerous implications, though her face gave no evidence of discovery. I took a drink of the bourbon I had poured, and said, "Well, she's a delight."

Martha said, "She's as sweet as can be, and crazy too, but in a good way."

"Amanda's better than most company we see, and that's a fact," I added with perhaps too much emphasis on her qualities as a guest.

Quickly I added, "Randy's a little dull. If only he came around, it would get a little tiresome. He tries too hard. That's it."

Martha let out this loud groan, "Gawd, with a mother like Estelle who wouldn't be awkward? The woman finishes your damn sentence when you're with her."

Then Martha was silent, looking at her folded hands.

"You knew all about that stuff at Auburn, the Virgin Mary story, right?"

Lying in this case, I told Martha, no, I hadn't heard that and what was it about? I was curious to learn what Martha's interpretation of the bizarre tale might be, maybe a different perspective.

She repeated pretty much everything I had already heard from two others, so long ago that I hardly remembered who had told me. I only remembered that it was during the wedding week at a friend's house who were an older couple hosting a celebratory dinner for the two of us.

Amanda had been chosen as a bridesmaid, naturally as she was Martha's only female cousin. During those otherwise sedate festivities, Amanda began dancing on a table drunk. Someone had shared the damning college story with me as part of the explanation for what I was watching. She had been wild and unbridled in her dance and had this primal ecstasy etched upon her alabaster face as the man told me that unnerving Birmingham Christmas saga.

While he spoke I simply nodded and continued to watch Amanda as I couldn't take my eyes off of the gorgeous young woman with the long, black hair across the room as she swung madly and then abruptly jumped from the table to a leg split on the oriental carpet amidst the crowd cheers.

Martha finished the Birmingham story with shrugged shoulders, and said, "Amanda's Amanda, there's not much more to say, really," and she smiled.

I shrugged my shoulders in unison.

"Amanda's an amoral creature," Martha ventured further. "She's not like other women. She's capable of most anything, though her life seems simple enough as a doctor's wife."

My eyes followed her closely anticipating the accusation which I thought would soon come, and I asked, "Why do you think so? Her life seems normal enough to me."

"She could work for one thing," Martha added, "you know, more than all the volunteering." At last I thought I had found her reason to discuss Amanda. As there was some lingering resentment, I encouraged her.

I pronounced this hasty analysis. "Amanda wants to be a society woman but she's already there. She's only missing the two children and they'll come soon enough."

"No, that's not what I mean," Martha continued, "Honestly, it's as if she doesn't know the line between right and wrong," and she gave me examples of a few things over the past few years.

"Martha, for God sake, she's young." I said, "We all do stupid things, and I've had my share, things I'd wanted to undo."

"You don't understand." she insisted, "It's alright in Amanda's mind to sleep with a friend's husband. She'd do it if she felt like it."

I gave her this sarcastic laugh, and felt a tenseness take over my whole body and said, "Oh, you know someone Amanda's sleeping with?"

"Well no, I don't, and it may never happen. But if it did, she wouldn't have any guilt. That's how Amanda is, amoral."

"Martha, Martha," I called out, "that sounds plain silly. Amanda's headstrong but she's not going to ruin her marriage for some unnamed fling."

"Look, I've known Amanda her entire life, and the idea of right and wrong doesn't exist for her."

"Okay, it doesn't exist, but I still like her anyway," I added, perhaps with too much of the disingenuous and I checked myself from saying more.

"Are you to disinvite her from the lake?" I asked, almost curious.

"No, I'm not going to do that. I love her too much," Martha explained. "It's just that she's an amoral woman. That's my point."

"I understand," I said and asked her with a nod if she wanted another drink, and assuming she did I went to refill her glass.

"You think I'm being mean," Martha called out to me as I was getting ice from the refrigerator. "But I'm not."

"Oh no," I shouted. "It's an observation of someone you've known forever. I get it, alright, you can hold any opinion you want. Maybe I'll see Amanda as amoral too, could be."

"Enough on morality," she tossed out, laughing. "Where's my drink?"

"Served now to her majesty," I said, mimicking a royal chamberlain to the queen.

The brief conversation was all about Amanda, and not why was I sleeping with her cousin or why did she constantly insinuate herself, and sometimes her dull doctor husband so often into our otherwise tranquil lives.

We sat there for hours looking into the blazing fire. Martha talked about the cases she expected to prosecute, and now as a seasoned trial lawyer, win. I was happy to listen, though maybe desultory.

The thing about Martha was that she was a curious woman, and she had spotted the orange moon in the winter sky. We walked down to the lakeshore and saw that it was conjunct with the planet Venus.

I'd asked her what that meant to astrologers, and she laughed, saying, "It's a time of love, heightened emotion. And maybe time for a child."

We held hands loosely, hers holding my splayed fingers, as we walked up the bank toward the house. I was furtively thinking to myself to inhabit that moment in front of me, whatever it may be, because there's nothing else.

When I stepped into the office on Monday morning, Wyeth was beside himself. The editorial board of the Commercial Appeal had taken him to task in the Sunday newspaper. It published a half-page expose of why Memphis had become a crime-ridden city. They clearly laid the blame at the feet of the incumbent mayor who had two terms in office to get it right, and he obviously hadn't.

Cowboy tactics of the city police belonged in Deadwood, not in the South's second or third largest city. Black street gangs now controlled vast sections of the city. Thugs dispensed their own brand of justice through killings and torture and not the municipal courts any longer.

Memphis had lost its war on violent crime. You only needed to look around and it became painfully evident on every street corner. No one was safe: women, children, and the elderly were in constant danger.

The article was perhaps the most damaging description of a city that I have ever read, and the only thing I could say to Wyeth was, "My God, they went overboard. Who in the hell allowed them to do this?"

"Scripps Howard, the owner, that's who," Wyeth said. "They're sitting on the West Coast and they don't give a shit. We're all a bunch of crackers to them."

"But it's bullshit, unwarranted attacks." I threw out, "The editors live here, and they know better, c'mon. This is a set-up."

"I don't know what it is, but they've handed me my head on a platter," Wyeth continued looking glassy-eyed. "The city council will be running for the tall grass, and we can forget about their help. We have been hung out to dry."

"Can't we call the television stations? Get some time for our side of the story," I laid out excitedly. "Harry Tucker's a friend, and he's got the biggest station."

Wyeth got up from his desk, and looked out the window at the city complex parking lot, and confessed, "I didn't think they'd stab me in the back."

They had done just that, though Wyeth was complicit in what he hadn't done to stem the street crime in the city. He thought it was only about cops on the street, not about any dialogue between the haves and the have-nots. About half of the innocent blacks in the ravaged neighborhoods lived under this continuing, though unacknowledged boot heel of segregation. It was in the schools, the workplace, and in the hearts of whites who lived in that particular South of forty or sixty years ago, and it continued. In the small towns around Memphis they even lynched blacks.

The recent turmoil that had taken place in the black ghettos in Los Angeles, Detroit, and a handful of other cities, had been averted in Memphis for the most part. The dam hadn't broken so there was no reason to offer an olive branch. This obvious concern of an armed rebellion, the attacks on police, and random white killings by these enraged black radicals troubled the mayor.

Wyeth thought mayhem in the streets was possible and feared the potential slaughter of innocent people. He couldn't embrace the philosophy of his police commissioner that this horrible conflict had already started. The recent raft of burglaries of sporting goods stores, and the dozen stolen rifles didn't mean radical blacks, or Black Panthers had become rampant. They wouldn't murder whites in cold blood on Memphis streets.

That was Holston's fear, and it wasn't shared outside of the city police department that he ran like a feudal fiefdom. This unquestioning loyalty from some of these officers mirrored that of some besieged and battle tested battalion bracing itself for the enemy's final charge. It was the battle of Corinth that the South would win this time.

The simple fact that Wyeth couldn't control, or even talk rationally, to his own police chief made matters that much worse in this fearful river town. The sensible thing to do was to replace Holston with a more moderate, less contentious administrator. Then reach out to those beleaguered neighborhood blacks, opening a dialogue where there might be some real trust, and defuse those awful confrontations on the street that left people dead. But, for some unknown reason, Wyeth wouldn't do it. Instead, he continued to butt heads repeatedly with an irascible Holston, and nothing was accomplished.

When there was a new break-in at some West Memphis sports store and guns were stolen, Holston went over the top and you could hear him shouting behind closed doors.

Through the office door you could finally hear the rarely angered Wyeth shout, "Dammit, I'm not going to arm your cops with machine guns. This isn't Vietnam."

Holston had yelled something back about dead cops on the sidewalk, and making little headway with Wyeth, had stormed out the door, letting it fly back with a slam. Everyone on that part of the third floor had stopped what they were doing as they watched the commissioner punch the elevator with his stiff fingers, and frustrated at the elevator's slowness, had cried out an expletive and started down the nearby exit stairs.

The deputy mayor was useless, as he had little to add. He was a city councilman who had been promoted to his highest level of incompetence. It was one of the more glaring mistakes of Wyeth's second term to have this sycophant as part of his inner circle. His sole function, it appeared, was to chair the city council if the mayor happened to be out of town.

He was a short, fat Jewish clothing store chain owner who had represented a midtown section of the city where two of his stores were located. To me at least, Jacob Cohen was as anonymous a city government executive as you might ever invent. This ridiculous caricature of a pants salesman who wore the worst cheap ill-fitting suits. That he eventually would become a US congressman of an exclusively black district seat, defied my imagination in later years.

It wasn't that Wyeth wouldn't listen to other people's opinions, or entertain any sort of reason which might have might have prevented his eventual sacrifice and political demise. Wyeth had conducted his whole career with compromise. His lawyerly talents were always significant and had usually been correct, though this time, they weren't. He let the circumstances that occurred define his solution, and that never worked, certainly not for him.

Why Wyeth chose Cohen to open up this meager city initiative to empower black neighborhood committees who would meet with police on resident safety was beyond me. It achieved nothing more than supplying cold chicken lunches at city hall for the black participants. He then wanted to cater them in the respective black neighborhoods, which would cost the city another $20,000, which only enriched a caterer acquaintance of his who later became a campaign donor.

The Federal Community Action Agencies set up by Washington as part of Johnson's War on Poverty, were opened

160

within six months inside three Memphis black high-crime neighborhoods. Cohen competed with them for black community attention. Without the deep federal government pockets, he had almost no presence there. It was a failed program, and Holston had only grudgingly cooperated with him by rescheduling his patrol officers.

These Community Action Agencies inflamed the more radical black political groups, who saw these CAA staff positions passed out to blacks who cooperated with the white political structure: first with the federal money masters in Washington, then with local black city councilman who wanted this patronage for their poll workers, and for a few friends.

Wyeth had failed on all sides to bring together blacks and whites, and particularly the police to any mediation or community discussion table, or even to engender any goodwill from a city government standpoint. The mayor was 'the man' to these poor and working-class blacks. He was just another white boss in his glassed-in office to crush them underfoot should they ever get out of line. His white cops would do just that.

The crime rate shot up that hot summer, and lasted into the winter, while there was an awful tenseness that enveloped the entire city. No one I knew would drive downtown in the evening for fear of being robbed, raped, or even brutally murdered.

* * * * * *

The annual Cotton Carnival held at the Peabody Hotel, became the artificial white garden party while surrounded by a sea of hostile black faces. The carnival was carefully watched by double, or triple, the usual number of uniformed policemen on the downtown streets.

It was a mock coronation, protected by the Queen's household cavalry, but without the horses. A celebration was replete with a white-complexion middle age cotton merchant king and his young princess who would be chosen to be queen out of the other ladies in waiting at a lavish party in the Peabody ballroom.

161

The separate black celebration, The Cotton Maker's Jubilee, was referred to by the young white dinner jacket crowd laughingly as the 'cotton picker's' jubilee. Those Negro-only parties were hosted at some nearby commercial hotel not frequented by whites.

It was as it always had been, perhaps since Reconstruction period, I stood in my own white dinner jacket in front of the Peabody waiting for a late Martha to arrive in her gossamer finery. Contempt was evident in the blank faces of the blacks who valet parked the freshly waxed cars, or carried bags for those carnival revelers. They traveled from Mississippi or Arkansas plantation homes and would stay the weekend at the hotel. You could feel the resentment in those hard set black eyes, and even if a smile flashed for a moment as you greeted the uniformed bellman, you knew deep inside he loathed you.

At least that's what I felt, though Martha would later tell me I was dead wrong. Unless I'd grown up in this same South, I'd miss those nuances which she accused me of doing.

"You don't get it, and you never will." Martha had scolded me, "So don't try, and stop your stupid judgment." She told me this forcibly on the way home from one of those secret society parties she liked so much. It was the Memphis ball, the same carnival society where her mother had been Duchess a decade before.

Martha confidently sashayed into the carnival dinner dance as a high-powered woman lawyer from Smith in a stunning floral summer gown. She still hadn't gotten those same male glances her prettier sister had evoked even as a teenager.

As we started up in the elevator to the rooftop ballroom, Martha knew most everyone inside the narrow car. She sang the praises of an older woman's finery, which had been bought in Paris almost thirty years ago. And how she still looked like that same long ago princess. That sort of pleasant elevator banter brought a wave of gentle laughter and coy smiles from the perfumed women onboard, and the pungent smell became an aphrodisiac to male nostrils.

162

Once inside the ballroom, we found our table which had place cards, and Martha greeted one couple after another until we finally found ourselves on the roof, where a bar had been set up.

I brought her our customary gin and tonic. We walked over to the small rooftop garden that had a seating area with couches and stuffed chairs, and joined another couple already there. Martha knew the couple, and although he was perhaps a decade older than Martha, she attended school with the man's younger sister. He had divorced his first wife, and was there with his new and much younger wife. This urbane man, a well-respected eye doctor in town, was perhaps in his early or middle forties while his wife was barely over eighteen.

When they had left, Martha whispered to me, "It's as you can see. That new wife probably finished high school this year. His old one was ahead of me at Smith and could at least carry on an intelligent conversation."

I tried to feign interest in what the gossip was, and nodded.

"I'm told she couldn't have children, and that it ended the rather short marriage then and there," Martha added with a downturned mouth. "Where he found this child he immediately married is anybody's guess."

"He's that crass," I noted, "No kids and adios."

"Hah," she uttered almost in a gasp. "They've got money and brains, but the family's classless. Drunk and worse. The father and his two sons are awful. The daughter's a little nicer."

"Uh-huh."

"Oh, I remember now," Martha exclaimed. "The new wife comes from a plantation in the Arkansas Delta, Osceola, I think. He met her as a debutant last season at the Country Club."

Martha said the girl was going to go to school at Fayetteville, or some other depressing place, but got married instead. Maybe she was nineteen at the oldest.

I added, "She has a pretty face though."

"Please, he's too disgusting," Martha continued, "and her family probably thought Metcalf Boone was this great catch. At least, she wasn't some truck stop waitress."

We tired of sitting and walked to the edge of the roof where you could see the activity on the street below with the cars depositing women in gowns and their escorts. Martha had this beatific look on her face of complete approval.

I looked out over this small riverfront city and the smell of the humid air that reminded me of Asia, and that part of my life.

"Standing on this roof makes me think of Saigon. I don't know why that came to me. Maybe it's the heat, and the noise from the street," I said to her quietly.

Martha started, "What a strange thing to say. I can't imagine any comparison. But I guess it's how you look at the world." With that, her mouth turned down.

At that point, a squat middle-aged blond who served as the newspaper society editor, called out to Martha, waving her fingers in the air.

"Martha, come over here with that lovely man, and tell me all about crime," she literally cooed across the roof. "Is Jim Latham treating you right?"

"Jim's the last gentleman left in Memphis," Martha told her.

The woman put her hands through her short blond streaked hair, and exclaimed, "You are so right. He's a prince among most here tonight."

She greeted me with a ladylike handshake, and without missing a beat in the conversation said, "I see you've met the good doctor's teenage wife. It's a scandal, honestly." And after elaborating on the entire family's questionable character she was soon gone.

The ball was lovely and the Cotton Carnival king and queen made an appearance. They had the first dance of the evening to polite applause from the seated guests, then the tables emptied to join them on the dance floor.

I danced with Martha, and we moved through the couples as she smiled at those she knew until I got this sharp punch in the back.

Turning in a half circle, I noticed Amanda in her powder blue gown being swung around by husband Randy who was clearly enjoying himself with his head held high. As they moved across the chandelier lit room, Amanda turned toward me and stuck out her tongue then vanished with the other couples on the crowded floor.

How long would this craziness with her continue? I said to myself. I gave my body over to the music and finished the waltz that came from the bandstand.

Amanda was on the other side of the ballroom, and I told Martha that I could see her cousin, and we waved across to her. In a moment, Martha had left the table and pulled me along with her to go over and speak to Amanda.

I hugged Amanda after Martha did, and we changed partners for the next dance. Randy led Martha onto the dance floor and behind them, I brought a petulant Amanda. Once we started dancing, she began to whisper things to me that made me uncomfortable. She spoke about when we'd next be together in the same bed and how it was time to leave those two people dancing in front of us.

The dance ended, and Martha and I returned to our table as dinner was being served to the guests. We engaged the couples surrounding us in affable conversation, and finished the evening on a festive note.

On the way home as I drove, Martha mentioned, "I love this life. It's so different from the twisted families I visited from Smith. None of them enjoyed anything. They had no traditions, only money and that's it. Every set of those parents were so 'fucking' miserable."

The flight of profanity had surprised me, and I laughed, as it was so unlike Martha. Had Carolyn ever heard that from either of her daughters, she would have died right on the spot as this type of unladylike behavior was intolerable.

It was something that I had come to embrace about the South, the real South, and not the Atlanta suburbs with their armies of transplants that held the show of mock aristocracy that never really had one. However, compared to the ravaged coal town of my childhood with generations of miners and their wives and families, the layer of the richest cream in this Mississippi River city had an unfamiliar atmosphere of casual privilege. I had become a willing participant in the grand scheme of garden parties, cotton carnival balls, fox hunting, and polo game picnics. It seemed that there was little reason for anything to change around me, though it would, slowly and inexorably.

The area had a strange layering of the races. The bottom layer consisted of negroes that had lived here their entire lives, as well as the generation before when the plantation economy had collapsed and they had escaped servitude. However, this was the South in the Forties and Fifties with demarcations of strict racial roles, and even the overwhelming prosperity that much of America was experiencing, it hadn't changed Memphis.

All the racial tensions around me were held in seemingly perfect balance. Yet, now, the unseen force that preserved the earlier order was being tested, first within the blighted northern cities where there weren't clear barriers separating blacks and whites. Here, those differences were obvious with segregated drinking fountains to bus seating to the colored bars of the neighborhoods.

Throughout the carnival ball night, the entire service staff was black, the bartenders and certainly all the waiters, and the white-coated men slicing cheese and Virginia ham for revelers. It was as it should be, and the Peabody Hotel prided itself, as did the city country clubs, with their gracious black staff. I was told they were very well paid and had worked for generations in these service positions and passed them on to dutiful sons.

Martha's family had several black women who had worked for them for many years as well as a white haired Negro gardener who was in his late seventies and could hardly bend over, but was beloved. I was told of them all, affectionately by

Martha. I had no reason to think it was strange for this particular place so I had accepted this subservience as commonplace.

What went on in much of Washington, and in Lyndon Johnson's efforts to change the unique character of the South, seemed woefully misplaced. The handfuls of anti-poverty agencies he had created had been for his own aggrandizement and Great Society legacy he sought to leave behind him. I believe he had mismanaged the Vietnam War. His draft and escalation wouldn't solve the basic issue that Vietnam was a civil war with constantly changing characters on the side that we had chosen, and that it may not be won. There was no reason for me to believe he could do any better with his so-called civil rights executive orders. That was the purview of carpetbaggers from Boston and New York and Washington with little appreciation of the society they sought to change, and then destroy.

I never talked to Martha about any of this, certainly not the Vietnam thing. There was no reason, really, and as intelligent a woman as she was, she had no understanding of what I had seen. Why would she?

As for Johnson, Martha, in her southern heart of hearts, didn't want anything to change around her including the people she knew or the city she lived in. She treated him and his initiatives with innate disdain.

Carolyn was getting worse, and it seemed that she was totally out of control. Though he loved her, Alfred eschewed entertaining at home, or meeting friends downtown for dinner with Carolyn. The chronic alcoholism had taken her over, but yet, he ignored seeking medical treatment. He treated it almost as a medieval madness to be hidden in the castle tower. He wouldn't intervene with any proactive rehabilitation, although he certainly was sophisticated enough to know she had become seriously ill and in time, it got much worse.

The upshot was that we hardly ever saw Martha's parents except for holidays and for never more than an hour or two that might involve exchanging gifts. They became isolated in their own home. Alfred continued with his law practice and met with clients and close friends downtown and poor Carolyn lived through her boozy days and nights.

Martha's sister had divorced the English hunter. She returned home for longer and more frequent visits, which served to escalate the tension in her parent's household. On the last visit, she had been given a school friend's furnished pool house on a spacious Germantown horse farm and decided to stay for several months, which exasperated those involved. She was dating and had been seen at restaurants with an unsavory developer who had come through a rather messy divorce himself, and lost custody of his two young children. They had that particular bond in common, and I don't know how often Carrie saw her son, but my guess was not often. She came back to recover from the divorce, and Memphis was a town where she had friends, and felt comfortable.

Martha invited her to dinner once, and the table conversation was neutral. It seemed that I was forced to do most of the talking as the sisters had little to say to each other as an impenetrable wall seemed to have been erected between them.

There was an awkward moment after dinner when Martha had lost it and yelled at her sister, "You're such a self-serving bitch," and I held up my hand to diffuse the anger and bring us back to normalcy.

For most of the two months Carrie lived in the Germantown house. We didn't see her, and only learned about what she did or didn't do from others. Her first ex-husband wasn't any friendlier or cooperative than the last brief visit. The acrimonious behavior between them continued. When she finally left for London, no one was sad to see her go. I felt sorry for the little boy who was torn between two warring parents.

Amanda was a frequent part of both our lives, including that secret part of mine that she continued to occupy. I found that I couldn't get her out of my mind and heart, and no longer tried.

Randy continued to press her to start a family, and since he was a doctor, the usual subterfuges of difficult conception wouldn't work. Amanda simply told him she wasn't emotionally ready for motherhood, and he accepted it with benign patience. On the other hand, his mother had come to loathe Amanda. It was difficult to get them all together around a table without harsh words, so we became the single couple they were closest to and usually spent the holidays and weekends together. The intimacy with Amanda continued. Although we were careful, we both agreed that if we were caught, it didn't matter.

Why didn't Amanda and I leave together? It was the history with Martha perhaps and my own dysfunction. In my soul, I feared that somehow I couldn't last with Amanda. She could as easily mistreat me as she did Randy, as someone to be manipulated, and then discarded. I feared what she might be capable of, and though we continued this secretive romance, and celebrated the intimacy we enjoyed together, I didn't trust her enough to leave Martha, who was a safe haven. Did that make me a coward? Probably, though I couldn't see myself as that desperate, though what I didn't do, defined me.

Mercifully, Carolyn died quickly of an aneurysm of the brain, which had been caused by her years of alcohol abuse. It came, initially, as a slow seizure, then three weeks later she died in the hospital without regaining consciousness. The doctors said the death was exacerbated by the severe damage done to her liver and other organ functions. The body simply couldn't function any longer, and she passed away.

She was buried in a small cemetery off Central Avenue where she and Alfred had purchased plots several years earlier. The memorial mass was said at Holy Communion Church, next to St. Mary's Episcopal School where Martha and her sister had studied. It was painful and tragic for everyone concerned, and the funeral brought a great many friends to pay respects.

Amanda's parents from Jackson had come into town and stayed with Amanda and Randy for the duration of the services and the burial. Spending time around her mother, Louise, was a real eye-opener. It was apparent even to a casual observer that she was a lunatic. She was attractive, soft-spoken, honest, mannerly, and intelligent, though, nevertheless, a lunatic. You could see where Amanda had gotten her rather erratic personality, classic features, and her distinctive view of the world. You only needed to be with Louise for a few minutes to know. Her friends (not her family) called her Lulu. Louise commanded whatever space she occupied, whether it was a church pew or standing next to an empty grave or having tea in someone's living room. Wherever she was, that particular small part of the known world belonged completely to her as well as everyone in it for the expressed purpose of her pleasure. She had coal black, fast-moving eyes of the mad Charlotte Corday in Marat's asylum, and she stared right through you. Mostly, Amanda ignored her mother rather deferring to her father on occasion, but wasn't really warm to him either. When the funeral was over, her parents started off for Jackson, and Amanda gave them a furtive goodbye which was purely cinematic in its distance. As they left the residential neighborhood where the young couple lived, you could imagine that Amanda had muttered, "Good riddance," though, that may be unfair.

Chapter 13
Jones

Holston continued his way of attrition with those who opposed him in city government, and with each passing week, they became fewer and fewer as the city crime numbers went through the roof. There was talk that Memphis had more murders than New Orleans, a far larger city, and that troubled the populace who heard it reported on the six o' clock television news. It was mostly blacks killing other blacks, but there had been some cars stolen as they idled at boulevard stoplights. A teenage girl had been killed on Central Avenue, not far from First Presbyterian Church, who had resisted having the family car taken. A witness had seen a black man escape with the car. It was eight in the evening and students were crossing the street nearby to attend university night classes, yet it had happened as they walked nonchalantly across the half busy street.

Wyeth had wanted to replace Holston and his critics on the city council. The press mushroomed, and he became a mayor under siege. The city had failed in all its efforts to get people downtown. All the money that they had spent on revitalization hadn't gotten anyone to leave the relative safety of East Memphis residential neighborhoods.

After the recent cotton carnival, Sheraton had announced it may even shutter the Peabody. The hotel block had become a target for black criminals. Two St. Louis businessmen had been robbed and badly beaten in the dim alley light across the street from the hotel returning from the Rendezvous Rib restaurant.

Wyeth had pleaded with the Sheraton executives, and for the moment they had taken a wait and see attitude on whether to unload the hotel property. He had subsequently called one local developer who still had some civic pride, and he had told Wyeth he might consider buying it from Sheraton to save the landmark. Without the Peabody, the downtown was dead, and it would indeed become another Beirut. The elegant Peabody and its legacy

171

and ducks were part of the glorious city history and now it would implode into dust on Wyeth's watch.

Wyeth went from one of the most popular mayors in the city's long history to a pariah: mistrusted and loathed for his miscues. There was nowhere for him to hide, and the city's reputation suffered immeasurably.

I could do nothing more than keep a loose watch on police activity for him, with a cursory outside surveillance which produced little insight into Holston's motivations and his skewed strategies against undetected black conspiracies.

The city government was falling apart. It was evident wherever you looked, and it wasn't for lack of trying. Wyeth became the convenient scapegoat.

The previous year, the National Conference of Mayors had made a sincere effort to hold its annual meetings in smaller cities across the country. There had been a great deal of interest and some talks about possibly selecting Memphis. It was believed to be this dynamic city of the New South that had initiative, however that had evaporated. Now, the only news heard about Memphis concerned its contentious racial politics, and high crime rate.

In truth, Memphis was probably under siege, though, it didn't seem so. People still played tennis on weekends at the University Club, drove all the way down Lamar to Justine's for dinner. On a summer night there may even be an outdoor concert at Tom Lee Park on the Mississippi with the symphony playing Broadway show tunes. Nevertheless, trouble lurked in the dark shadows.

The sanitation worker's contract was at an end, and it hadn't been renewed. The AFSCME had tried to intervene with Jones, but was unsuccessful, and the new local president wanted a general strike. One morning, that was just what he did and the garbage collection throughout the city stopped.

He had other plans including inviting national labor organizations with large black memberships to join him. There had been talk of a march through downtown of striking workers to demonstrate solidarity, and to have national coverage of this

172

new black empowerment. Jones would bring Wyeth and his flaccid Memphis city government to its knees, and the labor shutdown would accomplish that, and quickly.

The older local AFSCME leadership had counseled slower action, though they had been largely ignored. Jones now possessed the power and support of his workers to do precisely what he envisioned: to crush the white establishment underfoot.

Jones did make an appearance at several arbitrations, however, he had no intention to settle. All he thought about during those tense meetings was for an army of thousands of blacks to march through the Memphis streets ending white domination of their miserable lives forever. 'Power to the people,' slogans resonated within his feverish mind, and he saw black labor marches across the entire South. He thought, 'We'll reduce their great cities to chaos, and disorder.'

Wyeth knew this loathsome strike would occur, and the mayor demonstrated what executive strength he could muster in its wake. He also suggested to Holston that at worst, his police officers might serve as interim garbage workers, though only until the crisis could be settled. Holston had laughed in Wyeth's face. He said he would never force any law enforcement officer to pick up somebody's driveway garbage. Their task under the charter was to keep the peace, and protect this city and that's exactly what he'd continue to do.

His police tactical operations had gotten far more organized. Holston had developed three teams of four officers. Each of them had been trained in Nashville by former combat units of the National Guard who had returned home after combat service in Vietnam. These Memphis police officers had been trained in the same hunt and kill methods Army rangers employed against the embattled Viet Cong.

The weapons complement these officers had received from the department was much different from the rest of the uniformed officers. Now, they were armed with automatic carbines and the latest hand grenades. The counter terrorist units also had Claymore mines which could be set up against impenetrable houses that black radical groups occupied. Ideally, Holston wanted an armed attack helicopter. That was impossible for a small city police department. After all, Memphis wasn't Da Nang.

"Hell, it could easily be," Holston thought to himself, and was satisfied that these select men were ready for the deluge when it came.

The anti-revolution police units Holston had created were officially assigned to special duty. They spent a lot of time at the shooting range honing their weapons skills. Each officer was an expert marksman, and he could take down the black radicals in a split second with a high-powered rifle thwarting a hostage situation. He had a veteran sergeant in charge of his paramilitary section he trusted and had been brought up as a rookie. The man's loyalty to Holston and the larger purpose as well as his silence were unquestioned. He would deploy these men when the unseen enemy finally showed their murderous black faces. The police would eliminate them once and for all, keeping the streets safe of the scourge.

'Let these lieutenants and precinct captains think they're in charge and shuffle around their meaningless papers', the unit sergeant reasoned. 'Those commandos of mine are the front-line, hard-stomached killers in their own right: not some bunch of goddamn tired administrators with paunches waiting for their pensions to kick-in. They're fishing out at Horn Lake with the grandkids every Saturday. They had become too soft, all of them.'

Holston's small guerilla force came into being without the knowledge of the mayor or anyone else in the Memphis city government. They carried out their training mission in secret. No other high-ranking police officer in the department except Holston knew they even existed. It was masterful.

Wyeth had a continuous bane of bad publicity to trouble him. The same could be said for a lot of other city executives as a tidal wave of black discontent and their increased activism flooded the urban centers where they had been forced into segregated city ghettos.

You saw angry black faces shouting into television cameras every night from Los Angeles, Detroit, and New York, followed by some of the smaller cities like Charlotte and Richmond. It continued on, encouraged by the hands-off treatment from Washington. As long as no whites had been hurt, or killed, they could continue their unchecked dissent everywhere in the streets, and they did. They started with tiny crowds at first, and then in much larger conflagrations. It was protected by the Constitution, the right to march in the street, and that's what the blacks did while being supported by a handful of renegade New York and federal government lawyers.

The loudest of these voices came from firebrands like a part-time black university student who had talked of non-violence through protest to achieve equality that they already had. Others wanted Negro repatriation back to the African homeland. A few more saw armed revolution in the streets.

Memphis didn't have any of the so-called black Messiah's as local leaders had always gone along with the white establishment. The fortunate blacks at the top had always enriched themselves with city contracts. They wielded political power inside those blighted neighborhoods, owning the funeral homes, convenience stores, and the Negro taxi companies.

Jones knew that he would need a visible outside black face to get the national news down here in order to be interviewed by NBC in New York City and send the message that things for blacks were changing across the country. He paid no attention to the voices of the union leadership.

He had stopped taking the head Jew's calls pleading for calm, and some sort of quick compromise. He became unavailable for Wolfson and the AFSCME minions, period. This was the moment where history would finally be rewritten, and Jones knew he was a torch for change, and reveled at the power that enveloped him.

In two weeks' time, the mountains of Memphis garbage would begin to pile up on the streets. Two weeks after that, rats would be scurrying around residential lawns chasing white children. He laughed at that prospect. He couldn't appear weak, or recalcitrant, and he decided to meet one more time with Wyeth and his labor negotiators to show the world that he had really tried to settle this strike, but the white powers were immovable.

'This time', he thought to himself, 'I'll act as if we have some smidgen of a deal on the table, scrutinize and ponder their pathetic offer, and after that, we'll get up and leave the table.'

It would be dramatic as he left the city conference room. There would be reporters outside waiting to learn the results of the meeting. He would speak to them, telling the newspapers and television stations that the AFSCME had tried, but its poor black workers deserve a living wage and some small guarantee of a doctor's visit.

The meeting ended just as Jones had predicted with a stalemate between the city and the union. He walked out the door proudly knowing he had seized the day. There were two reporters from the Commercial Appeal he knew and Jones devoted five or six minutes to answer their questions.

He then turned to WMC, the local NBC affiliate, and had a long on-camera interview with their woman city beat journalist. She first asked Jones to start the interview inquiring if he, as the union president, had come to an agreement with the city on the present contract.

Comfortable in front of the camera lens, Jones leaned closer to her hand microphone, and he had cleared his throat. "The sanitation workers in this city are troubled that the mayor and his administration refuse to give them a living wage. We have met several times in good faith with the mayor, and he continues to treat us like he's still on the plantation."

That remark received a few gasps, but mostly breathy sighs from the cache of reporters who had heard this stinging reference from other blacks in public life numerous times. They knew they had entered familiar territory in this acrimonious black and white dialogue.

The woman reporter asked Jones "At what point did the strike talks break down?" To which he merely laughed.

"Janet, it's very simple," he said calmly with that same smile on his face as a moment ago, "Poor black working people only want a living wage, nothing else," then his voice rose in an almost stentorian manner.

"My own father was a day laborer, a ditch digger with no education, and he worked himself into an early grave. He had no health care, or wasn't paid decently either." Now he raised his deep voice and turned to the other television cameras.

He commandingly said, "That man I loved. My father was broken by those same people who should have helped him. He never asked for a handout, or did he miss a day of work no matter how sick, or tired he was. He had no union to protect him. My task in this life, in the memory of that same man, my dead father, is to make sure men like him are treated fairly. Nothing more. Fairness. "

The circle of reporters moved closer to Jones, writing down his words.

"I promise you this. I will see that these working men who have elected me to represent them can feed their families."

After delivering the last line, he had glanced over to the open conference room door where Wyeth's disgruntled labor deputy stood watching and Jones gave the man a knowing grin.

Jones thought at that instant, "You want war, well, you'll get it...and lose."

He thanked all the press people milling around outside the conference room, and excused himself for other pressing engagements that day.

Jones was followed closely by his two assistants who were heavy-set thuggish black men and completely out of place alongside the slim well-dressed sanitation union leader. No one would ever mistake who was in charge.

Jones was a light-skinned Negro, and his mother's family had the telltale strain of white overseer blood in their veins as they all had aquiline straight noses and narrow faces. These features had certainly served him well as a young man with attractive black women, and his own wife's complexion was as light, or even lighter, than his own. His two young daughters already looked like magazine fashion models as most people noted when they were seen walking down the street as a family.

His wife, Cora Nell, had been in the top five of her graduating class at Humes High School. She had won an academic scholarship to the all-black Tougaloo College in Mississippi. She had passed an idyllic freshman year excelling in both her studies, and her passion, sacred music. Unfortunately, she became pregnant and had to drop out. She returned to Memphis and was later joined by her child's father, Willy Taylor, who had also been a student. They moved in with her parents in the Orange Mount projects into a tiny two-bedroom frame house where she delivered a healthy baby girl named Charissa.

As with so many relationships with children early on, Willy found the role of father and provider too much for a young unskilled black man. Confused by responsibility and rebelliousness, he didn't want to be the day laborer his father-in-law or his own father had been, and he left one day never to be seen again.

Of course, like so many young black couples with children, they didn't bother to marry and with Willy's disappearance, whatever small amount of money he'd contributed to the family's support vanished with him.

Cora Nell was on her own, and shortly after the little girl turned a year old, she met Jones at a church holiday supper. They began to see one another. After some time dating. Jones insisted on marrying Cora Nell in a proper church wedding. Her daughter Charissa carried the bride's bouquet to the altar for the couple.

They now had two daughters who were both beautiful and lively and gave Jones so much pride. Both girls had grown tall and slender with exquisite caramel skin color and their long hair was almost silken and rather straight.

He was a family man, and he had never entertained the thought of another woman besides his lovely wife, and only occasionally might he drink a beer at a picnic or sporting event. Their church life was important to them, and Jones was a long time deacon at the AME parish three blocks from his modest Southside home. One Saturday each month he volunteered to serve hungry black families, cooking half the day in the church basement kitchen. Twice this past year, the minister of Blessed Jesus Church and his wife had been guests for dinner in their home. They prayed and sang joyous hymns. Jones, his wife, and their two daughters had rarely missed a Sunday worship service. His wife was a soloist in the parish choir, and he would look after the girls two Wednesday evenings each month, sometimes more as the Christmas season approached.

Jones was an ambitious man and he had positioned himself to push out the tired AFSCME black leaders at the top who had become mere lackeys for the mayor's conniving people. When the time had come for him to assume the helm of the union, Jones had placed his supporters in those key positions to nominate and elect him president.

He had hobnobbed with Wolfson's sleazy Mafioso lieutenants in New Jersey and was becoming well known and respected for his unwavering loyalty to labor movement principles. Jones believed in labor's seminal role in building this country and thought the working man had led the way for the path of greater equality for blacks. The union workplace was the cradle for all integration, where blacks and whites working alongside each other, on the docks and in the steel mills, could receive a fair return for hard labor.

During this adult life, Jones had never cheated his employers out of an hour's work. He was among the first on the job and went from the back of the garbage truck to dispatcher then onward to union steward, president and, finally, its chief negotiator.

The sanitation union president was not a man to be trifled with. He could not be bought cheaply, or at all, as he was a man of strict morals and believed in the dignity of labor by working with a man's hands.

If Jesus truly had been a carpenter, then certainly Jones could work with his own hands on some stinking garbage truck.

He remained unashamed of the sometimes menial labor he had performed for fifteen long years. Jones was unlike many of his fellow laboring blacks that could be bought at any price. It was a painful lesson Wyeth had learned during the days of the strike. No one would remain the same after it was all over.

In a last ditch move to save face, Wyeth had submitted to a television interview and went on far too long on camera about the intransigence of the sanitation workers. The mayor suggested that outside influences were to blame for the failure to renew a 'more than fair' contract, and he called on other city labor leaders to bring them to their senses. However, they were the white police and firefighter unions in the city that had little in common with the striking garbage workers. No shared arbitration would occur between the disparate factions as the police or even firefighter unions shared common purposes.

* * * * * *

Another unplanned visit from Carrie came and went, and this time she had been pressing her ex-husband to allow the son to travel on his own to Britain. He would be watched over by airline stewardesses, but pulling him out of school to come back with her for a time was a ridiculous request in the first place.

There were nightly telephone arguments that we couldn't escape. Carrie asked to stay with us for the week she was here. We had reluctantly agreed. Except for the telephone rants, however, it was a mostly emotionless visit.

She had found another man who had proposed marriage. This time it was an Oxford-educated art restorer named Reggie, who owned two London galleries, which meant he had some money. He had worked for Buckingham Palace and in the past, assisted in the restoration of the Queen's vast painting collection. The man was fourteen years her senior and had never been married. Up until this past November, he'd kept a flat in Sloane Square but had decided to reside in the country. Carrie met him at a National Trust event where she'd done the event organizing that

180

had become her specialty. He was at the buffet table at the Surrey manor house when they had struck up a conversation and seemed to like one another. Demur to a fault, Carrie had passed on her business card, and told him of her great love for British painting, particularly the Joshua Reynolds portraits. Three weeks later, he had invited her to a Reynolds exhibit at some country estate, and thus launched the romance.

From his photograph, he resembled an older square-faced Alec Guinness, though not nearly as attractive, and he seemed to nurse the start of a double chin.

Naturally, Carrie shared her good fortunate with us and Alfred, whom she asked to give her away at some country parish in Britain, but alas there were so many things to decide first.

Even after the announcement of Reggie's new role in her sister's life, I could see that familiar look of disdain cross Martha's otherwise smiling face, though she didn't roll her eyes.

Martha chirped, "Oh, that's so wonderful," and she jumped across the table to hug her sister and shower her with kisses.

When we finally got into bed that night with Carrie safely asleep at the other end of the house, Martha went into her tirade.

"Serial marriages, is that the game?" she spat out, and threw her paperback novel to the foot of the bed. "He's probably some tiresome joke, like the last one. My God."

I interjected, "Well, the last one was a little handsome, and he had that West Country brogue. That counts for something."

"Oh please," she hissed and turned over showing me her narrow back. Then she abruptly sat straight up in bed.

"At least, she won't live here. That's the one saving grace." With that, she turned back over again but this time turning out her bedside lamp and covering her head with the sheet.

It was my turn to look for a book to glance at before bed so I had picked up a new spy novel that I had found at a mall bookstore, and opened it to the first chapter. I finished the end of the first sentence of the book when Martha once again straightened up against the bed headboard.

She asked furtively: "Tell me. Am I selfish to want my goddamn sister out of my life? Be honest with me. Am I?"

"Martha, she's had her difficulties, alright, and maybe life is easier without her for you, certainly," I tried to explain unsuccessfully.

"You think I'm self-centered, don't you?" she asked, insisting again that I be completely honest with her.

"No, you're not," I reassured her. "Look, there's been a lot between you two, and maybe some painful things were said, but you seemed fine together at dinner."

Martha was now pointing her finger at me, and said, "She's been the awful bitch, not me. Look how she treated Momma and Daddy. Like shit."

I told her that the first divorce and hasty departure to England may have crushed her mother, but Carrie didn't make her an alcoholic. Carolyn was well on that path long before her daughter even considered marriage.

"Why do I feel so guilty?" Martha asked, and I pulled her toward me for solace.

We could hear her sister closing the second bathroom door, and I suggested that Martha go into her room, sit on her bed, and try to pretend they were both sisters and friends.

"Imagine you're fifteen and she's just turning thirteen, and you've got a secret to tell her, and only her," I counseled Martha. "Try that again. March down the hall into her room, stretch across her bed, and be kids again."

"Dammit, I will," Martha said jumping out of bed, putting on her robe and then skipping to the bedroom door. But she stopped there and shook her head.

"The hell with her," she whispered with a twisted mouth and came back inside the room.

Martha had few close friends any more, and the next week she'd gotten a call from her oldest friend from school, Elizabeth Collins, who had returned to Memphis with her husband and two boys.

She and Elizabeth were inseparable as schoolgirls and the only ones in her class to attend college outside the South. While Martha had gone to Massachusetts and Smith, Elizabeth had gone to Boulder where she'd met her husband, a fellow Colorado university student. By the third year in Boulder, they were living together when Elizabeth found herself pregnant with her first child, and they quickly married.

Buzz was a doctor's son from the Pittsburgh suburbs, and continued with college during the pregnancy and doing odd jobs around Boulder, which never provided enough money. He didn't want to ask his parents to support them, so he joined the Marines and was commissioned a fighter pilot within ten months.

They finally married just before their first son was born, and were stationed at the Marine air base at Twenty-Nine Palms in the Mojave for another few months.

Then came Vietnam, and he was away from Elizabeth for more than a year flying sorties across the jungle in F-2 fighters, and had clocked something near fifty missions, when he figured he had enough. They went back to Boulder where he finished his degree, and a second child was born. That was when they decided to move to Memphis.

Elizabeth came from a wealthy Memphis family on her mother's side, with boarding school educations and cottages on Martha's Vineyard. Her father was a Yalie who had met her mother when she was a girl at Pembroke, and they married.

By the time Elizabeth and Buzz returned, her parents had divorced and Elizabeth's father was quickly remarried to a local widow, Nancy MacIver. She had been a Rockefeller before she came to Memphis as the wife of the MacIver cotton broker family. The husband, Mickey, had died young and she had been alone for a decade before she had married Elizabeth's father.

They had been staying at the mother's large home for a few days before Elizabeth called Martha, and we had gotten together as couples.

The women thought that Buzz and I would fit neatly together based on our common Vietnam history, though it doesn't quite work that way. Each man from that country had a unique perspective that sometimes had nothing to do with another man's experience, even if they were placed side by side in the same battalion. Most likely, Buzz had been forced to fly too many combat missions, and the nervousness and anger still lingered below the surface and caused his exaggerated movements, like the annoying tapping of his foot at the dining room table during that first dinner. That awful anger was buried inside him, and though he was pleasant to Elizabeth around others, he was hopelessly lost in some unrecognizable place.

He had tried, initially, to work at her grandfather's seat cover factory as sales executive. After a month he had begun to argue daily with the uncle who was the present company director, and he quit. Soon after, a family friend with a food truck service had hired him as a management trainee; taking out one of the vending trucks out for a week but Buzz had been robbed while he was taking a cigarette break.

Finally, Elizabeth's mother had pulled strings at the First National Bank, and they had agreed to hire him in management, though they sent everyone through a battery of psychological tests conducted by an outside expert first. Buzz had failed the battery miserably and the psychologist conducting the tests told the bank that he had dangerous aggression tendencies, and would be a terrible candidate for banking.

That was the final straw for him, and when he was informed of the test results, he went to the psychologist's office and threatened him physically, pulling the man across his desk and slamming him back in his chair. He yelled that he was a child molester to the secretary and the patients in the waiting room. Apparently there was another psychologist with the name of Atkinson, not Addison that had been arrested for pedophilia. That doctor had worked as a public school system counselor and the crime had been exposed that past week in the newspapers.

Martha saw a lot of Elizabeth, and though I did sometimes enjoy Buzz, there was so little common ground we shared, however, I didn't object to seeing them regularly.

In the middle of all this domestic angst, Martha decided we would all take a vacation to Cumberland Island. It was a Georgia sea island where the new Rockefeller stepmother's family had a home. It wouldn't cost anything but the airfare, and we planned a visit to the island. We would fly into Jacksonville where we would hire taxi to Fernandina Beach and then a small boat shuttle across the inlet.

Martha had let it out to Amanda and she insisted on coming, though it was impossible for Randy to readjust his patient schedule and join us. The five us of flew down to Florida, and at last got to the island where we were met on the weather-beaten dock by the gruff island caretaker, Roger, who took us all crammed together with bags in his rusty jeep to the sprawling seaside home.

It somehow worked marvelously for three days and nights, and only once did Buzz have what could be called a meltdown. He was screaming at Elizabeth in their bedroom, which was so loud, no one could ignore it. Elizabeth had told Martha on their walk, that if he didn't get some kind of therapy, she had no choice but to leave him. Of course, he hadn't physically abused her or their small boys yet, though she wasn't certain that wouldn't happen.

Amidst this turmoil was the unnerving spectacle of Amanda swimming topless in the surf. In truth, it may have been the only thing that amused Buzz who would watch her around his beer can while she danced on the beach half naked and was constantly laughing.

At dinner the second night, Martha asked, "Amanda, do you have to, you know…" and Amanda shot back, "Show my tits."

"Yes that," Martha continued, and Amanda only grinned sipping her white wine.

"Does that offend you, Buzz?" Amanda asked, turning to him where he was seated next to her and in mid bite of the fish that I grilled for dinner.

Buzz wasn't without a sense of humor, and he quickly added, "Oh no, Amanda, I quite like your tits," and burst out snickering.

His laughter somehow helped the tenseness of this juncture of the trip, and everyone at the table started to roar with laughter.

Amanda did find an excuse to walk with me down the path to the end of the island, and insisted we make love in the sand to which I complied.

As she pulled on her panties, I searched for my shorts and underwear that were partially hidden in the dunes when Buzz appeared from nowhere. The strange battered ex-fighter pilot looked at the both of us half-dressed, and made a zipper motion across his smiling lips, and told us, "The secret is safe with me. I'll never tell, don't worry." With that Buzz vanished along the windy path and onto the main island shell road. As far as I knew, the youngish man who was seasoned in the worst of unimaginable circumstances was true to his word. I don't believe he ever told a soul what he'd seen that day.

Elizabeth divorced him, or at least filed for divorce, six months later and someone told me that he returned to Pittsburgh, hopefully to heal his awful wounds. I had always figured him to be a fearless fighter pilot and comrade-in-arms. He was, perhaps, only another in the legion of walking wounded from that merciless conflict, and I wanted his life to end happily.

Martha continued with her childhood friend as a confidant and touchstone, and Amanda was simply herself.

There would be a last visit to Cumberland with a single Elizabeth, this time without Amanda, and four years after that, the three families that owned most of the island, The Rockefellers, the Carnegies, and the Coca-Cola heirs from Atlanta, all agreed to sell their holdings for a dollar each to the park service. It was a move to thwart the poorer and now more avaricious Carnegies from unloading the robber baron island to Marriott for thirty million dollars.

Martha and Elizabeth stayed close. I was delighted that she had someone to talk to beyond me and a woman to talk with about womanly things.

* * * * * *

Jones received a telephone call from Wolfson who had insisted on flying immediately to Memphis to discuss the upcoming strike and there was little Jones could do to discourage the national AFSCME head. He would see Jones at his headquarters around lunchtime the following day.

Inside the union offices, the brash Wolfson came right to the point, "You think you can fuck up everything we've done as a union?"

His language had surprised Jones, who remained passive during the rough tirade, and began to form his considered, thoughtful reply when the union boss continued:

"If there's any violence in this goddamn strike, I'm going to see you out on your ass."

Jones responded with his usual calmness. "There won't be any. This march will be led by church people."

"What are you talking about?" Wolfson exclaimed, thinking that when he finished with this guy he should see the Memphis mayor for a last ditch try to settle.

"Four pastors will walk with us for the march," Jones added, "as a Christian protest, to undo the wrongs done to blacks."

"Oh yeah," Wolfson hissed, "And they'll deliver you a new contract? What absolute bullshit."

Jones patiently explained to the man his strategies for allying the black workers with their own churchmen, and how that solidarity would undermine the city's immovable attitudes.

Wolfson wasn't convinced. He'd spent his working years in organized labor movements, and never had churches been of any value in achieving their goals. It was always talk. The tired platitudes mouthed to the masses from the pulpit. He had seen those holy priests cavort with the bosses who filled their collection plates, and gave the parochial schools money.

This nascent strategy Jones had developed called for the enlistment of prominent national ministers from outside Memphis. These pastors were leaders of the burgeoning civil rights movement to empower blacks throughout the South, and they had been successful in many cities in moving the worst of the racist mayors toward compromise.

Wolfson sputtered with an unconvincing laugh: "This shit won't get you a contract. It'll get you a crack on your skull."

He stood rigid at the small conference table and told Jones that as the head of the AFSCME, he had an obligation to talk once more with the mayor, trying for some eleventh hour contract settlement.

Jones said thoughtfully: "Do what you believe is right. And we'll do the same in Memphis."

On the way out the door, Wolfson muttered something over his shoulder to Jones which was mostly inaudible, and left the building.

Jones picked up his telephone and began to dial a number. He introduced himself to the woman who answered on the other end.

In the next moment, he asked, "May I please speak with Doctor King."

The union president leaned back in the cheap office swivel chair, and took a deep breath, then exhaled in a rush of air. He was ready.

"Thank you. I'll be happy to wait a few moments, until he's off that call, yes."

The other man, in a dark inexpensive suit in Atlanta, picked up the phone and asked Jones to explain how he might help. Jones spelled out his vision for black working men in the city. He said he, like Martin Luther King himself, believed non-violent acts were the only way to achieve this needed change. He had conceived a labor march downtown that would be led by several Memphis pastors, and had hoped King would join them.

Jones told King that he was also a Christian and that in his own lifetime, intimidation had played too large a part. Within the labor movement itself, black men beat other black men, all for an extra piece of bread. Angry white policemen often did the same in this evil atmosphere of vengeance.

The Atlanta clergymen listened patiently to everything Jones said and told him he was pleased to hear that Jones eschewed violence or hate as a solution.

"It was this painful past that we inherited out of fear," King mentioned, and told Jones that he had already seen the smallest glimmer of hope that a change was possible.

"Yes, it would come, though slowly," King continued. "Men's hearts can be softened, and universal brotherhood will at last reign."

The brief phone conversation, at first, sounded as if it were part of a Sunday church sermon, and King's voice, even on the telephone had a strange resonance. The inevitability of what he said was what struck Jones. King unquestionably believed that this brotherhood he spoke of could be achieved, and in their lifetime, maybe in ten years, or even sooner.

"Even the worst sinner can climb to the high ground of salvation," King had told him.

"We will march with you, Mister Jones, and together achieve what these black men and women deserve, this freedom from want," King pronounced, asking Jones to call him that next day or the one after to provide him with details for the trip. He would need accommodations for himself, and perhaps as many as four other colleagues. Any modest nearby commercial hotel would be adequate. It was really unnecessary to house them in other people's homes, as some folks often suggested. The motel would be easier to come and go.

"You'll like Reverend Harris, who'll join us," King said ending the call. "He's been with me from the beginning. You should hear him from the pulpit." And with that comment, he gave out this gentle sigh, saying goodbye.

Jones grinned to himself at his success. His fellow sanitation workers would march across this city as a black-faced army, calling attention to the long abuse they had suffered from the terrible working conditions to the low wages that they were paid, and the world would finally notice. This conflagration of oppressed men would be the largest gathering of black workers in the history of the entire South. It would come as a shock to Memphis.

There was much to do in order to ready things for King's arrival, so Jones walked to the office door to summon his staff for the planning. Even if they tried to settle the contract dispute tomorrow, Jones would find a way to balk and put them off by examining the fine print. He would have his march and nobody could thwart him. History had better remember his name. He would see to that. In his mind, this crusade had become a battle of fierce wills. His vision for this change, like that of Reverend King, would prevail.

He didn't care if King brought along the East Coast liberals that always followed him around who consisted of mostly slogan-chanting Jewish New Yorkers and a few Catholic priests.

His was an uprising of the purest black souls, his own people moving that much closer to the promised land, as trite as it had sounded. He didn't care what the college students said or did as they were useless and indulged. None of them had any idea of what it took to put food on the table because their lawyer fathers would send them a couple hundred bucks each month. If there was a revolution, it would come from the workers, the men who labored for their daily bread as it had in Russia.

He pondered over his thoughts after his staff had left him. This protest is the true revolution of working black men. They alone would stem the tide of white politicians and the wealthy bosses who crushed them underfoot. Jones could be a rabid Communist if it came to that, but the power should begin with the people at the bottom, not from the top down.

But first, he had to deal with the city and get the parade permits from City Hall, then arrange for motel rooms for Doctor

King and his staff. He would do all that tomorrow himself since he couldn't really rely on his small staff. The young men were so limited in their myopic visions. They only wanted to get drunk on Saturday nights and sport around the Southside in some flashy maroon Bonneville car.

Could he become a Communist? He thought pensively about that idea but quickly dismissed it since they had burned churches and said there was no God.

Who was this Stalin character anyway? Some horrible monster who had killed millions, and for what reason? They were barbarians. Even white workers had been murdered by their bosses and henchmen during the long Depression. Jones knew all about that tragedy and believed that organized labor was a right all men embraced together. He had traveled to New Jersey for a week, and the union leaders and intellectuals from New York City had taught him about the labor movement, and its crucial importance. He knew the name, Samuel Gompers, and of the sacrifices.

There was another thing too, and as a black man, it became less about earning decent wages on those garbage trucks, and more about simple human dignity that had been missing from all their lives. The same twisted slavery mentality persisted.

* * * * * *

Martha's work seemed to mushroom during a three-week period. Suddenly Jim Latham treated her as his closest ally and seeming to trust her acumen over the more experienced and seasoned lawyers on his staff. It hadn't gone unnoticed, of course, but Latham wasn't a man to cross. He had the deadly sting of a scorpion and his venomous words could end promising legal careers.

I had imagined this was discussed in passing by the staff lawyers who stopped for drinks after work and some resentment developed as a result. But it was Martha's career, and she was a big girl. I felt it wasn't my place to offer her advice when my own

191

endeavors seemed to become putting one fire out after another behind Wyeth.

Every week brought a different attack on him from some new quarter. He had clearly lost the confidence of the city council, and rarely saw the chairman gracing Wyeth's office anymore, or even the usual supplicants. The path to the mayor's office had become a minefield, and he had lost a lot of would-be friends who avoided him.

The last city council meeting had been a shouting match, and he had been called weak and soft on crime, and unable to act as a chief executive on any policy. The more vocal voices on the city council were seconded by the bad press the two newspapers had heaped on him. It took the afternoon paper, the Press Scimitar, perhaps two months before they joined the larger morning daily attacking Wyeth, and they also enumerated his many failures in city government. A continuous deluge began to drown the otherwise honorable mayor and it became a powerless position.

Wyeth had met with national AFSCME leader Wolfson who had lent his support to the successful settlement of the upcoming garbage strike, though nothing was done. Jones chose which of his many calls to return and the strike became inevitable. When the request for a single day parade permit was made for the garbage workers' proposed march downtown, the city officials had called the mayor for his assistance.

They had made excuses to Jones on delays involved, but within a week, outside attorneys had questioned their legal right to withhold the permits and the city was forced to grant them. There had never been any violence associated with the AFSCME union. The city attorneys had scrambled for reasons to not grant the permits, however, they weren't able to find any.

In the meantime, as the city administrators waited to act the ACLU and the Southern Poverty Clinic lawyers began filing their briefs for cause on the delays, and a legal morass began to form, so Wyeth was forced to grant the permit.

The estimated number of people who would march downtown was thought to be around three thousand workers, but in reality, when it did happen there were more in the two-mile-long march. Wyeth was able to delay issuing the permit for a single week then the dam broke, and he finally ordered the city office to issue the paperwork.

Not surprisingly, police commissioner Holston had opposed this march from the very beginning. He had attacked the mayor for granting permission thereby risking the public's safety which, in turn, would most probably result in deaths along the route. Holston charged Wyeth with gross neglect, contending that now the mayor could count on these black radicals murdering innocent people.

"You're going to have blood on your hands," Holston warned him. "You've consistently undermined police efforts to prevent this slaughter. On your watch."

It was reckless on the city's part to allow the thousands of blacks to run wild in the streets, Holston conjectured. They would end up destroying property and the whole thing would turn into a riot. At best, a few people might be killed though the commissioner feared the radicals would turn the event into a turkey shoot.

"Look, there aren't enough police officers to protect people," Holston spat out with vehemence. "Call the governor and have him station the National Guard along the parade route. A few tanks too."

Wyeth began to lose his usual composure, and threw out, "Dammit, I'm not going to put tanks on Memphis streets. That's bullshit."

"It'll be too late when the shooting starts," Holston muttered sarcastically. "My hands are tied." He held up his two meaty hands for effect.

Wyeth did call the governor who was worried about the containment of the crowd, and was persuaded to order four hundred National Guard soldiers to Memphis for the march. Two hundred of these men would come from the existing city units and the balance would come from Nashville. The troopers would be armed with rifles and would carry live ammunition which could be employed if violence occurred during the march. The governor also ordered his most senior general to command the troops, and suggested to both the general and Wyeth that no preemptive action would take place with the soldiers. They would be held in strict reserve to back up Memphis police should they be needed to intervene.

The fact that both the police and the Tennessee troopers possessed weapons which could wound and kill people troubled him greatly. Only the ultimate decision to protect the public had motivated him to act. Naturally, by the time these orders had trickled down to the lowest level, all the soldiers ordered to Memphis were carrying loaded firearms.

It was possible that any individual soldier or police officer could fire into the marchers if provoked, or not, and create bedlam and certain death. This situation had become a powder keg ready to blow at any time as Wyeth made final provisions for the deployment along the parade route of armed men.

Wyeth was a man under pressure. As I sat in his office listening to him outline more of the problem and not the solution needed, or any workable solution, I saw he was doomed to fail miserably.

My stealth with the police department had not uncovered much. Holston had created his tactical paramilitary units. We knew that he had armed them with far more firepower than the rest of the police department. When they weren't scouring the rundown black neighborhoods or meeting with their paid informers in some back alley, they were all at the Police Academy firing range blasting away. Or they were huddled in the situation room that Holston had created in the basement of police headquarters.

This was the counter radical, or strike force, the commissioner had formed, and Wyeth and others in city government were only vaguely aware that they even existed since they generally were hidden. They looked like every other cop on the force. Holston hadn't bothered to dress them like Green Berets or commandos, preferring instead to not call attention to their existence. If the other police captains knew about them, they never mentioned it, so in a sense these men were of little interest to this hierarchy of cops.

The white sergeant in charge of these tactical units had been in the Korea conflict. He was considerably older than the others, and in some unmistakable manner, half crazed. He had been wounded twice and later decorated for bravery at the Chosin bloodbath where the Chinese troops surrounded the Americans and began to eliminate them with their vast numbers, battalion by battalion. It was a disgusting failure of American military strategy.

For some strange, though predictable, reason, the man seemed to loathe all blacks he encountered. His racist language in the most inappropriate moments reflected that ingrained hatred. He didn't bother to hide it, and perhaps for that police department, there was no real need. Certainly Holston didn't care. The sergeant had once been questioned on an arrest where he had almost killed the black suspect. Though he'd been exonerated, that unpleasant record of excessive force had followed him.

The other cops who were more reasonable in their response to the common black criminals didn't much like the man. I was told that later when I made inquiries about him. However, this was a veteran police officer, and a decorated soldier, which ended any negative conversation about the man.

In those days, no one used the term 'police brutality'. The beat cops were simply tough customers as you had to be on these streets.

The suspect the sergeant had beaten, never recovered his health. There had been some brain damage done with continuous blows to his head with a blackjack, or service revolver. The man had been blinded in one eye from that nighttime arrest, and was unable to work, except for the most meaningless tasks like collecting empty soda bottles for deposit. In the official report, he'd been detained for something as minor as vagrancy and supposedly had assaulted this sergeant while being detained for questioning. His partner had gone along with the sergeant's account. Later he claimed he had been around a corner in pursuit of another suspect, and only returned for the final blow to the downed miscreant.

Perhaps this particular sergeant had been the perfect choice for a police unit targeted to find and arrest, or kill, black radicals in this city. He had the persona of a dangerous and unreconstructed racist. He was the perfect man to pull the trigger if these uppity blacks gave him the smallest excuse, which undoubtedly they would.

Holston didn't believe he had much to hide with me. On several occasions he brought me down to the basement, and briefed me on the progress of his tactical units. There were five or six large charts with lines, circles, and pins on them denoting something, and he felt compelled to carefully explain it all.

Once the sergeant was present. Holston introduced me as the mayor's messenger which had gotten a laugh while I forced a half grin. Taking over from Holston, the sergeant explained all the neighborhood areas of reconnaissance they had staked out. He told me how they used this informant information to track the most active of these black radicals while monitoring their every step. Most of these blacks had criminal records, though some were of a higher class who had been enlisted by outside agitators from Detroit and elsewhere.

There was a permanent tactical unit placed near LeMoyne Owen, the exclusively black college where they'd learned some radical elements on campus were now organized into neighborhood recruitment tools. They had picked up one student that informers had fingered as a leader. Police had managed to arrest him on an illegal weapons charge, and brought him in for further questioning.

He'd proved to be a smart ass, using his tired revolutionary jargon to answer the questions the officers asked him. Finally, one of them had smacked him in the nose a few times, and his arrogance seemed to disappear. The black student had done little beyond passing out radical literature someone had sent to him from Chicago. It was a mimeographed twenty-page magazine calling for the armed rebellion of blacks against their white oppressors. However, the radical brochure was written in a style that few neighborhood blacks would understand.

The gun police found on him was an ancient 22 caliber pistol. This subsequent charge for possession would keep him in the county jail for maybe eight months. To them, it was one more revolutionary out of the picture.

During the basement interrogation which lasted for three days, the man had finally given them other names under duress, including the Chicago source. The officers had called the Chicago police to pull the individual in for questioning.

Typically, this arrest was like most of the others Holston's officers made. These dime store black radicals had little or no intention or wherewithal to bring down the white establishment through armed action. The arrests were for the usual illegal gun traffic that supported street mayhem, and petty theft, and none of the blacks they interrogated seemed capable of these larger crimes.

Chapter 14
Twenty Thousand Blacks

On a chilly overcast morning, the Memphis mayor left his bed the last time at four am in his Chickasaw Gardens Georgian brick home. Wyeth had been pacing around his spacious house since one-thirty that morning filled with a dread over this massive march which would begin at nine o'clock and probably involve twenty thousand blacks, and who knows who else.

It was the largest event of this kind in the history of the city and what had started as a simple negotiation over a city labor contract renewal, had taken on monumental proportions. It had become this grotesque unmanageable circus of out of town news people, with their camera crews and powdered star-quality television reporters that he had been plagued with for days now, and he was already exhausted.

He sent his wife back to bed twice as she asked if he wanted coffee, or something to eat, or to talk to someone, and he'd said no. There was nothing to say anymore. He had done all this talking but to no avail.

Wyeth had gone back three times to the local AFSCME management and they had turned down all his offers, and finally refused to speak to him. He tried to get the union head in New Jersey involved, though nothing had come of it, and the Memphis garbage workers had dug in their heels for a general strike. The strike wasn't the real issue any longer. It was now the grandstanding of Jones who had enlisted the SCLC, and the radical preachers who inflamed local blacks to riot in the street for a so-called freedom that they already had.

He pondered over his tepid coffee. For God's sake, the civil war took place a hundred years ago and all these things have long been settled. Blacks had representation on the city council, and a black federal judge had been named two months ago by Johnson. This march had become something else.

What had been strictly a home town labor problem, a simple city contract to pick up the garbage, became this blinding international spectacle. It had attracted destructive blacks and their supporters who were here only to cause trouble. They called themselves ministers, but were they? They would create violence in their wake, and refuse to shoulder the blame.

Wyeth's wife sat down in the den in the stuffed leather chair next to her husband of almost thirty years, and asked, "What are you thinking about?"

"I have a bad feeling. This march today could be something awful, and I don't know what," Wyeth told her calmly. He looked at her and smiled.

"It's for show, isn't it, really," she said to him, "putting those black preachers on TV, so we all look like a bunch of rednecks."

"Some of that, sure," Wyeth agreed. "What worries me is people getting hurt and fired up, and that's never good."

His wife stood and reached for his coffee cup ready to go to the kitchen for a refill but Wyeth told her no.

"Well, you have the police," the wife added in the doorway leaving him.

Wyeth said, "That may not be enough."

Sitting quietly as the yellow dawn light poured into his comfortable den, the mayor believed he had done everything possible to prevent this whole thing from happening. Perhaps, it had been inevitable. If this particular march didn't happen with the striking black workers today, it would be six months from now with some other group of disgruntled blacks, or the next year. It had all become too blatantly political with the charade of failed anti-poverty programs, and the mayor blamed Johnson for this heightened polarity between the two races.

Five of the storefront Community Action Offices had been opened in Southside neighborhoods and fifty million dollars of Washington's money had been funneled into their hands, and what had been the result? Crafts programs for preteen black girls, and a few after-school basketball leagues at the public schools.

Had crime or poverty been decreased? Hardly. The needle hadn't moved.

Wyeth had received telephone calls yesterday and the day before from the Justice Department informing him that federal marshals were being sent to the city to ensure the march was peaceful. It had the President's attention.

Well, this mayor had a police force to ensure that, so what could a dozen of these suited G-men possibly do? The answer, of course, was nothing, except to report some unseen infraction back to their masters on the Potomac. Again, the ridiculous history of race-baiting.

Holston refused to cooperate with the marshals, and he told Wyeth that he had informed them so himself. His responsibility was to protect the city, not chauffeur around these fresh-faced lawyers who pretended to be real cops, which they clearly weren't. They were on their own in the city.

The National Guard units from Nashville had arrived. They were to set up around the perimeter with the Memphis troops behind the police cordon along the march route. They would remain as far in the background as was possible for men dressed in camouflage uniforms carrying assault rifles and ammunition belts. Thankfully, the suggestions to employ tanks or cannons mounted on jeeps had been dismissed, and the Guard was only deployed as an assurance factor.

Wyeth had told the governor this wasn't necessary even though Holston had welcomed their presence. However, the mayor didn't push back very hard and went along with the executive order. It had been increasingly difficult for Wyeth to pick these battles, as he had been attacked on numerous fronts.

The Memphis mayor was a beleaguered public official, and the river port city he oversaw was in turmoil, though some might deny the damage had gone that far. The dark green lawns and the century old elms in the finer East Memphis neighborhoods were still the same, and life was unchanged.

Wyeth's daughter, like her closest friends, attended Miss Hutchinson's School or St. Mary's where integration wasn't much of a factor in the privileged schoolrooms. The forced busing and the integration orders destroyed the older public schools like

Central and East High. Though for the wealthier, this wasn't really their problem as they had always preferred the more established academies.

He lit a cigarette, and after he had finished, it had come time to shower and prepare for the difficult day ahead. As Wyeth crushed the butt in the ashtray, he thought to himself, 'I'll come through this, like before.'

Holston, in a four-bedroom brick ranch house in another less grand neighborhood in East Memphis, readied himself for the day and the march.

His commissioner's blues were immaculate. He had all his uniforms professionally laundered. His brass was polished, and his black ankle boots had been shined by a black shoeshine man near police headquarters who had done it for years.

The policemen under his command were ready to be deployed in their tactical units along the parade route, and the so-called advance party of marksmen were in place. He had spread three units of these marksmen on several high rise rooftops along the march route. They were readied for anything untoward. The officers were crack marksmen, and they had long range weapons and powerful scopes which allowed them to take those difficult shots, if it became necessary.

He had placed four of his black police informants within the parade posing as union workers in the scheduled march. These men weren't armed, but he had provided each with a stylish men's leather shoulder bag where they had hidden radios keyed to police frequencies. If, for any reason, they needed to alert his officers, these men could leave the crowd of marchers, and quickly use the radios to alert the police.

Along the downtown parade route at critical junctures, Holston had placed groups of uniformed police officers, and they were charged with crowd control and safety. On several of the side streets leading into this route, police cruisers were now parked to block traffic, and to prevent an attack on the marchers by a speeding vehicle. The Air National Guard that was allied with the army contingent, would have two helicopters in the air to monitor the march, and carried Memphis police officers who would keep on the lookout for dangerous activity from the air.

It was believed that the march was scheduled to terminate at Tom Lee Park on the Mississippi River, where the crowd would be addressed by its leaders. Holston had two police motor launches already in the water to move up and down its banks and keep a careful watch on the protesters.

The single thing that concerned Holston the most was the National Guard. He had little confidence in the weekend warriors, and thought their military training was too haphazard and often deficient, particularly their experience with firearms. He didn't want any of these soldiers to somehow panic and start shooting innocent people simply because they heard a noise. Their NCOs and officers didn't have enough control of their troops, and Holston worried that some unpleasant incident might occur because of lack of training.

This was the initiative of the ridiculous governor who was trying to show off his executive prowess. Generally, these same Guardsmen were never the right men to rely on in these types of tense situations which required the clear thinking of experienced police officers. They would remain in the background where they belonged.

For today at least, the commissioner would carry a sidearm when he usually didn't, and he found his favorite Colt 45 with the pearl handle and slipped it into the leather holster. He would put on the cartridge belt later when he arrived at the staging ground and carried it out the door in his hand to his shiny black unmarked police cruiser.

He started his car ignition and noticed his worried wife at the kitchen window watching him. Holston gave her a broad grin, and touched the brim of his commander's field cap with its gold braid as a gesture of acknowledgement that everything would be alright.

* * * * * * *

Martha's schedule had gotten hectic lately. Part of it was a sudden rash of carjacking and the subsequent arrests of the poorly organized street thugs who held on to the stolen vehicles and had been spotted by police. She had three cases to prosecute although two of them there were guilty plea deals for reduced sentences.

The living room table and the bed were covered with legal briefs, and half a dozen manila folders stuffed with depositions, forensic reports, and official police reports. It looked more like a law office than a home I told her jokingly. But true to form, she took exactly what I had said to heart. That unleashed a rant about women with important careers, the tragedy of her own mother, her best friend Elizabeth's reluctant divorce, finally the absence of children in this house. At the finale of her breathlessness, I was completely lost.

Her legal job created too much pressure on Martha and even her own lengthy description of what Latham wanted from her seemed too ambitious.

I asked her to tell him to back off on the assignments, at least for a while, until she could right herself. I didn't want her suffering a nervous breakdown for a misguided need to escape the self-esteem Carolyn had planted in her head over the years.

Martha was obsessive. I could almost accept that trait of hers, and gradually over the short marriage, it had eased a bit. For the past year, it had constantly made no sense. I had pushed back hard, and there were outbursts of anger and frustration from her, but it had to be done. We couldn't continue as a couple without some meaningful change and she made some small changes in how she acted, though not nearly enough. Sure, it was a ridiculous contradiction for us with the presence of Amanda in my life, and the unsuspecting behavior that was going on between us. Of course I didn't have a leg to stand on there.

We agreed that the compromise was that the legal papers were confined to the bedroom, and Martha would put them back in her briefcase after working.

203

Wyeth had me practically living at police headquarters once the sanitation workers talks collapsed and the march of black solidarity was announced. The nagging fear that the worker's protest might end in violence and death plagued Wyeth's nights, and most of his administration as well.

Memphis itself was an untamed sprawling city. Illegal guns in the hands of angry black marchers stirred up by outside agitators seemed a distinct possibility. They would probably use the weapons on white policemen who might challenge them inciting a bloodbath on the city streets.

Holston's department had been in close communication with the FBI, and not only the small Atlanta regional office with a handful of agents, but also with J. Edgar Hoover's top aides who voiced concern with the presence of Reverend King and other radicals involved in the Memphis protest. The FBI had found damning evidence of numerous examples of their questionable association with King. His staff consisted of mostly black clergymen that followed him to Detroit, Birmingham, Selma, and wherever else he had sought to disrupt peaceful order.

In this constellation of men there had been contact with renegade governments and guerilla movements such as the IRA militants, which sought to overthrow the British government, and had become gunmen of women and children. It was on the record.

King himself was caught on camera in a restaurant in Boston where he had been educated at the Boston University seminary talking with two known IRA functionaries, one of whom was a suspect in the recent bombing in London of a pub, killing twenty-one innocent people.

The IRA had a checkered past of supplying illegal arms to individuals and movements that it supported. They were believed to come from the Soviet Union and this concerned the FBI. Together with Soviet intelligence agents, it was feared that their revolutionary intent would be spread to radical American blacks.

What made the association even more obscene, for King, was the proliferation of terrorist bombings that had taken place in the past six months resulting in the death of hundreds of innocent people, including small children. Perhaps the innocent weren't really the IRA target, however they had been among the awful casualties which resulted.

A tea shop in a Protestant neighborhood in Belfast had been obliterated with explosives on a Sunday afternoon killing ten women over the age of sixty.

It was criminal to watch the violence. Many of the so-called Provo's had escaped jail, and currently moved across Northern Ireland itself, or found their way across the border into the Irish Republic.

There had been IRA involvement in Chicago as reported by the FBI presence in that city. But they had been shielded by the large Irish population, many of whom supported an armed resistance against the British. Public meetings were held in Chicago's Irish bars and restaurants monitored by federal agents where tens of thousands of dollars had been raised, possibly more. It was passed on to the IRA for suspected arms purchases, though that was never mentioned at these rallies. Instead within this circus, they tended to be all about lauded Eire, and what all those distant Irish brothers shared. It was sentimental and without accountability for the funds.

Repeatedly, the IRA and its loose association with revolutionary blacks had been examined. There had been clear connections with King and its more militant cells. The FBI director himself was convinced the IRA would most likely supply weapons they had received from their Soviet friends with the purpose of encouraging a racial war and a full scale revolution.

Hoover had trailed King's many movements. He had his telephones at the SCLC headquarters in Atlanta wiretapped, as well as at King's home. He suspected the minister and activist had become a surreptitious and ever present danger to the country.

Sitting rather uncomfortably in Holston's office on several occasions, I had heard in excruciating detail all about King's unsavory and suspicious associations that were taken from FBI files and surveillance. And what a risk these people presented. Holston told me he believed that King was a communist being groomed as a Soviet provocateur not unlike the traitor, Alger Hiss.

The other men surrounding King were no better, and that included those double-dealing liberal Jews from New York, who were self-proclaimed civil rights lawyers whom Holston particularly loathed. They were all hypocrites.

Holston thought, 'They didn't know anything about this place, and the hard lives people had lived. A lot of us are from some dirt farm in the Ozarks or some shit Mississippi town without a stoplight.'

'These same country boys barely escaped poverty inside an army uniform with trembling hands pulling at a jammed rifle on the side of a hill at Iwo Jima or maybe half-frozen in Korea. And they didn't come back to Memphis with the Olds car dealership or running the MacDonald's franchise business for three states. That went to the people who already had the connections, whose families had been the planters or cotton brokers on Front Street, or had a fleet of river barges. People like Elizabeth's grandparents who had a ten bedroom Tudor stone house midtown. Who the hell needed that many bedrooms anyway?'

'I know how these people think,' Holston believed. 'Lyndon Johnson's afraid of these black preachers, and of Martin Luther King and what the man represented. King could get a lot of people to do his bidding and the federal government just stood looking on. They broke the law when they thought it worked in their favor, and the lessons of history went out the goddamn window. They disappeared, and overnight one hundred years vanished into thin air.'

Holston had looked at the King files, all of them. Who was the IRA murderer King met with? It was a cop-killer from Belfast that the British released in trade for civilian hostages, at least that was the story and they let the bastard go.

There was never a shortage of weapons as they had a ton of automatic assault rifles, ammunition, and boxes of explosives.

The IRA had the Kremlin get weapons to them on ocean freighters and unloaded the boats at night in the Irish Sea.

They would teach the blacks how to blow up elementary schools, or maybe police stations, and white churches, then give them the explosives. They were sophisticated murderers, and the radical Negroes would learn from them. The days of the stupid street criminal had abruptly ended. The country would have mass killings, and the IRA and King conduit needed to be stopped in its tracks and eliminated.

Holston didn't share with me all that he had learned from the FBI and the CIA as he had hinted.

"People who know think communists are involved. This march might have been infiltrated and we're too late," he added after a long explanation on the need for increased police power throughout the city.

"Wyeth doesn't want a war zone, commissioner," I finally explained to him after skirting the issue halfheartedly. "He believes it's best if the police are less visible to these marchers and in a situation where they remain in the background."

Holston went on the attack himself, saying, "That's not how you stop violence. You demonstrate this heavily armed force, show people your resolve, and that prevents a riot before it starts."

By this time, Holston had risen from his desk chair and addressed me from different locations in his office as he nervously paced. He delivered that last important soliloquy as Hamlet might have done, with his hand raised and an open palm.

There was no point arguing with the commissioner, certainly not as a low-level mayor's mouthpiece. I simply reviewed his written report of police department preparations for the labor march and carried it to Wyeth.

It was rather detailed. It was fifteen typewritten pages and three additional graphs which identified the police units and their deployments along the parade route, as well as where we might expect the National Guard units to be placed.

At home that evening, I had confessed all of the day to Martha and she listened patiently without interrupting, which was unusual.

With the rare cigarette lit in her hand, she said smilingly: "That bastard wants some black to pull out his pistol so that the cops have a reason to mow them down, all of them, right there in the street. Teach those niggers a lesson."

"Martha, we're trying to stop that from happening. It's about having some controls in place and preemptive actions that can be taken."

I found myself defending Wyeth when I knew I didn't need to, and continued explaining it to her. "Look, if we minimize the amount of armed police that confront marchers along the route, and put them at strategic points along the route, hopefully that keeps the hotheads out of it."

She said: "Somebody's going to get shot, mostly some blacks. Bang, bang! In front of everyone. He'll spit on some cop. And you know what? He'll be shot dead for it just as fast."

I shook my head, and looked away from her for an instant, exasperated.

"They don't charge cops with brutality in this town." She threw at me, hardly waiting for an answer. "You don't believe me? You should."

I told her she expected the worst from this march, and that didn't necessarily have to follow, there were plenty of peaceful protests around the country, lots of them.

"Not in Memphis," she stated, adding her confident smile to the comment.

Without any real common ground in this conversation, we simply ceased talking. The evening pretty much ended so not five minutes afterward, she excused herself to the bedroom with legal paperwork to do, and I turned on the television set to some mindless drama.

I had neglected to mention Holston's recent FBI talks to her, and his belief that there could be conspiracies involving King.

She probably would have laughed at me anyway. It was difficult to persuade her away from anything.

When I came to bed, she had turned out the light, so I undressed and slipped under the covers. She reached over to me and rested her hand on my bare chest.

"The black and white thing here is so complicated. I just don't know where to start. When you live here, you see it with a different set of eyes."

I caressed her hand in a show of acknowledgement.

"I know you, and you'll do the right thing. Make the right decision," she whispered, but didn't elaborate on her meaning.

For a moment she seemed to be talking about something or someone else, and it made me think about her cousin Amanda, and what we'd done. But eventually, sleep overcame me.

In the morning over coffee, she laid out her day while looking at the day timer she had opened on the table. "It's a bad week, I guess, for both of us. I've got the two trials and there's the march."

I outlined what I knew the mayor expected of me. Wyeth wanted me to join the labor deputy for a last ditch visit to the local AFSCME office and see if there was anything we might do toward an eleventh hour settlement.

Wyeth had caved in, and said he would find the money for the garbage worker salary increases somewhere. All he asked from Jones was to call off the march, and Jones could shout to the heavens that he had won the labor war. But Jones had no intention to do so. He would never call off the scheduled labor march. It was the most important event in his otherwise lackluster life. He would willingly link arms with the Reverend Martin Luther King Junior and walk past the scowling policemen with their vulgar catcalls, and enter history.

We sat silently for fifteen minutes outside of Jones' office when finally, a staffer came out of the inner suite. She apologized and told us that Mister Jones had been called away on an important appointment and regretted that he couldn't see us now.

The labor deputy started out the door in a bit of a huff muttering under his breath, though it appeared to me that we were accepting the inevitable.

He drove us back to the city garage in his beater car and crossed the invisible line in his criticism of the mayor and his mishandling of the sanitation contract talks. I didn't bother to answer him, and remained mute.

* * * * * * *

On November 15 and 16, 1967, the Thursday and Friday before Thanksgiving, the Reverend Martin Luther King traveled to Boston to speak at the Hale Theology School, his alma mater, where he had been granted his doctor of divinity degree and briefly taught the faculty afterward.

For two nights he had stayed with friends in nearby Cambridge. The first night he was hosted at a dinner in a small neighborhood restaurant by school faculty and other friends. On the second night, he was seen at a noisy Greek restaurant in the rundown Boston neighborhood of Dorchester, meeting with two unknown white men who were initially unknown to the two FBI agents who had been closely trailing him. The two federal agents were dressed in casual clothes posing as regular diners, both covert operatives with powerful directional microphones. They managed to record the conversation King had with the two men at his table. The accent of one of the men identified him as being from a Soviet satellite country, most probably the Ukraine. The second man was largely silent during the whole dinner and he deferred to the other. Though when he did speak, it was in their native Russian.

When the meal was served, it was discovered that one of the men had known King from before. They had discussed some earlier event in Atlanta where the two had been present, and the Ukrainian man spoke of the 'nice' dinner of southern home style cooking that he had enjoyed with several the SCLC staff members, and even asked about the health of one of the black ministers.

It appeared that the Russian-speaker was originally from Kiev. He currently resided in the United States and made his home in Stamford, Connecticut, a small city outside New York considered a bedroom suburb.

He had been with King on another occasion in Harlem where King had addressed the congregation of the Ebenezer Baptist Church and later had talked with residents of the surrounding neighborhood alongside the black congressman, Adam Clayton Powell.

Powell was known in Washington, not for his position of black empowerment, but more for his lavish clothes, spending, and his employment of the spoils system. At the time, King had been subdued with Powell beyond being American blacks in a country which had denied them full citizenship, they shared little in common. King was always circumspect with his various hosts, and was plain-spoken.

Quite animated, the squat man from suburban Stamford had been born to Russian parents who later emigrated to the United States during the deadly Stalin purges. He was a minister in the Methodist Church and had been trained at the seminary at Wesleyan University. His Russian parents who lived in the rural Ukraine had been protestant missionaries in the once Catholic country where they had been persecuted. Somehow they had survived it all and had been allowed to emigrate as they were considered religious undesirables.

This man who laughed at the table with King was also a member of the Russian intelligence service, and his task was to open a dialogue specifically with King and others in the SCLC. He had been trained in Moscow as a young man by the KGB and other agencies of the Communist government. He had been allowed to rejoin his parents in the United States as a man in his mid-twenties, and had been subsequently granted asylum along with his missionary parents.

Alexsey and King had both said a brief grace each when the meal was served, and then the table devolved into a moment of silent prayer.

211

The Russian didn't speak of the Soviets supplying guns to the SCLC, or anything as revolutionary as the arming of blacks for organized resistance in city streets. Rather, he addressed King's greater philosophy of employing the non-violent principles of resistance to force peaceful change. Though the compelling reasons for the loose association with the Atlanta minister and resistance movement leader were far more sinister, and included the deeper infiltration of Soviet intelligence into American life.

There was little direct involvement thus far between the Russian government and King. It had encouraged the IRA's more radical elements whom it had supplied arms to advise King's lieutenants and their operatives who might act with violence. King set an unquestioned tone for his non-violent philosophy and with other ministers he endeavored to lead these protests and marches across the country. Not everyone associated with the Atlanta minister subscribed to those same principles. Yet his was a top down leadership of more radical Christian principles, not remarkably different from what was happening across Central America, particularly in El Salvador with the Catholic priests.

There were many unhappy young blacks ready to abandon King's not always effective results. They'd take to the streets with armed gangs such as the Black Panthers whom were widely feared and thereby respected. They ruled the black neighborhoods in Oakland and Los Angeles, and especially in Chicago where wary police rarely entered those sections of the city.

The Russian minister talked of his missionary parents' experiences in the Ukraine and of the sometimes conversion of Soviet authorities to accepting religious thought, and granting wider freedom to worship.

King listened intently as the Russian talked. Then he himself spoke of his greater vision. It depended on those poor blacks refusing to live with the unfair segregation thrust unwillingly upon them, and with it the loss of simple human dignity especially in this Christian country.

It was this same opinion that the Russian minister had heard before and hoped for the obvious fissures that might be widened. The Soviets were ready to supply weapons to King or others in the splinter black radical groups, and had already achieved some success infiltrating black student associations at several universities in the larger cities.

They left the restaurant together and another agent followed as the Russian dropped King at the home of the white Cambridge minister with whom he was staying.

Later review of the recording had raised suspicions of more widespread Soviet involvement with American blacks, although there was little of a specific nature that led the FBI to act. Still, the agency continued its investigation of King's behavior. In the future, the Russian minister would be monitored closely and all his activities would be duly noted by Hoover's field men.

The aging and paranoid FBI head had reluctantly agreed to involve the CIA in this as he was required by law to do. They had requested a greater role in the King case, which he had subsequently discouraged.

Remember, this was the same man who single handedly ambushed the notorious criminal John Dillinger. The CIA people were a bunch of limp wrist Ivy Leaguers who sipped schnapps in West Berlin restaurants showing off their facile German language skills. He would ignore them as he had before, and conduct the investigation of King on his own terms.

Hoover had heard reports that King had been with numerous women, who were not his wife, on his many trips across the country. There had been multiple photographs taken of them as they were leaving his motel rooms in the morning.

One of the black women had told them that when she and King had sex in a motel room, it was their second time. He had been in Selma once before where they had met, and he later invited her to his room. He had insisted on having intercourse so she ended up spending the night with the Atlanta minister. She swore that the account was true, and had written a statement to that extent that was given to the interrogating agent who had promised not to prosecute, or make the incident public.

The fact that King was of dubious moral character had already been established, and his tasteless adultery had been repeated several times, according to the investigation. So much for the man's Christian pronouncements.

****

With the formidable racial storm cloud over the city and the lives of those people who watched it closely with fear, Martha's sister Carrie had decided it was time to return with her recent British husband. She would introduce him to friends, those of her family that cared which probably now only included Alfred, and the larger society of which she once was a part.

They would stay with Alfred, arrange for a welcoming buffet dinner and visit the clubs and restaurants she had frequented in the past. She might even see her son who was now a gangly sandy-haired young man at the Presbyterian Day School. The boy was painfully shy with few interests or friends, it seemed, and would later enter into years of rebellion against an overprotective father that he couldn't understand.

His father had remarried and his new spouse came with a daughter who was a few years older. This particular mother had, unfortunately, showered the girl with most of the attention, and though perhaps loving, couldn't connect with the boy. The son grew up with this unresolved hostility and became terribly withdrawn, so much so that the father had decided to send him to a military school. The place was mostly a popular depository for unruly children from wealthier parents who could afford Webb's ten-thousand-dollar tuition.

It was a four-hour drive toward Chattanooga in a rural mountainous region, and this academy had developed a reputation for dealing with difficult sons. The boy would live uncomfortably at The Webb School for almost six years off and on with calendar holidays, like Christmas, and the summer months spent at home with his father in Memphis. He would see his mother on her annual, or perhaps bi-annual, visits. And it wasn't

214

until he reached eighteen that he would be permitted to visit her by himself in England.

For the visit with the new husband, the welcoming flag had been raised. Martha's sister Carrie was particularly proud of his elegant European manners, and knowledge of the international art world. It seemed Reginald had lived in Paris for a time, and naturally was an expert on all those modern French painters who were in great demand on the world market.

He had curated several important museum shows in London, including one featuring works of Jean Dubuffet and his awful toilet sculptures. His conversation was incessantly about the important people he knew in the art world. The tiresome man assumed a condescending approach with most of those he had met in Memphis because, apparently, we were the unschooled natives. He clearly couldn't contain his own hubris enough to placate his wife, or even make an attempt to enjoy her family and friends.

Carrie was rather proud of his Oxbridge mannerisms, and that's what it amounted to. He had a patently false veneer of an upper class British accent and made some few contacts over the years. He was the youngest son of a travel agent for BOAC and lived in the meanest part of suburban Wimbledon. He had been sent to a Catholic boy's school in concert with sons of other Irish fathers. His mother's father had been a steward on the Cunard line, and he had never risen above that seagoing waiter position. There was a physician brother among the large Irish brood who had found his way to Harley Street, however, the others were either tradesmen or sales representatives for insurance schemes.

In deference to their collective ambition, his elder brother had been at the London School of Economics, and later became a broker in the city. Their wits had indeed propelled this family forward. They were both distasteful, overbearing men. I would have the unfortunate experience of meeting his brother on an extended tour through the country with his pasty-faced East Indian wife before the end of the year.

Martha's sister's visit wasn't without harsh words, and at one dinner she literally pulled Carrie by the arm away from the table to berate her for some off-putting remarks at Alfred's expense. I sat there with the art dealer and listened to him disparage the paintings around the dining room. He had called them, "Rather dull American primitives."

The couple departed without fanfare. We asked them to taxi to the airport themselves since we would be far too busy to drop them off. We said our goodbyes at a round of drinks at Alfred's, and even by the end of the rather short visit, the brother-in-law's disingenuous manner hadn't much improved.

Honestly, I liked Carrie for her panache, yet I couldn't stomach this new husband who represented everything that British upper class pretenders tried to be, yet did so unsuccessfully.

Chapter 15
To the Mississippi

The first indication that the sanitation worker's strike had started came on the morning of February 13th, when two hundred garbage workers didn't show up for their morning shifts.

Instead of taking the sanitation trucks along the usual routes, the small contingent of the larger labor force walked en mass from their union hall to the city offices and met with the mayor in the city council auditorium who, by this time, had conceded to their demands.

However, the meeting rapidly fell into name-calling and threats initially from the white union officials representing other labor groups. It was followed by the heated black workers responding by attacking Wyeth himself, and all the white city administrators.

The next day, a similar solidarity trek to the downtown city offices took place. But the number of black garbage workers doubled, and this time there were teenage sympathizers as well in the all black ranks that marched along.

Two blocks off Union Avenue at an intersection monitored by Memphis police officers, there was an incident of rock throwing and the wielding of baseball bats or sticks. Within two minutes, a Memphis police officer had fired into the riot with a shotgun killing a sixteen-year-old boy who had been part of the march.

This was the first casualty and the larger labor march hadn't even begun. The black crowd ran amok after the shooting and the police used tear gas and clubs to disperse the angered protestors.

That night there had been an immense rally of blacks at the largest downtown CME church, and local ministers had called for resistance against the police at whatever the cost. This was said to be an undeclared racial war, and many blacks in the audience vowed they would rather die than submit to the continuous oppression they had encountered their entire lives.

Holston had his first black death from the strike to explain to the frightened Memphis public. It appeared that a young white officer, who was barely twenty-one, may have acted without enough justification and quickly gunned down an unarmed teenager who posed little threat. This brutal police response went far beyond the perception of any real threat as there had been none. The heavily armed officer had become caught up in the numbing paranoia of what he thought might be happening.

There was shouting and chanting and pushing and a cacophony of loud voices as a thousand black men crowded together. No black marcher had attacked him. No one had threatened this cop's life, and he had reacted as Wyeth and others had feared might happen. He panicked and killed an innocent man.

When the news of the shooting finally reached Wyeth, he had called an emergency meeting of city officials, but first he had wanted to confer with his staff, and wanted Holston to appear and answer questions on the incident.

As the commissioner left the elevator on the executive floor, there was a staffer waiting to direct Holston to the conference room where the mayor and others were waiting for him.

No sooner had he been seated when Wyeth began his rapid fire questions for Holston: "How in the hell did this happen? Tell me, commissioner, why would one of your officers kill an unarmed black teenager?"

The commissioner's face was taut, and he prepared to speak, but Wyeth continued in his tirade, and gave him no chance.

"I'll tell you exactly what happened. These men are permitted to shoot anyone on the street that they want, including any black, like goddamn cowboys."

The commissioner held up his hand, and he said calmly, "Wyeth, are you going to permit me to speak, and answer the questions you asked, or do you just plan to continue this tantrum?"

"Damn, damn," shouted the mayor as he pounded his open right palm on the conference table, which sounded like a shot itself, and everyone tensed in the room.

"Please enlighten me then, commissioner. Tell me all about the shotgun blast at the march."

Holston had interlocked his fingers and put his hands in front of him on the conference table before speaking: "The incident is under internal police department investigation. This is the procedure for all shootings where a policeman is involved and we don't know all the facts just yet."

"Oh, your officer didn't shoot an unarmed sixteen-year-old black kid giving him some lip? That didn't happen, did it?" Wyeth threw out still consumed with anger at the horrible event.

"Wyeth, be reasonable. I wasn't there. I didn't see the shooting. I can only trust my people to determine the facts. That officer has been suspended until we know what happened. That's the procedure."

"Alright, let's get on to the next subject," Wyeth continued. "What will you do to see this doesn't happen again because there will be more blacks in the street tomorrow, or the next day? I'd like to know that."

The commissioner cleared his throat, and coughed before answering the mayor's question. "We have set up stricter crowd control procedures, and the unit commanders have repeatedly cautioned their subordinate officers against the use of excessive force. We want this to be the single, unfortunate casualty as the result of these marches, either the protestors, or the officers themselves."

"A thoughtful little speech, commissioner," Wyeth added with unmistakable sarcasm in his voice. "So you'll put a leash on your men from now on until this mess ends, right?"

The commissioner stared at Wyeth, his eyes hardened. "I have the utmost confidence in the officers under me if that's the answer you're expecting. But I do caution you, this is not over yet."

Since the strike had started a few days before and the daily marches of black workers varied in size, generally getting larger each time, the garbage began to pile up on the city streets. After a week, more than 15,000 tons of fetid black plastic bags overflowed onto the city streets, creating an odorous nuisance and health hazard.

People in the white residential areas were predictably irritated with the towering refuse piles in front of their homes, though most didn't recognize this strike as a precursor to death. It was simply a thorny negotiation with rowdy black city workers, and would eventually be settled by the mayor's office.

The local AFSCME stopped all communications with the mayor's office. Wyeth had authorized the hiring of non-union sanitation workers who were strikebreakers and often battled on the streets with the club-carrying union men. This behavior eventually spread into the quieter city neighborhoods.

At one point in the middle of the second week of February, Reverend King came and spoke at Clayborn Temple. He urged the striking workers assembled, which perhaps numbered five or maybe six hundred blacks, to continue their resistance. That was the first King visit during the strike, and he would return once before the month ended after speaking at several black Memphis churches, and then several times again in March.

King's pulpit rhetoric to the anxious crowd had been powerful, though he had discouraged any form of violence from striking blacks, and spoke of this philosophy of nonviolent protest several times in the address.

"Do not seek to harm your fellow man, black or white, for any reason, it is wrong," he had pleaded from the pulpit. He lived his principles.

* * * * * * *

Howard Burnett, a polo player and lawyer friend of Martha whom I had met, had invited me to hunt for birds with him and a group of his friends. We visited his grandfather's large sporting goods emporium and found a shotgun for me to lease. Howard brought along the store manager whom he had known all his life, and he more or less directed the hunt by finding the fields and supplying the hounds.

We drove out to a farm on the other side of Ames Plantation, a landmark where the National Dog Field Trials were held each year, and hunted for three or four early morning hours. We did pretty well and filled quite a few bags.

It was considered off-season hunting though we had a special permit just for the historic plot. And I felt rather good about being able to join the local Memphis men on the hunt. It was great fun to be out in the open fields, and shoot the game birds with the few dogs. The Memphis sporting goods store manager that came with us even told us of a curious story that happened several days before.

It seems that the day before I went to York Arms to lease the shotgun, there was a man shopping there who told the store manager he was a hunter. He wasn't looking for high-powered rifles because he already had one. Instead he was in the market for the best of their binoculars. He spoke glowingly of the optics that the Germans had perfected, however the Zeiss price tag was far too high for him, and he had hesitated. There was a tall, gaunt-looking man with him who then pulled him to the side. They walked across the showroom floor to the gun racks while having a spirited conversation. In a moment at the large front window it appeared that the man had handed this customer a pile of folded bills and motioned him back to the counter while he stayed and examined the rifles displayed in a glass case.

This second man then returned to the counter as the customer handed the clerk the bills to pay for the expensive set of binoculars. The other man picked them up and examined them by focusing outside the storefront windows on the Winn Dixie grocery supermarket across the street.

He had made comments to the first man that were almost inaudible to the store manager, but had heard something said about 'how tight the site line was,' and some sort of humorous remark that drew chortles from both.

The customer said he wanted to see some handguns. He was shown a military service Colt and a Smith and Wesson 38 caliber revolver. He took his time examining the weapons, and held them in a firing position aiming at the rear of the store. He told the manager he liked the Colt best, but might buy it on another day when they were less pressed for time.

He also looked at the boxes of ammunition in the cases, and asked the manager what he recommended for deer rifles. He wanted bullets with the most effective stopping power because he sometimes went out West and hunted Elk.

They were darn tough to bring down as they were big and muscular. You needed a bullet that would drop them to their knees with a single shot because you would be hard-pressed to find another in that mountainous country. This man sounded country and maybe even a little foolish.

He also talked about hunting white tail deer in the Mississippi Delta, and how you just waited in those freezing swamps for them to show up to feed, and then, Bang! You couldn't miss with them. The other man with the binoculars didn't say much as he stood behind the first man at the counter, though he finally touched his arm and with a head jerk motioned toward the store front door.

One of the two men was clearly in charge, the man with the binoculars. And though he didn't say much, this second man's odd accent confused the store manager. It didn't seem to be from anywhere really. It wasn't Southern or from a place like the Midwest or maybe Boston. The York Arms manager couldn't tell you what it sounded like, and that was unnerving since he been asked that same question later. In general, the men wouldn't have made an impression on this manager, but he couldn't stop thinking about that strange accent.

* * * * * * *

Inquiries about the garbage strike shooting of the black sixteen-year-old and the officer involved had found its way to the Attorney General's office. What would normally languish as an internal affairs investigation plodded its way toward some resolution of justifiable homicide and the controversy had been discussed with the prosecutors. At least Martha and the other lawyers had been alerted of the killing and the circumstances surrounding it.

There were hurried staff conversations about exactly what steps might be taken, and informal talks opened by Jim Latham's suggestion. Latham knew this had already become a political football with Wyeth and the feds, anxious to be kicked through the uprights by either side. He had wanted to prepare for a possible bill of indictment, just in case.

Two more days of strike marches downtown produced no new killings. The worst that had occurred were perhaps a dozen disorderly conduct arrests of rowdy blacks and two incidents of assaulting a police officer which was impressive from a crowd of many thousands of shouting strikers.

Holston had, in the mildest of terms, passed the word down the chain of command not to engage in excessive force if it might be avoided in managing the demonstration. Though at all costs, the public safety must be ensured.

He had never used the words, peaceful protest, because he believed that they had been created through unwanted agitation, and influenced by outside malcontents. To him, Martin Luther King was the worst kind of pariah and his malicious motivations were hidden behind his thoughtful pastoral manner.

It was a mixed message to the Memphis uniformed officers, but what might be expected from a police commissioner that feared a widespread conspiracy of radical and armed blacks threatening his entire country.

Holston told Wyeth point blank he suspected that before this was finished, there would be some officer brought down by sniper fire. He had prepared himself for the worst, making certain that his tactical team had secured all the high ground along the usual march route. That was the least he could accomplish. The shot could come from anywhere, and he cautioned an already weary mayor who was now smoking two packs of cigarettes a day non-stop.

Wyeth had called Wolfson at AFSCME national headquarters several times and Wolfson explained that his hands were tied as he was powerless to intervene. He candidly agreed that this had become far more than a labor grievance. It was now about blacks, and what their place in this city had been, and what changes they wanted. Wyeth understood that much.

At dinner that evening, Martha wouldn't talk about anything but the strike shooting, and she all but convicted the cop for murder.

She said: "I'll bet this kid just called him a, 'Motherfucker,' or something. That's all it was. Showed him a fist. Street shit."

"Maybe, I don't know the circumstances," I said, figuring I'd lose the argument with her anyway and tried to avoid that unpleasant journey.

"The cops panicked, got trigger happy," she went on.

I explained that from all the many meetings I had with the mayor, he believed that anytime you had thousands of angry blacks and edgy white cops in the street, things might get nasty. He had done everything he possibly could to prevent this.

"Oh stop defending Wyeth," Martha said.

I stood up from the table and walked to the sink to empty my watery drink, and thought about getting another.

"What happened could have happened anywhere," I insisted as I got the ice tray out of the freezer and found a few cubes.

"Maybe he could've been wiser, and figured that it would be better to give in early on, and not try to play the tough guy."

She grunted her disapproval, and gave the slightest laugh. Martha didn't really care for Wyeth, and it was perhaps something from the past, some slight I wasn't aware of. Maybe his larger law firm had turned her down for an associate position, telling her to her face, "We don't hire women," or something else equally insulting.

"Has Wyeth done something to you?" I asked her, curious.

"Not really, aside from saying stupid things at parties when he's had too much to drink."

I pressed her, "So there's no one thing he's done that makes you hate him?"

"Look, I don't hate Wyeth," she explained. "He's just typical of the men who run things here, and his arrogance pisses me off."

Martha loved the traditional southern show of gentility, though on the other hand, she wanted some other interpretation of how things were done here and couldn't resolve the two things in her mind. Her own sister had broken the rigid mold that had encased Martha. She had behaved in the most outrageous and self-absorbed manner while leaving bodies strewn everywhere.

Wyeth, as so many men before him, would either be made by those responsibilities they had sought or destroyed by them. He would most likely leave office with some unpopularity in his wake. It probably would end his political ambitions for governor, and even for a local congressional seat, though I can't imagine why he'd bother with that at all as it would be a step down at his age.

He would weather this storm, and settle with the union after weeks of these shows of black solidarity, and the city would continue as it had been. In fact, he had told me that he felt the local AFSCME people, particularly its president Jones, had already received their moments of glory and it was time for everyone to settle down to business with a favorable contract. Wyeth had no intention of seeking vengeance for those months of widespread anger and fear. It served everyone's interest to move forward with these changes.

Maybe Wyeth and Martha had some kind of intimacy in the distant past, a moment of passion between a teenage girl and a forty-five-year-old man. It seemed there was something certainly personal that she wouldn't share with me, and I wanted to know what had happened.

Over the course of days and weeks, I would introduce Wyeth into conversation, and watch her flare up. After multiple outbursts, I finally resolved to ask her about it. "Enough, I want to know the truth about you and Wyeth. Why this hatred, and what is it about? I have a right to know."

She didn't answer me, and just stared into space. She looked out the window and folded her arms defensively.

I finally spoke with some anger: "Martha, tell me what this goddamn thing is with Wyeth. Well? Were the two of you..."

She sang out, "No, no, that's not it. It was my mother."

"Carolyn?" I said, confused.

"Are you dense, or what?" she added quickly followed by some false laugh. "Wyeth had an affair with my mother."

Then she yelled out at the top of her lungs: "They slept together for Christ's sake. And under Alfred's roof, in his fucking bed."

At last she sat on the sofa and told me the story. They all had been close friends in the same Cotton Carnival secret society once and one year Wyeth's wife was the society duchess, then the next year Carolyn was chosen.

"It was incestuous, wasn't it?" she'd said unconvincingly, and filled in those sordid details that she had known. It might have lasted for as much as a whole year, but she wasn't certain. Though she had seen Wyeth coming out of her parent's home late one evening when Alfred was in Charlotte on business. It was a chancy encounter for Carolyn. They had taken a big risk, and that's when she had known for certain.

Martha had gotten a ride from her law school in Nashville, and didn't have the time to call as she was dropped off on the street. It was eleven at night and Wyeth was backing his car out of their driveway when she saw the light in her parent's bedroom go out with Carolyn standing at the window. Martha had gone into the house screaming and had confronted her mother with what

226

she had seen. Carolyn calmly told her the truth, made herself a scotch, then sat in the living room and confessed the infidelity.

Carolyn said they were finished and that this was the last time. Wyeth had been bold enough to come to the house, which he would've never done before, only to hold her in his arms one last time and they had made love.

"Now you know how I feel about Wyeth. That man makes my skin crawl and he's a monster," she uttered not so much in anger as disgust.

There was little more to say to her, and I felt no real need to know if Alfred ever knew about it, or if it had pushed Carolyn deeper into alcoholism. As long as I worked with or even knew Wyeth, I had never brought the conversation up about his involvement with Carolyn, nor did he, even as we sat next to one another on long plane flights. Why would he? I didn't talk about Amanda.

The internal affairs investigation took less than a week, and the police board exonerated the officer of any charge of manslaughter, or culpable negligence in pursuit of police duties. He was given a two week leave of absence to collect himself after the ordeal, and visited an uncle in Arkansas.

Martha said that Jim Latham was furious with the decision, and had taken great pains to have Holston review the findings, and order a second investigation based on the facts interpreted by the District Attorney. But it was a soft request, meaning that Latham wouldn't, or couldn't, legally pressure Holston to look for an excessive force charge. It would be buried in the department files.

"A goddamn shotgun," Latham had complained to Martha when he'd heard the police board findings. "Blasted this unarmed black kid point blank with a fucking shotgun. And that ain't excessive force?"

When Latham made that remark to Martha, the fourth garbage workers' march had started at the door of the Clayborn Temple, and eleven hundred blacks were making their way eight abreast down Union Avenue toward city hall.

The day before there had been a brief clash between police and marchers when a police cruiser had been kicked by a handful of passersby on the route. Twenty cops had roughed up blacks who ended with some injuries.

After that first shooting incident, Memphis appeared over the worst of the violence. It was an eerie time.

Increasingly, a hungry national news circus had found its way to Memphis. The streets along the route had reporters and cameramen from LA, New York, Chicago, and even as far as London. The men and a few women would weave in and out of the crowd for quick interviews during the marches.

They were not quite out of the woods, but Wyeth reasoned that the strikers couldn't continue this for much longer. The popular black worker interest for a much longer standoff had already diminished. How many times could these people march to city hall, demand an impromptu meeting with city officials, and then hurl insults?

It couldn't continue, though somehow it did. The black ministers fired them up in the pulpit and sent them shouting into the street for some elusive freedom, that delved deeper than the original dollar and fifty cents an hour raise. The whole exhibition in the streets became a cause celebre. It inflamed the civil rights conscience of more and more sympathetic whites.

Soon there were Quakers, Seventh Day Adventists, and a coalition of Episcopal clergymen. When the anti-war protesters who had been consumed with Johnson and Vietnam joined, the entire atmosphere changed almost overnight into something so much larger than a garbage strike.

Each day was as fraught with chaos as the next, though Wyeth kept his focus, usually with five hours of sleep at night if he were lucky.

One chilly morning, he slid into the leather seat of his Buick Electra, a new car he had treated himself to, and put the key into the ignition. The powerful engine immediately started. Wyeth pulled out the car ashtray and was about to reach over on the passenger seat to take a cigarette out of the open Marlboro pack, when something happened, or rather, nothing did.

His instinct was to reach over with his right hand, the one closest to the open pack, and then take out a cigarette. That's what he wanted to do, but something was wrong. He couldn't move his right arm across the seat from his lap. It wouldn't move, nothing on his body would.

He thought to himself, because he could still think, 'how was that possible? What's happening to me? Why can't I just reach over and take the cigarette out of the pack? That's crazy. Am I in some sort of hallucination state from the drinks from last night? Was I drunk last night, and didn't realize it? No, I just had two drinks, and I always have two bourbons.'

He squinted his blurry eyes, and he could see his red brick house in the early morning light. He also saw the front of the driveway and the green boxwoods on either side that had grown waist high this past summer.

"What's wrong with me? " he muttered to himself, but Wyeth didn't hear those simple few words aloud as his mouth didn't seem to work.

'I spoke the words, I know that, I formed them clearly in my mind and then I tried to say them and nothing came out. Why can't I speak? Am I having a fainting spell? Maybe my high blood pressure has soared through the roof with the constant strike chaos. Is it making me groggy?'

He tried to move his right leg and his foot which had been resting on the accelerator. Wyeth struggled, or thought he had struggled, to remove it from the gas pedal though nothing occurred. His right foot sat exactly where it had been.

'This is crazy,' he thought, 'My mind works, but it can't direct my legs to move,' and he tried to move his left leg and it seemed to move perhaps an inch. He began to lift his left hand, and he was able to move it a few inches above his leg and it dropped to his lap.

'Something has happened to my body and I don't know what it is,' he thought, and a panic had started to overcome him.

'It's a heart attack, that's what's happening. My heart is trembling and ready to burst like a dam. I can feel it beating fast inside my chest for all its worth, and the blood isn't going through my veins. There's some obstruction, and my brain is being starved, and I've got to get help, or I'll die in this front seat.'

When he managed to tone down his excruciating fear of death, he started to count backwards from one hundred, and this act calmed him enough to think more rationally.

He would open the Buick car door and try to make it to the house to wake up his wife who had gone back to bed, and she would call for an ambulance. That would save his life, get him into an emergency room, and open the clogged heart valve. Otherwise, his brain would suffocate, and that was slowly happening to him.

Wyeth raised the left hand to the door handle but his fingers couldn't grip it and they sat on the metal handle flaccid, and useless. He concentrated on bending them around the handle but his hand wouldn't obey his brain, the connection had somehow been broken. Would he just die in the Electra this morning?

The mayor began to think of the life that had passed, and the memories from over the years. They all sped rapidly through his consciousness like motion picture frames, hundreds or thousands of them speeding through his vision, and then they would stop. He saw himself driving to Mary Baldwin from law school to see his young bride, and eight years later they had a beautiful blond daughter. He saw the moment when he buried his irascible Judge father, recognizing that they'd never been close, or even liked each other.

He'd had a successful career, great friends, a few loves, and for the most part, this life had been kind to him, more so than other men, and he'd felt thankful as he looked back through the years.

What would he do differently if he never left the car seat this morning? If he could turn back the clock. How would he change his life, would want he want to change? 'No, I regret so little. Almost nothing.' he thought. 'I've lived fully and well, and I've been a good and decent man, well, mostly. That nagging human imperfection.'

Wyeth saw the morning light become brighter, and figured that he spent hours in the car, when in truth, he had only been there no longer than ten minutes.

'Should I pray?' he wondered, and quickly closed his eyes silently praying to a God he doubted existed, though he obeyed in most things.

"I'm a Christian, I am" he said silently, hoping to believe those same words.

Trying desperately again to encircle his fingers around the door handle, he now had two fingers that were partially closed around it, and he thought he could press his body weight on that arm and force the door open.

In an instant, he moved with all the strength he could find in his shocked body and his buttocks rose from the seat. The door flew open with the pressure of his torso, and Wyeth fell out onto the concrete driveway.

A neighbor leaving for work a couple doors down had seen Wyeth lying on the driveway motionless from his car window and slammed on his brakes and rushed to the mayor's aid.

In another fifteen minutes, an ambulance had appeared in the driveway as the mayor's wife stood speechless in her cloth coat and bedroom slippers, and climbed into the back of the ambulance and rode with him to Methodist Hospital.

The first tests the emergency room doctors conducted indicated that Wyeth has suffered a brain aneurysm that had become a full-fledged stroke. He had temporarily lost his ability to speak coherently. He could make certain word-like sounds, but the left side of his body had been paralyzed and there was only partial movement in his left leg.

The doctors had learned all this and more before the end of the mayor's first day in the hospital. They had done x-rays of his brain and located the blood clot which had caused the stroke. But the only possibility they saw to prevent complete paralysis and loss of most brain functions, was to remove the clot and open the normal blood flow to the brain.

They could accomplish this by sending a tube up through a vein in his groin, although this was a relatively new procedure. It had worked in numerous cases, though it was risky and sometimes a patient died on the operating table.

A decision was made to do the procedure and they did it that night. Two surgeons performed the surgery and it was a success. The pressure on the brain had been relieved. Wyeth would retain many functions, but which ones remained to be seen with the passage of time since this was inexact science.

In the interim, the deputy mayor took command of the city. This mild mannered accountant had been a city councilman first before being selected by Wyeth to join his second administration. He was terrified.

Jacob was mostly timid as well as a sometimes stutterer and he probably was the worst choice to lead this city under attack. Yet, fate had chosen him and the rotund, black-haired man sat in the mayor's leather chair, meeting with myself and the other staffers, readying himself for his first press conference and his own bloodbath.

The conference could've been worse. The interim mayor stammered his way through a barrage of questions and he seemed clearly ill fitted to save this beleaguered Southern city. But those who watched it all, including myself, had hoped that God protects fools and small children because this man was the former.

Holston would eat this man alive, and he would continue to do whatever he wanted, which seemed his modus anyway, but now probably more than ever.

In the conference, local reporters asked the predictable questions about the nature of the strike settlement but the out of town press aggressively attacked the interim mayor on the city's history of civil rights violations because they had done their homework. These questions were painfully specific, and the result even before the man had attempted to find an answer, was damning. They wanted to portray Memphis as a corrupt and racist town which repeatedly violated human rights for fifty years or more with no change on the horizon.

The garbage strike instead of being a strictly local problem had become an international human rights crisis that probably required federal government intervention. One journalist had spoken about the imposition of martial law to save the city from further deaths on its streets.

There was no way that the city could walk away from this press conference with any confidence that the attacks against this administration would diminish. The present Memphis city government would become a pariah in the eyes of the entire world as racist and brutal as the South Africans.

I could see this interim mayor's hand shake as he reached for a glass of water in the pressroom. He had this terrified look on his face that I'd never seen before. It lasted twenty-one minutes, and he had survived the first onslaught, though barely.

When I visited the hospital to learn more about Wyeth's condition, I met his wife in the hallway outside his room and she was filled with optimism. He had regained his ability to speak almost overnight, but he spoke with some slowness in his sentences even though it was obvious to her and his doctors that no permanent cognitive damage had occurred.

It was indeed Wyeth in the hospital bed. He had made conversation not terribly different than usual, nothing short of a miracle, actually. He had, however, not recovered the use of his legs, and his physicians pondered the question of whether he would walk again, either assisted by a cane or perhaps confined to wheelchair living.

Inside his hospital room for five minutes, I was amazed at how Wyeth had bounced back. He laughed with me over one or two ridiculous things I'd brought up, and vowed that he'd be back shortly even if it meant being wheelchair bound.

"I have every intention of coming back," Wyeth said in his weakened voice, "and some things will have to change." Seeing what I recognized as exhaustion on his face, I cut the visit short, pleading piles of work at city hall.

"Try to help him as much as you can," Wyeth said in parting. "He's so goddamn pathetic." He let out a gentle laugh that sounded so much like the sense of humor that was part of the mayor.

"Jesus, you're so right," I had said to him, and was laughing too as I found myself walking down the hospital corridor.

I guess it was nothing short of a miracle what those doctors had done. I always reasoned that if you had a stroke, you were finished and on the way out.

The strike continued through March and by the fifteenth of the month, Wyeth miraculously made his way back to city hall. By this time, he was confined in a wheelchair, though with sound mind, and no noticeable change in his speech.

He would sit in his office with the wheelchair flush against his desk and conduct city business. If he had to use the bathroom attached to his office, he had two canes that he would use to hobble into the bathroom. Wyeth had enough strength in his arms to pull himself up from a sitting position to stand, then slowly walk with the canes to the toilet. He knew what he had to do to walk again, and was determined to do so.

His long dead mother had spent her last years in a nursing home with a broken hip from a nasty fall at home. Wyeth had watched her get enough strength through sheer resolve and the assistance of a physical therapist to spend her last years walking to the facility dining room by herself for meals, sitting content on the sofa in the common living room, and he had decided to follow her example of courage.

The mayor used metal canes that people with cerebral palsy often employed with safety handles and wrist guards that made them easier to maneuver. He started to walk around his city hall office with the use of the two canes by the second week, and had a bicycle device under his desk that he would pedal throughout the day as he worked. It strengthened his stroke-weakened legs, and his steady recovery was visible to all.

By the middle of March, the strike had lasted well over a month and there had been nearly a dozen marches of black garbage workers downtown, though thankfully, mostly without the violence of those early gatherings. It had gained national attention, and civil rights groups arrived daily in Memphis to join the strikers trailed by a crowd of reporters and the national television coverage continued.

The interim mayor had no thoughts of continuing as city chief executive after his short, but brutal, introduction, He gladly turned over the reins to Wyeth. The man disappeared into the woodwork with his numerous small projects as quickly as he had emerged. Jacob would appear now in his too-tight sport coat at staff meetings with his porcine smile, and only occasionally might Wyeth deign to defer to his opinion on any topic.

The first city council meeting the mayor called after his return to city hall had developed into a shouting match between white city councilmen and the few black members about the garbage strike. Wyeth finally had to yell to invoke any order in the proceedings. It was a useless forum for the city under siege and threatened with the outbreak of violence at any time.

This awful burden was Wyeth's to shoulder. Its solution could only come from him and the forces opposing him which had been steadily gaining strength.

I had asked Wyeth when we were alone once if he was in pain. He told me that sometimes it was almost too much, and pointed to two white bottles of pills that sat on his mahogany desk.

"Good Christ, I wouldn't know what to do without those," he said, motioning in their direction with his hand.

After news of the stroke had reached Jones and his strike organizers, they wrongly suspected that it would lessen the mayor's courage to continue to face them. That in fact emboldened them to become more outrageous in the demands that they had enlisted the press to proclaim publicly.

Jones had chosen the court of public opinion to make his case. It was now about black empowerment in the United States taken through the prism of what was happening in the Memphis streets. So instead of the marches leading to settlement talks with the city, they increased on the streets unabated.

His was a familiar face on the Clayborn Temple steps next to its fiery minister passing out box lunches before the marchers commenced. Jones often spoke through a megaphone to the burgeoning crowd of garbage workers that had evolved into interested blacks from across the city and fifty or sixty white civil rights sympathizers.

There was a sea of printed signs and banners passed out to the waiting crowd. It began with a loud chant as a dark-faced leviathan of protest began snaking its way through the downtown streets.

One of his favorite subjects wasn't the poor wages, rather the accidental deaths of two black workers who had been crushed on separate occasions in one of the large trash compactors which was a macabre tale almost inexplicable in its horror.

Had they been drunk, or was it simply negligent? Such a thing might occur once, but to be repeated twice was unthinkable, though it had. Two men had been mutilated in the city garbage compacting equipment, and both had been officially termed as accidents after a safety investigation. The incidents were uncanny.

This utter disregard of blacks by the city and the larger white society that it represented became a rallying point for Jones. His rhetoric burned the white establishment's disregard for black lives, their safety, and their very existence.

"To them, we're the garbage on the streets not those stinking bags," Jones shouted out at the milling protestors on the church steps. "We're less than people, and we're tired of that disregard they carry for us, the black man."

Angry vows came from the swelling crowd, and expletives were shouted from hundreds of blacks. They began their loud chanting of defiance toward the so-called masters who smashed them underfoot.

Jones knew exactly when to stop, and he urged the marchers to non-violence, and told them in both Reverend King's and Christ's words, "Turn the other cheek. Let them drown in their own hatred." He had become a disciple of the Atlanta minister.

Slowly a long black line turned the narrow corner and spread across Union Avenue and within ten minutes, stretched back for a half mile as it trod toward the bastion of city government.

Even with the constant pain, Wyeth maintained his position to not capitulate to the marchers who weren't interested in the fine print of the sanitation contract, but to the spectacle of what they joined, and he dug in his heels.

He would wait out Jones and his recalcitrant union people. Wyeth also believed that this earlier fear of radicals and revolution, and its attendant chaos was false.

The unfortunate police shooting at the beginning of the sanitation marches had been the result of overreaction by a poorly trained police officer. Though he probably should be prosecuted, Holston let him go. There would be no bill of indictment passed on to a grand jury. It had already ended with the internal affairs decision.

Wyeth's labor negotiators proved useless, and even with the sweetened offer to the sanitation management which met almost all of their demands, they would have their black march. The mayor was destined to watch. Three of his calls to Jones to resume these talks had been ignored, and the union president didn't bother to return a single call of simple acknowledgement.

It became a waiting game for city hall. The police department continued its high alert on the streets as march after march passed under their noses with few confrontations. Oh, there were some arrests, that's true, but they were for misdemeanors and the blacks that were taken to the police precincts numbered around a dozen out of the thousands who demonstrated.

In fact, there were others involved too. The police ended up arresting two white Quaker students from Philadelphia who refused to move from a roped-off area near city hall so they were arrested for trespassing.

Also, there was a photographer from Reuters who claimed one of the cops had grabbed his camera and had broken it as he was taking shots of the crowd. That charge went unsubstantiated though it had gotten out of hand as the photographer supposedly pushed the officer away from his equipment, and a confrontation had resulted. He was restrained by two nearby officers, and handcuffed. These types of incidents became commonplace on the streets as the strike entered its sixth week with still no resolution on the new sanitation contract.

Wyeth had tried enlisting the help of the two blacks on the city council to possibly intervene in the settlement, and become part of the negotiations. They had wisely backed off, refusing to be seen as the mayor's dark-skinned pawns.

Alas, the mayor was sadly on his own, and it was a lonely and friendless place to be. He couldn't turn to his police commissioner for succor whose philosophy of confrontation was to shoot the strikers in the street.

During all of this craziness, only once did Wyeth ever talk to me about his stroke and that was maybe a day or two after he returned to the office in a wheelchair. We were the last ones there around seven o'clock, which was late for me, and I stuck my head in his office to say goodnight.

He had motioned me to sit down, and we talked about many things for perhaps fifteen minutes when he finally broached the subject of his stroke.

"You know, I thought I was dead when they first put me in the emergency room." he said slowly. "And I was dead, really."

A sad smile came to his face, and he took a deep breath, and slowly continued what he'd told no one else.

He explained, "That ER nurse tried to get my pulse on my left wrist and then my right one, and in desperation touched my jugular with her long fingers. And in a panic, she pressed a blue button and the heart team came running to shock me back to life."

"You didn't have a pulse?" I asked him skeptically.

"No," Wyeth said shaking his head. "You understand, my heart had stopped and I was already dead, for, I don't know, maybe four minutes."

My eyes followed his face as it turned to look out the window at dusk.

"And when I was dead I was surrounded by all these people I knew: my grandparents, my cousin killed in Korea, and all the people I knew as a small child. They were standing in a circle around the hospital bed."

He laughed, and continued: "And I asked this man next to me if this was heaven, and he said, yes, it was, and that I could enter if I liked, and only needed to go right through those double doors, and I'd be inside. Forevermore, I imagine."

"Wyeth," I said, interrupting him.

"No, let me finish," he said, holding up this hand.

"I told the man I wasn't ready to go to heaven, and he said, 'Are you sure?' and I told him yes I was, and he said 'Alright.'"

He put his hands together and intertwined his fingers almost as if he were praying, and added, "At that same moment, I opened my eyes and I saw this man in white with two metal shockers ready to restart my heart, and I came back to consciousness."

Wyeth asked the man in the white hospital uniform if he'd been dead, and the man answered, "It took me three times to bring you back."

Each march brought with it the real probability of dead bodies in the street though that hadn't occurred, lately, but it wasn't a bloodless strike.

After the first damning accusations against Wyeth appeared in the newspapers, the press had waited for a bit. During the month that followed, it had seen the absence of violence from the black protests, and ended up praising the restraint of city police, and of the mayor for remaining firm.

His report card from the local media became considerably better than what was written and said about him in New York, Chicago and Washington, where he had become another caricatured figure of the segregated South.

This simple fact that Wyeth had suffered a serious stroke, and against all the odds, had quickly rebounded from almost certain paralysis coming back in a wheelchair to direct the city had earned him widespread respect. There was little doubt as to his courage under fire and against great pain.

When Wyeth and I finally talked at length, he had expressed surprise that Holston had demanded the restraint we saw on the Memphis streets from his officers. I had to admit that it shocked me too. It was almost as if Holston had found his enemy elsewhere. Maybe he found them in some communist cells organizing a mass bombing of the city water system, or planning to blow up the police barracks.

Truthfully, Holston had focused on King and his minister lieutenants and had the support to do so from the FBI's highest levels. Holston had talked several times on the telephone to Hoover himself about what they both perceived as this King threat, not only with this prolonged garbage strike but nationally too. This man was a menace to the United States.

The tactical units and the infiltrated officers Holston directed saw little organized resistance outside of the few national civil rights coalitions that found their way to the city and had attempted to recruit locals but unsuccessfully. There was no evidence of arms or explosives finding their way into black hands beyond the normal illegal gun trafficking. You would see those cheap handguns and a few shotguns make appearances in the usual criminal hands. That's all.

King made his repeat visits to Memphis with his national media entourage during the month long sanitation strike. After that it became apparent to both Holston and Hoover this dangerous black minister was the one they had to stop.

His sole existence was to undermine the present order across a wide swath of this country. King was determined to enlist

240

tens of millions of disgruntled blacks in the South to turn that peaceful region toward an eventual race war and into a nightmare of killing.

Hoover found a sympathetic ear for his theories with Holston who had profound respect for the agency director and his methods. Holston himself was the beneficiary of the reams of incriminating evidence the FBI collected on Martin Luther King Jr. There had been photographs of women leaving King's motel rooms in the cities that he visited and most or all of them were black, but one of them was so light-skinned she might have been white, and that thought alone had disgusted Holston.

As the fallout from the standoff between the sanitation strikers and the crippled mayor persisted, it had taken its toll on me. I had ended up trailing Holston and his officers, trying to anticipate some egregious move that they planned, then warn city hall. There was none.

At home, the constant stress from the war torn mayor's office had taken its toll on Martha and me. We became distant, and the angry undercurrent made me say sharp things to her usual sarcasm. I regretted what the marriage had become, and with that emptiness I turned more toward Amanda.

For about five months we hardly saw one another, except perhaps for some accidental passing at the university club, but never together as couples, and never alone. Amanda was at arm's length, never near.

In the void I experienced with Martha, I began to rethink what I wanted for the rest of my own life. The constant routine of Martha's obsessive control, and the mendacity of her well-defined world. That burden was followed with the inhuman and ponderous moral responsibility of the law on her slender shoulders that simply became too much.

So I decided I would try to escape somehow with Amanda. Maybe it would be for the moment, or even forever. I couldn't decide which, but escape I would.

We had lunch downtown at my invitation and she looked like a dark-haired wisp in powder blue as she ran into the restaurant fifteen minutes late, breathless.

"I had to get the new yard man situated. He's trimming all those overgrown bushes and planting new monkey grass so the place won't look like a truck stop anymore," she told me, running her hands through her thick hair.

"How are things with you?" she asked, "Frankly, I was surprised to hear from you. I thought you were finished with me, or something like that."

"Amanda," I told her, "look, I don't know what to do with you, that's all."

"Oh, now you're doing something with me," she continued. "Well, that comes as news to me. Not one damn phone call in how long?"

"You could call, you know," I responded.

She didn't answer right away and reached across her empty plate to take a long drink from the ice tea glass the waiter had put on the table.

"It wouldn't matter if I loved you, or not, would it?" she said with a serious face.

Letting out a long sigh I reached across for her hand but she moved it away as soon as she felt my touch.

"I'm angry at you," she whispered, though there wasn't venom in her soft voice, "but now maybe we can cross that next bridge, huh?"

I confessed that she'd become so important to me that I couldn't let go of her, and I wanted the two of us to walk away from the life we lived here.

"Jesus, stop being melodramatic," Amanda scolded. "If you got divorced tomorrow, I'd do the same. Then we'd move down the damn street to another house, and who cares, honestly?"

It was a matter of innate courage of conviction and emotion, and I readily admitted to her that I needed her strength to take those next steps.

"Alright, we'll start by seeing more of each other, and I'll arrange that. You push Wyeth around in his wheelchair and get the garbage picked up."

I asked, "Are you sure this is what you want?"

Amanda gave me this wide grin, "With a life as boring as this doctor's wife one, I'd probably hang myself in two years, for God's sake. No, it needs to be us, period."

She leaned in closer, and whispered, "And fuck them."

We ordered from the familiar waiter I knew and afterward we talked about many things, though none of which had to do with what was going on several blocks away as a thousand chanting blacks made another journey down Union Avenue demanding some unheard of freedom.

Toward the end of the lunch Amanda did ask me about the marches, and how long did I think they would continue?

"Why don't you just give them the two dollars an hour, and get it over with?"

I explained that it had gone beyond the wage settlement stage, and it had taken on a political life of its own with the blacks on center stage marching across television screens.

Yesterday a five-man crew from NBC had come to interview Jones for its national news broadcast with a panoply of titanium lights and television cameras in the local sanitation union offices resembling the Today Show. There had been no call from anyone to Wyeth to explain the city's position in this garbage strike, and over the past few weeks both Jones and the already well-known Reverend King had become television darlings.

With the interview of Jones completed, this NBC crew had gradually followed him downtown as he led the swarming crowd of blacks toward city hall once again.

In the later television broadcast, Jones had taken on a theatrical persona of a modern day black Moses. His words were replete with familiar Bible quotes that inspired viewers with impassioned pleas for social justice. At one point, Jones had stared directly into the camera and then looked up into the heavens for guidance and uttered, "I'm a humble, uneducated black man, brought here by Providence," with an almost mystical ring to it.

Not surprisingly, this was the perfect moment for that rich rhetoric both Jones, and certainly King had mastered. Those few television clips of King speaking to the assembled sanitation workers at Tom Lee Park and in front of Clayborn Temple were magical. King's sonorous language went to the heart of the matter. He spoke not only to all the disenfranchised blacks listening, but to everyone everywhere in need or suffering. The rather simple lessons for a more inclusive humanity that he articulated were profound.

Of course, Jones saw all of this. He was a poor substitute for the monumental intellect and the vision of Doctor King, and he willingly stepped aside because it was time.

Now King assumed center stage in Memphis as the apostle Paul did on that dusty Roman road to Damascus. King's message appealed to all the downtrodden and misused black men and women in America. He prayed for a deeper understanding in the painful shadow of this difficult history of enslavement they both shared. In two speeches, he had occupied the higher moral ground.

Amanda and I began to close our circle of involvement. I think I finally had admitted to myself that Martha and I were doomed as a couple. We were a mismatched pair from the very beginning.

Slowly I began to search for the exit to our short and unhappy marriage and focus on the woman that I'd chosen in her place who had been brought to me through the most bizarre of circumstances. We had an unspoken passion born of some lunacy from the night of the wedding rehearsal dinner. If I had really searched for any higher ground, it had eluded me and instead I followed some derangement born from an inexplicable night shared with a woman who embraced the same insanity. Why do men do these things to themselves and make decisions that haunt them yet seek to undo them?

That evening King was once again in Memphis. April had begun but there seemed no finish to the garbage strike, the longest lasting in this city or even the state's history. The days plodded along, each similar to the one before.

King was scheduled to speak at the South Memphis Tabernacle and there would be an overflow crowd. It would likely be covered by the national news networks, since he's become the face of the strike and all black empowerment.

As usual, Holston had employed his army of gendarmes to protect the church and prevent any counter-terrorist action. Though I doubted that he even cared if someone blew the church full of blacks and King off the map.

He might have to chase a racist bomber across town, true enough. Although that itself wasn't the real threat, but rather his irrational fear of black radical encroachment and their potential for killing innocent whites.

Almost on a daily basis, Holston talked with several Chicago police chiefs and they kept him informed on Black Panther clashes with their own police. He learned how these officers had thwarted the loathsome criminals with preemptive thinking and quick action. There were five Black Panther gunmen dead in the Chicago morgue who had misjudged the police resolve.

King's church address was delivered without incident to thunderous applause, and later he had been interviewed for CBS national news in a fifteen-minute broadcast aired nationally that weekend.

Holston's officers had escorted his entourage of clergymen in and out of the church, and surrounded the building with armed officers during his address.

There was some pushing incident in front of the Tabernacle between one of King's staff, a young minister from North Carolina who had played college football, and some older white man, who was quickly thrown to the ground.

Holston's men had quickly diffused it, and took the white troublemaker into police custody for the assault, and didn't detain the King people for questioning.

The Atlanta minister traveled with a half-dozen staff members, almost all other black clergymen. The unlikely cadre of ministers with King's Southern Christian Leadership Conference generally rented four inexpensive rooms at an all-black motel downtown about two or three blocks from the Mississippi River.

King always had his own private room in these commercial motels as their entourage leader, but the other ministers would share accommodations to reduce expenses. They had done this regularly for the past year, and it seemed a prudent choice, allowing them enough independence of movement rather than staying at supporter's homes.

At the Tabernacle that evening and other King assemblies, there were always at least one or more FBI agents. Also there were other paid black and white informers, located strategically in the audiences to monitor King's activities and those of his people. They usually weren't identified to Holston and possessed a different agenda concerning King.

Since the beginning of the Memphis garbage strike and the continual appearances of King as a spokesman, Hoover had increased his agency's presence there. He sent as many as eight agents from his special counterintelligence group in Washington in order to watch the movements of the Atlanta minister closely. He also had King's downtown Memphis motel room telephones bugged and the hours of King's conversations had been recorded for over the past month.

They were analyzed by Hoover's domestic terrorist team in Washington who were looking for a clear pattern of criminal intention and possible espionage.

Hoover had been aware of King's association with several known Russian communists and a handful of murderers from the IRA who had become notorious gun runners in a few American cities, and King's involvement had been implicit.

Hoover had shared with Holston some of these concerns for compromised national security and told the Memphis police commissioner that he would personally support any armed preemptive action from the police that might be necessary involving King's questionable activities.

To Holston, that sounded like a green light to follow his own instincts, and much of it had never found its way to Wyeth's ears, so the mayor continued to operate within his cloud of relative ignorance about his own police force.

I passed on whatever I had learned from Holston to Wyeth, but it wasn't much. From the outside, it appeared that Holston's officers on the street had been restrained. The debacle of the first tragic shooting had disappeared.

There were no radical black revolutionary cells to surround and capture. Holston's role had been to protect the sanitation marchers and the gawking whites on the sidewalk from each other's stupidity and occasional felonious assault. He had been successful with the strategy.

This strike had continued from the middle of February into the first week of April. Wyeth still hoped for some negotiated settlement. At some juncture, it would be obvious to everyone involved in this dispute that the garbage workers couldn't continue marching to city hall each afternoon with no real purpose beyond the abstract idea of a new black empowerment. Eventually, there would come a negotiation and contract renewal and all this would finally end.

Chapter 16
April 4, 1968

Wednesday, the fourth of April, the morning was overcast. I had started the day with a heated argument with Martha and she yelled for me to just 'fucking' leave as she slammed the door with her briefcase in hand on her way to her car.

In two minutes, she had spun out of the narrow driveway and headed to downtown Memphis to the DA's office for the morning and then to court for an afternoon trial with Latham. It was a homicide case that had looked like a sort of horrible spousal abuse where the wife had been killed with a blow by the husband. They were both white.

He was a municipal bond trader, and she worked for the Chamber of Commerce in an administrative capacity. Both were educated with bachelor degrees from the local university, and were from decent families.

Someone in the pretrial testimony blamed cocaine for this man's constant rages and three weeks ago at nine in the evening he had hit his wife in the throat with a single punch and shattered her larynx killing her immediately.

This man was over two hundred pounds while she barely weighed a hundred and ten. It was a grisly domestic case, and though he had pleaded not guilty, somehow all the evidence seemed to insure his hanging.

Maybe he could plead insanity from drugs and they would convict him for involuntary manslaughter. In either situation, he was going to spend most of his life locked up somewhere away from the world. That was her case anyway.

We were in the third month of the sanitation workers' strike, and all the charade from New York, Los Angeles, London, and even as far as Berlin, had come and gone. King had made his point, and his name has become a household word for many.

At the office, Wyeth had his usual quick staff briefing which we did since the city was still under siege. I pushed his wheelchair back to his office, and he'd invited me inside to talk more about Holston because he was still unsure of what he might be capable of doing.

The police commissioner had not really been out of line lately, and it seemed that he'd kept most of those officers on the street on this tight leash. There had been no further incidents of excessive force and I breathed a sigh of relief at that fact. Right now it was a waiting game that would play itself out with the blacks.

Wyeth didn't have much to add except the AFSCME national head Wolfson had reintroduced himself into the settlement negotiations, and was in Memphis scheduled to meet with Jones later this afternoon.

Not without some thought there was yet another march. King had been in town for the past two days and had held several rallies in black neighborhoods on the Southside and was now at some soup kitchen meeting with community organizers.

For today at least, I didn't bother with Holston and did the reports I had been asked to do, writing out the various categories in long hand. Finished I gave them to the staff secretary to type them. With these, I would be caught up in my paper trail and expenses, and I could safely continue to be Wyeth's bird dog with the police department.

The tension with Martha had been building since last Sunday when we'd had another shouting match. Emotionally I'd been drained for days so much so that I left Amanda alone, and hadn't called her.

I left the office right after five, and stopped off at a nearby Sheraton hotel bar for a drink with one of the other staffers, a man I actually liked, and we had a few laughs before I drove the fifteen minutes' home.

Martha was probably still in court, and the house was empty so I made myself another drink going out in the yard to get some air because the day had been humid with a hint of spring.

By ten to seven, she still hadn't returned. I sat in the living room half bored going through familiar magazines on the coffee table. She loved Southern Living with all its comfortable summer

249

seaside cottages, and restaurant reviews, and I read about the South Carolina low country for twenty minutes.

The phone rang and I assumed it was Martha, so I trudged over to the hallway next to the dining room, and picked up the receiver.

It was Wyeth, and what first came out of his mouth was, "Goddamn, unbelievable, how could this happen?"

I asked him what was unbelievable, and exactly what had happened that he was talking about, but he continued in this rant of expletives.

"What are you talking about?" I asked again, and his voice finally lowered and he told me what he had learned about eight minutes ago.

"Holston called me from the Lorraine Motel downtown, where King and his people usually stay," he said with some hesitation.

"And?" I pressed him.

Wyeth let out this interminable sigh, and in a quavering voice said. "At six o'clock this evening King was shot. Holston said he was pronounced dead by the fire department medics ten minutes ago. That's what."

I uttered, "Good God, how can that be?"

The mayor answered that all he knew was that King was at the Methodist hospital. The Lorraine Motel had been roped off by Holston's homicide detectives, and now they were searching the immediate vicinity for signs of the suspected assassin.

Someone had finally made good on the threat to kill that so-called 'black bastard' whom so many had misunderstood and hated, mostly from fear.

I asked Wyeth what I could do, and he said nothing but to wait until he learned more and then we'll see what's next.

"There needs to be some kind of a press conference, not tonight but maybe tomorrow morning. I've got to make an announcement concerning the shooting along with Holston. I'm leaving for the motel when I hang up. Call the deputy mayor for me and tell him to inform the rest of staff about this, Okay?"

250

With that short conversation I learned that Martin Luther King, Jr. had been murdered.

Chapter 17
The Second Man

The second man at the sporting goods store with James Earl Ray had a slight German accent when he spoke. Though in truth, it was closer to Dutch because he had been an Afrikaner from rural Transvaal for a good part of his thirty-eight years.

He had handed Ray the four hundred dollars in large bills to buy the Nikon binoculars but had made his own presence in the store almost innocuous.

As a teenager he'd been in the South African army special forces fighting the black rebels organized for armed resistance by the outlawed African Congress movement. Then he had been a guerilla fighter in dozens of pitched battles with the black enemy and even crossing borders in pursuit into Angola. This man killed a dozen men up close where he could look into their dying eyes.

By the time he reached twenty-eight, he had been exhausted from the fighting and the tide of the resistance against the white government had escalated into a full scale war as UN sanctions crippled the South African government.

In 1965, he was recruited by another ex-South African who had been a captain in the United States Army special forces, the so-called Green Berets. He was one of two hundred foreign soldiers with combat experience from various parts of the globe who formed the earliest core of the military unit. They were charged by the American government with unusual covert operations in Vietnam.

These men were often employed as assassins, and had eliminated twenty-two high-ranking military officers and civilians in the North Vietnamese communist government, by mostly sniper fire, though sometimes with explosives.

Heinrich had been recruited in Johannesburg by this American army officer. He had gone through his combat training and indoctrination at a military base in North Carolina along with fifty others who included former agents of the East German Stasi, two Czech army intelligence assassins, some questionable men from the French Foreign Legion, and several Filipino marines who had fought the Muslim separatists.

A precedent for this foreign involvement had been set. Earlier we had also welcomed one hundred and fifty former Nazi rocket scientists with Warner von Braun to better the Soviets who were late to the space game.

The American government at its highest levels had approved the creation of this mixed cadre of dangerous men. It had turned its head to their colorful pasts and unorthodox former alliances with enemies of the United States.

Each foreigner who had become a soldier in the earliest days of the Green Berets had been granted American citizenship under a special proviso by the government. They were compensated at an advanced level, compared with the regular army enlisted men and officers.

In 1966, Heinrich was deployed with a small combat group to Vietnam, first in Da Nang, then relocated to Hue, and finally to the Cambodian border. He had been the leader of a squad dropped onto a jungle hilltop for reconnaissance of NVA encroachment across the border into protected sanctuaries.

When he was dropped by helicopter with three other men on this mountaintop, they immediately disappeared into the jungle canopy.

They separated quickly and Heinrich was moving alone along what appeared to be a worn jungle footpath when he had come to a metal trapdoor. To him, this meant there was an enemy nearby.

Opening the door easily, Heinrich lowered himself down a set of narrow steps and he found a NVA division headquarters in full operation.

Acting immediately, he killed everyone in the narrow bunker with continuous bursts of automatic fire. The lowest ranking of the dead North Vietnamese military officers were two captains. Heinrich had also killed three generals, two bird colonels, and four majors all of whom had been moving around maps on a conference table where they all had been huddled.

For this singular and selfless act, he'd been given an immediate field commission to second lieutenant and was awarded the Silver Star for extraordinary bravery under fire. This was the highest decoration for bravery in the United States forces under the Medal of Honor.

Later, as the American Special Forces transitioned to far less foreign military recruitment, he'd been encouraged to resign his commission and leave the army with a substantial paid bonus as others had. It was a sort of ethical housecleaning.

He had first returned to Johannesburg for a time, but seeing that that country couldn't contain its black armed resistance, he had found his way to the United States. After that, his whereabouts has no marked trail.

What happened since is unclear. He had been supposedly living quietly in Birmingham, Alabama, when he had met one James Earl Ray, a felon and an escaped convict, who supposedly shared some of his white supremacist beliefs. Heinrich befriended the unbalanced man, and found him an easy tool to manipulate.

He had talked with Ray for several nights over drinks about the widespread black threat to the United States, and Ray had confessed that he could easily kill any of those uppity blacks without fear for his own life.

Unknown at this point was who was the real sponsor of Heinrich in the first place. Yet Heinrich carefully encouraged Ray to fulfill his macabre fantasy to murder some prominent black leader.

"Pick the biggest black threat to American life, and then eliminate him," Heinrich had suggested to the man, and Ray had named Martin Luther King, Jr. whose expressive face had been a fixture on national television for months.

"King was in and out of Memphis urging the blacks to revolt during the garbage strike," Heinrich explained, and he told Ray that he would help him remove this scourge from the earth.

So Ray went ahead and bought a hunting rifle with a cheap scope and box of ammunition for it at Birmingham sporting store, then they both drove to Memphis the next week to plan the killing. That's when things get confusing.

After the subsequent visit to York Arms in Memphis to purchase a set of binoculars, Heinrich seemed to vanish completely as there was no trace of his presence in the city.

Had he stayed at some nearby motel before and during the King shooting? There was no record of this man at any local hotel or motel anywhere in the area, or in Memphis for that matter. Had he been seen around the Lorraine Motel? Why had he recruited a man with no firearms training at all to commit this heinous crime, and with such an ordinary weapon as an inexpensive rifle? Nothing about the situation had any logic for police and federal investigators who later followed the scent of the mysterious second man. Only a rather vague description from the manager at the Memphis sporting goods store who sold the binoculars to Ray. He was the only one who ever mentioned a second man in what was becoming a conspiracy theory.

Both the Memphis police and the FBI would lose patience with the store manager over the course of fifteen prolonged interviews, particularly Hoover's best trained agents, as they pushed the already shaky man into a nervous breakdown which required him to be hospitalized.

The manager had repeatedly told the FBI and others from Holston's department in those meetings what this other man supposedly looked like, using police artist sketches for reference. He had tried to mimic the man's tone of voice, and the slight German accent. This store clerk was sure about only two things concerning this second man: He wasn't tall, or short either, and he had close cropped dirty blond hair.

James Earl Ray, son of an Arkansas sharecropper, became a celebrity from his role in the infamous crime when he was interviewed by a national NBC anchorwoman on the steps of the municipal courthouse while television cameras churned. The killer suddenly felt very important.

Three days later, he recanted his earlier confession to the Memphis police, and denied murdering King. Perhaps the electric chair had beckoned and the fear of a painful death clouded his fevered brain. His defense attorney entered an innocent plea into the court record, and it was never changed.

Under persistent police questioning, Ray claimed he had thought about wounding King to teach him a lesson but that the rifle that he had bought in Birmingham had malfunctioned. The bolt action froze and it wouldn't move the round into the firing chamber. It was useless, although it had worked well enough in the store when he tried it.

After seeing King on the balcony and giving up on using his defunct rifle, Ray had heard another shot fired from above, and watched as King fell backwards from the impact of the round. In a panic, he had run out the door and left his own rifle, ammunition, and the binoculars in the room after quickly pushing them under the narrow bed.

Outside the rooming house, he headed down the nearest street toward the river and into a restaurant on the Mississippi dock that he remembered. He stayed there for maybe forty minutes while sipping coffee at the counter. He also bought a donut to fit into the small dining crowd and not invite any scrutiny.

Ray carried all his cash in a wallet in his back pocket, and decided to leave town with just the clothes on his back. He was frightened.

He had heard the wail of police sirens, and then he had decided to board a bus to Little Rock to escape suspicion in the killing. He walked four blocks to the Greyhound bus station where he boarded the next bus to Oklahoma City with a stop in Little Rock.

His gun, or the rifle he'd supposedly bought in Birmingham, was later identified by its serial number. The ballistic tests from King's autopsy clearly showed that the bullet that killed the Atlanta minister had come from that same rifle.

The hunting rifle, binoculars, a box of ammunition, and a blue sweater of Ray's had been found in a canvas utility bag next to a dumpster in an alley two blocks from the Lorraine Motel.

Ray's fingerprints were on the rifle housing and the barrel. Ray said he didn't put that cache from his room there, someone else did.

If he didn't actually take the shot, then who did? And where had it come from? In testimony he said he though it came from a nearby building.

One of the young ministers next to King on the motel balcony had seen a puff of smoke coming from a window in a vacant brick building next to the rooming house that had been condemned and padlocked by city inspectors. That front door lock had long been broken, and someone could have had access to its upper floors.

So, perhaps James Earl Ray had been manipulated and used for this heinous crime, and he hadn't fired the shot that killed King but rather someone else had. However, who on earth had organized this? Who had provided Ray with motive, money and enough support for him to be apprehended? Who set him up?

Ray was a terrible marksman and had no experience with any type of firearms. The man had never hunted, and was unfamiliar with even the ordinary deer rifle he admitted buying.

Did the second man make this shot? Did he, in fact, kill Doctor King which had always been the larger plan of someone else, and Ray had become their sacrificial lamb? If that was true, then the men behind this conspiracy moved seamlessly into the shadows safe from pursuit.

There was a high degree of intelligence involved, and Ray was little more than a country bumpkin. He was third rate criminal who couldn't even rob a convenience store without being caught. How could he conceive of all this, and then execute the cold blooded killing?

What gave him enough foresight to possess false ID cards? Or to find his way first to Toronto and once there, obtain a phony Canadian passport in order to travel to London unobserved? Ray was little more than a simpleton.

He had only worked at the lowest of labor jobs like changing oil at a service station or cleaning warehouses. Ray had been in and out of jail for the pettiest of street crimes.

Had the missing second man switched rifles with Ray who hardly knew anything about the weapon he purchased, and made the shot with Ray's own gun from the next building? Ray became a patsy for a larger organization. He had been set up to take the fall for this crime, but who had such precision of planning and movement to accomplish this murder?

It was rather an easy shot for an experienced military marksman such as Heinrich to make, someone who would have no trouble killing King with a single rifle shot even with the outdated scope. He had done it often and never missed his targets who were usually human.

With accomplices placed inside the rooming house, they had removed the rifle and other incriminating paraphernalia quickly after Ray escaped, and they later dropped it where they knew the police would find it.

Did Heinrich work for some foreign government interested in creating racial violence in the United States? It's possible, maybe probable.

Would this organization tip the delicate balance for what would become a shooting war in American streets between blacks and whites, tomorrow, or next week, or within the next few hours when the news of King's death had been learned? Would the Russians do this, or the Chinese, or even the South Africans, who thought this might move American whites closer to their own side?

That night Martha and I sat in the living room numb with concern. It was almost as if we couldn't speak. She finally said, "This means a race war, right here, right now."

I didn't wholly disagree, and told her I thought we needed to let the next few days pass and see what happens. That same evening Lyndon Johnson spoke on all the television networks and radio stations to the entire nation, calling for rekindled love and respect of all people regardless of skin color, and to move away from any reprisals for the unthinkable crime.

The president came to Memphis the next day and walked to the balcony of the Lorraine Motel where King had been assassinated. He got down on his knees onto the dirty concrete walkway and had prayed silently for his country's turmoil.

Wyeth had been pulled up the motel stairs in his wheelchair by two burly police officers, and bowed his head along with Johnson.

That night Wyeth called Jones. Jones had agreed that the strike needed to end and he would arrange for the contract renewal without unnecessary fanfare pushing it through the union membership. Wyeth had vowed to Jones that the killer would be brought to justice and told him he had enlisted the efforts of the local and state police forces, as well as the FBI to find this murderer quickly.

The entire country was shocked. That night and the next there were widespread fires and violence in the black neighborhoods in Detroit and Los Angeles with dozens of innocent people who were hurt in the outbreak of rage.

White and black clergymen in the city called for a peaceful summit. For the rest of the week they met in the downtown Episcopal Cathedral and at Clayborn Temple. There were over two hundred ministers and priests involved.

On Saturday, there was another march, not of black sanitation workers, but rather of concerned white and black clergy and supporters in the spirit of peace and reconciliation.

It was a sunny morning at ten when a dozen black and white Memphis ministers and priests linked arms then led a crowd of nearly a thousand of their congregants and other fearful Memphians down a deserted street to the river. There they would pray and call for a deliverance from the hatred that had overtaken this city.

In the diverse crowd was a local white Episcopal priest who had been working with troubled teenagers for a year, both black and white. He walked at the head of around a hundred young boys who had their gangly arms around each other, singing the Bob Dylan folk protest anthem, "We Shall Overcome."

Somehow this place where King had collapsed in a pool of his own dying blood, this same segregated city, had not exploded into uncontrollable slaughter between the races. Conversely, there was an unnatural calm that pervaded the hearts of almost everyone inside this city, and it gave cause for hope.

Riots like wildfire consumed whole neighborhoods in the largest American cities. There were beatings, arson, and in the maelstrom innocent people lost their lives. This eventually stopped because there was no more anger, only shame.

Resentment remained with some who sought to burn down the tenements and warehouses where they lived and often worked. But for the most part the white residential neighborhoods across Memphis were untouched.

Nothing happened where we lived, or on the other side of the golf course where Amanda and Randy had their fine red brick home. The week following King's shooting, there was an eerie silence that enveloped the entire city.

Johnson had called the Tennessee governor and had him mobilize the entire National Guard. They had patrolled the city streets in jeeps and camouflage uniforms behind their regular officers who watched the same streets.

Vacations were suddenly taken by some. Yet few people left their homes in the next frantic two weeks that passed. King's widow, Coretta, came to the city to lead the last march and nearly fifty thousand blacks and whites walked slowly behind her singing hymns in a peaceful procession of mourning.

Jones approved the city sanitation contract and the strike ended. The city barely woke from its horror and the wheels of justice slowly turned.

The second man in the sporting goods store was never found, and in the early days of that coming June, James Earl Ray was arrested by British police in London.

Initially, he pleaded guilty to the murder to the Memphis District Attorney James Latham with Martha standing at his side in a court hearing, though three days later Ray changed his plea to one of innocence.

That trial became Martha's entire life, and our own existence as a couple simply disappeared. I had imagined it was predictable as it was probably something we had both wanted anyway though were afraid to do.

I told Amanda I was leaving Martha, and that I had definitely made up my mind to end this forever, and she had nodded her head knowingly.

"Well, it's the two of us now," she said at the time, and added nothing more. She had no reassurances, or even showed the smallest excitement at the news.

Then suddenly she leaned closer over the table and whispered, "But do it right. Think it through."

During Ray's city police interrogations and that of the FBI, Holston had become a darling of law enforcement. There had even been talk of him joining director Hoover in Washington's inner circle and he beamed daily amidst the accolades.

On the other hand, Wyeth was never forgiven. The killing had happened on his watch as mayor, and he might have been able to prevent it had he settled the strike quickly. Instead, he remained stubborn and stonewalled against his union opponents figuring that he could wait the blacks out and be victorious when they would return to work on his terms. But it hadn't happened quite that way.

Few saw the courageous side of the man who had come back from a paralytic stroke and through his own unmistakable character. He had taken back the reigns of a troubled city government from an obvious incompetent, but his entire political career had died with King's assassination.

Still, Wyeth was an experienced lawyer with many friends who hadn't deserted him. This man would lose himself once again in the money making corridors of private practice, and watch his grandchildren play inside his spacious garden gazebo. There was no real tragedy in Wyeth's life save for his ambition of being more.

I had talked with a number of people about that second man. I knew the York Arms family well and they all trusted what their manager had said to the police.

Perhaps James Earl Ray hadn't done this alone, or he became someone's luckless pawn. Had Heinrich been an agent for the Central Intelligence Agency after resigning his commission with the army Special Forces, where perhaps he had been an assassin for operations of murder which even the army brass couldn't authorize? Later someone had suggested he was. His life was a conundrum.

He had spent the whole of 1967 in Vietnam, and no one quite knew why. Totally fluent in Vietnamese, Heinrich appeared on no one's official personnel roster, and there was no file available on him at any American government agency except for the army. Did someone in the American government want King dead? No, that was impossible to imagine, but what if it were rogue forces created by people of influence who were out of control and had the resources and people to do these things. It was absurd and unthinkable, yet was it?

The trial of Ray was easily prosecuted by the state as the evidence, the history of the earlier recanted confession, and his violent criminal past assured his guilt. It had all served to condemn him. The Memphis jury quickly returned a guilty verdict, and the judge sentenced him to a term of ninety-nine years for the King murder.

Martha had been in court for the entire trial, and had worked closely with Latham to prepare the state's case. The verdict elated her but left Latham cold because he saw no other outcome. Her serious countenance beside Latham had appeared a dozen times on local and national television and her career as a leading woman lawyer had been established.

The trial exposure had helped to erase her 'less attractive sister' phobia. For a while this new confidence had a calming and almost pleasant result in her demeanor, but then the obsessiveness took over and this time it became insufferable.

262

There would never be anything I did that was free from her constant scrutiny and barrage of criticism. I plotted my escape from her to Amanda.

I would continue with Wyeth for the balance of his term as he had been good to me and I liked him. Then I would leave government for something in the private sector. Friends in Chicago had called me on the telephone about a position with one of the larger public relations companies who handled mostly corporate work. I had broached the subject once with Amanda who had said she would just as soon leave Memphis and the whole South behind.

We could live happy and anonymously in a large city like Chicago blending into the woodwork without the prying eyes inside restaurants or on the tennis courts we would encounter here.

The FBI continued to talk with Holston and Wyeth both about the second man theory that hadn't been effectively dismissed. Naturally with a crime of this kind of international magnitude, the possibility of conspiracy was always a consideration.

Paper was passed between the various offices, and even more depositions were taken after Ray was imprisoned as more witnesses were called.

A former CIA station chief in Saigon claimed he had known a man named Heinrich Vorstadt who had also been with the army Special Forces. He said he had been on the CIA roster as an operative for Vietnam and perhaps elsewhere.

This man had never met the mysterious Heinrich in person or ever saw a photograph so he couldn't identify him. But nevertheless he had remembered some reference made to him as an agent with extraordinary 'elimination' talent.

After everything the only thing that had been established was that Heinrich had been one of the foreign soldiers recruited during the early formation of the army Special Forces. He had received a brevet commission for bravery in the field. Later he had been released from the American military upon the resignation of his commission as an army officer. That's all. There was no additional information about him except for the forwarding address of a post office box in Johannesburg which was no longer his.

It had become a dead end for authorities particularly as Ray had continued to voice his own innocence in the King murder. With this lack of any real evidence surrounding the second man who had been with Ray at the sporting goods store before the killing, the FBI conspiracy case was closed.

Martha and I finally separated. With time, strangely, she had become James Latham's third and last wife. The difference in age didn't much matter.

We didn't even argue once about the divorce as it made too much sense to the both of us. As a cynical friend of mine said later, we both cut our losses, exiting that bad stock. We had a brief history together and that part of it was painful.

Underneath it all, Martha was a decent woman, perhaps misguided and overbearing, but still quite nice. She was sophisticated too with all her neatly hidden kindness.

I took a temporary apartment off of Front Street down by the Mississippi that had been a cotton warehouse and converted to units that were essentially huge lofts with a view of the river. I waited for Amanda though that took longer than I'd expected. It wasn't surprising when you consider who Amanda was and that she was an unpredictable woman.

It took her more than a year to leave Randy, but when she finally did, she decided she didn't want to leave Memphis. He offered to leave her their large house on Cherry but she thought it would be better to join me in the loft.

The Memphis tongues wagged. And we were both readily vilified for supposed incest as Amanda was Martha's first cousin, though eventually that went away because it was ridiculous in the first place when anyone thought about it.

We didn't marry that first year together but by the end of Wyeth's term I had to decide if I wanted to remain in Memphis or go somewhere else.

Wyeth suggested I attend law school at the city university though I didn't have much appetite for jurisprudence, or the lack of it that I had seen in the courts. I let his suggestion pass unrequited. When I did come to that particular fork in the road, maybe a week or month after I walked out of city hall, I decided not to worry about the future.

Amanda had found a position with Memphis Magazine. Her job was to build up its home and architectural coverage while staying away from hard news.

We did go to the University Club on occasion because Amanda had a membership through her parents. We might sit courtside and have drinks while across from us on the other side sat Latham and Martha. It had happened several times, and to Jim Latham's credit, a veteran of several unsuccessful marriages, it really didn't matter much. He was the first to wave a greeting and to flash a ready smile.

Martha, initially, was more subdued until she got over the fact that I lived with her cousin whom she'd known all her life. Though she didn't forgive my choice in women, perhaps she tried to understand it. At least that's what I thought.

However, in the end, it was probably more about her much prettier cousin now instead of the more attractive sister, and for her whole life what I had done to her was unforgivable.

Since Amanda was neurotic and few would dispute that, she wasn't terribly concerned what people thought about what she had done. After all, she still was Amanda, and why should she be like everybody else who were so predictable and rather dull?

Once or twice, I had seen Randy around Memphis, usually at some social gathering and if he saw me or even us, he would quickly disappear. He dealt with the divorce by throwing himself headlong into medicine as it was a place where he could vanish without a trace considering the responsibilities that faced him.

In time, he would marry and she would be an ideal doctor's wife: fecund and readily child bearing and also demur though slightly humorless. I remember she had a pretty round southern face, and a very tight mouth.

Alfred had gotten much older, and without the burden of Carolyn on his back like a supplicant he had gone adrift. He became a solitary and isolated man. He continued at his law firm, and sometimes I would see him having lunch with a colleague or client at the Summit Club. Alfred would smile if he saw me, but he would rather not speak if he could avoid it because we would simply fall into some sort of meaningless and uncomfortable cordiality.

Though everything with Amanda was always uncertain, that beginning connection we had made from the very first moment I saw her persisted. I don't know how those mysterious things even exist, but each day seemed to have the glue that we needed, and we became more like everyone else around us. Now so many years later, Amanda and I have a precious and beautiful daughter Minna who's starting college this next year, and she wants to attend Auburn with plans to pledge a sorority right away as a freshman. Amanda thinks that's simply wonderful because it's such a great school.

Before I left the mayor's office, there had been a Department of Justice visit reopening the 'second man' theory. They located that same manager who still worked for York Arms, and interviewed him several more times. This time they had some photographs that were purported to have the second man in them, and wanted some kind of positive ID that this was the same Special Forces soldier they originally suspected. For the record, I can't remember how they came up with the Special Forces story in the first place. Someone from the FBI must have been responsible for the first allegation, and Latham had been consulted but had declined to take any further action because this evidence didn't really exist.

It was all mere speculation. There was only the single witness at York Arms who had seen the other man with James Earl Ray because no one else had. Could it have been just another customer Ray had met in the store, and talked up about

266

binoculars, or optics? Or was it someone he'd met earlier in Memphis as he moved around the city and had befriended him? The store clerk had seen money change hands, they appeared to know each other well, and there was that German accent.

To his last breath in prison, James Earl Ray said he didn't kill King, and maybe he didn't. Even later, the King family said they believed he didn't do it, as strange as that had seemed. The oldest King son had visited Ray in prison and he had asked him pointedly if Ray killed his father. Ray denied it.

Could it have been that man Heinrich, a South African given a battlefield commission, and decorated with a silver star? He couldn't have been working alone because it just wasn't possible. Even now, so many people think Ray himself was incapable of doing everything that he did without help.

I remember being in a conversation much later with an older lawyer from the Justice Department who never blamed Wyeth for his role in that acrimonious climate that invited King's murder.

The lawyer had mentioned a name that I had known, though he said the association led nowhere.

The Justice department official had asked me, "Do you know Lee Garrett?"

"Of course," I said. "Why do you ask?"

The man had his briefcase with him and put it on the top of my desk then opened it. He took out a manila folder then closed the case and put his file of loose papers on his lap as he leaned back in the chair.

"There was some earlier investigation that went nowhere. I'm not quite certain why this man Lee Garrett may have been involved. At first his name appears linked to the financing of this higher echelon of loosely organized militant civilians that leads into the government and then abruptly stops."

"I don't follow you," I told him.

He recounted that Lee Garrett had a meeting at his Germantown farm the week before Christmas in a rainy 1967. Some otherwise questionable people might have been involved with him at that gathering. A few were recognized from the federal government. There was talk about changing the misguided direction of this country and how that could be done. These men supposedly saw King as one of those threats.

"Alright. What came out of the Germantown meeting?" I asked the grey-haired man, and he returned this broad smile.

"I don't know," and with that he returned the file into the leather briefcase before closing it again and rose to shake my hand.

He turned to me at the office doorway saying before leaving, "Some things we're not meant to learn." and he laughed a hollow laugh.

A month soon passed and as I readied myself to depart the mayor's office for a new beginning, the same Justice lawyer called me out of the blue.

He mentioned a name to me on the telephone that I hadn't recognized, and asked me if I had ever heard of him.

I told him this particular name was unfamiliar to me but queried him a bit more and I asked him if the man were German. He said, no, the man was a South African, or that at least had been his original nationality.

"He's a horseman and plays top seed polo, I think," the Justice lawyer continued, and some dim light went on in my head from those days when I shared a guest house with Rusty on the Garrett farm so long ago.

"What did you say his name was again?" I had asked the Justice attorney.

The man used the name Vorstadt, he told me, that was the name from his army Special Forces days, and his first name was Gerhard.

"Gerhard doesn't ring a bell," I answered. The man that I remembered went by another name, not Gerhard.

"He could have used an alias if he were there," the Justice man contended. "Do you remember the name he used then?"

I stood up with the receiver in my hand and walked the few steps to the office window and looked out at the crowded city parking lot. There was a suspicious black man looking into car windows, but then I noticed he was simply putting handbills under windshield wipers hawking some automotive parts sale.

In a moment a uniformed policeman from the building had confronted him, and the bent over man had thrown his arms into the air with disgust. The older black man with this snowy white hair slowly climbed over a grassy knoll and disappeared into the busy sidewalk traffic.

At last it came to me all of a sudden. That polo player's name wasn't Gerhard; it was something else. It was Heinrich.

He'd introduced himself to me one summer afternoon on Garrett's farm when he and Rusty were training green mounts. They had run the polo ponies through this maze of quick turns, and had been watering the horses because it was so damn humid and the animals were exhausted.

"The man that I'd met then, his name was Heinrich. That's the name, Heinrich and I thought he was German."

I remembered he had a privileged status with Lee compared to the other foreign players who had passed through Memphis in those years. He often had lunch with Lee in the white portico home when none of the other players did. He was charming, that's true, and even Lee's sister Sharon had liked him and would talk to him if they were exercising horses in the corral in the evening. He wasn't the best of the players though. There were two Argentines that were far better which Garrett took all over the South on tour.

I can only assume there was some other reason he enjoyed that much of Lee's trust, perhaps something related to business, or they were close friends from an earlier time. I don't know.

With little more to add to the Justice official's conversation, I hung up the telephone without any more explanation from his end, instead only getting a strange silence as if he were writing something down, or maybe checking off a box on some government form. It felt unnerving.

I never heard another word from him again, and many years later James Earl Ray died of complications from Hepatitis in a maximum security Tennessee prison claiming to the end that he didn't kill King.

Garrett himself died very young and he had been gone quite a while. Lee didn't share much of his outside life even with his last wife whom we sometimes saw at charity events, or a summer garden party. Amanda knows her far better than I do. Being a prize-winning horsewoman in her day and now a show donor, the widow's usually at the Germantown Charity Classic sitting in her box each June handing out awards to the winners. She gives the Memphis equestrian spectacle ten thousand dollars most years.

Well, Lee's not around anymore to answer the Justice Department's questions about what happened at that meeting on his farm.

It must have been around fifteen years after all this happened with King and Lee had died during that time. The following year, Melissa his widow and Lee's sister, Sharon, finally decided to sell the big white house and the fifty or a hundred acres around it.

There was one last great party thrown. The house was pretty much as Lee had left it because he always called the shots anyway, and his wives concurred. At least it looked that way from the outside.

The party spilled out into the terrace and garden, and I remember taking my drink inside for one last walk through the house. I had wandered into Lee's office and den, rather masculine rooms with horse trophies, business awards, diplomas and maybe a dozen pictures of polo matches.

I stopped at one small photograph on the wall because I was actually in it standing in the back row beside Rusty. The picture was next to one of his father and Lee as a young man on his first polo pony.

It slowly came back to me. It was a sweltering summer day and Lee had returned from Point Clear with a silver trophy for having beaten the New Orleans and Point Clear teams in a southern polo final winning the whole Middle South championship. We were all spread around Lee: the team members who were staying at the farm, the grooms from the barn, and Rusty and me in the back row.

It was taken under the trees next to the corral. In the front, right by Lee was Heinrich, the German or Dutch polo player that I had remembered. He had these wraparound sunglasses on and you really couldn't see his face very clearly in the late afternoon shade. It had to be him, the same man with that ever ambiguous smile.

As I looked closer at the photograph, I noticed that he wore a men's square gold ring on his wedding finger. Not a wedding band, however, but a large distinctive men's ring with a stone of black onyx. I had admired the ring all those years ago and he had told me it had belonged to his dead father who had it made by an ancient goldsmith he had known. Heinrich had said that the jeweler had been one of the oldest Jews in Cape Town. Yes, it was Cape Town, and he had talked about the surrounding farms where he learned about horses. Who was that man, really, and what was his connection to Lee?

That last garden party was long ago when Sharon and Melissa got rid of almost everything in the spacious house and divided it among long lost cousins, some church friends, and a few Memphis relatives. They kept what they wanted of the parents and Lee. Melissa gave Amanda some horse print for Minna's room that had hung in the polo tack room. I think she still has it in her house outside Boston. Amanda would remember although she forgets things that don't interest her so easily, and Martha was always the horsewoman in the family.

What horrible act had this Heinrich really committed, and where had he gone? What could I have done to stop him? It was far too late for any answers. He had been a lonely Roman centurion who erected a cross for someone to die on.

Bruce Colbert is an actor, filmmaker and author. His stage plays have been performed Off-Broadway and in Chicago and Toronto. His newest play Fitzgerald, a biopic about the iconic Scott and Zelda, is now in production. He has appeared on the BBC, ABC, NPR, Discovery TV and in co-star film roles for HBO and Fox. His books include a short story collection, A Tree on the Rift, and three novels: Lombard Street, The Cairo Arrangement and Bosphorus. In addition to his fiction are five poetry collections, most recently Canary in the Dark